D1063368

High-Bred Rose

By Kate L. Hart

Cover by Angel Leya

Jacob Marley
PUBLICATIONS

© 2021 Copyright Katherine Louise Petersen
1-10346923501

Library of Congress Control Number: 2021907640

All rights reserved. No part of this book may be reproduced
or transmitted in any form or by any means without written
permission.

Other women's literature books by Kate L. Hart

Voices of Victorian Women Series
The Lark
The Basra Pearls

Contemporary Reality Show Series
The Reality Show
The Whole Package
Relevé: Erin's story

Contents

Chapter 1

I put a hand to one of the clustered columns, trying to find strength in the very structure of the building that promised such fortitude. Eva stood in front of the altar. The rector stood over her, and the huge golden statue of the crucified Christ loomed above all. In the dim light of stained-glass windows, everything glowed without edges, like I witnessed a living painting.

Eva wore a white gown enhanced by golden embroidery, remade from the lace and satin she wore when presented to Queen Victoria. Her dark hair and eyes contrasted dramatically with the gown and veil. She looked perfect.

Grey Chapel, a vast building of Elizabethan distinction over two hundred years old, was well cared for by the Grey-Hull Family, the initial patrons who still own the advowsons. I could not attend to the rector's passionate cries which echoed through the ribs of the great stone creature and vibrated upward through the hollow cavity.

As Eva repeated the vows, her face radiated joy. Why could I not reconcile this joyful beginning for her? Because it meant the ending for me. I had nowhere to go but to the home of my childhood. A shudder ran up my spine at the pain of memory. I felt so selfish to wallow at the end of this life when her joy was so complete.

Tears escaped my eyes. Lawrence noticed. He smiled at me. He thought my tears for Eva, not my selfishness. I lifted my mouth demurely in what passed for a smile. He winked most inappropriately for a marquess, then went back to watching his daughter – his whole world – make the vow to leave him behind. Yet, he smiled, unconcerned for himself. He loved her so much better than I; his love was unselfish.

When all was completed, Eva turned to me; in one action she gave me the place of surrogate mother for all her guests to see. We looked nothing alike, my light eyes, hair and full figure contrasted dramatically with her dark hair, eyes and trim figure, but I loved her as I would my own child.

I offered my congratulations, and I kissed her. I held her for too long. As I released her, I gave her to the future. I swore I would not burden her with the past.

"I love you, Myra," she said.

"I love you, too!" I said, soaking up the last of her childhood. "Good-bye Dearest. I must go now, but know how much I love you and how happy I am for you."

"I still think your brother is being unreasonable, but I will be back in a month and you will be ready to be home by then, I am sure," she said grinning at me.

For just a moment I allowed myself to be swallowed in her dream, her youth, her exquisite beauty. I smiled demurely at the idea she presented and touched her beautiful face, so caught up in the moment. I pushed back a straying ringlet from her forehead and said:

"Have a wonderful trip, my dearest Eva." I kept the mask of calm serenity in place to make her comfortable.

I allowed myself to be engulfed in the group of well-wishers, knowing that was the only way to disappear. If I were her mother, I would walk to the door with Lawrence and act as a bridge from her old life to her new, helping her up into her carriage.

But I would not embarrass Lawrence by assuming I could play such a role. Instead, I lingered behind them. I was not a part of them – the titled, the elite and their servants. I was neither titled nor should I be a servant. I quietly watched them exit out a side door lined with locals cheering and throwing rice and seeds to the tune of a brass band.

A fuss was made to help Duke Garrett's grandfather, Lord Devon, whose age made it hard for him to maneuver, into his Sudan chair. When Lord Devon was settled, Eva climbed into her carriage pulled by four white horses.

I tied my bonnet and walked alone toward the front of Grey Manor. There sat the glorious 125,000-square-foot Jacobethan estate, the home I was relinquishing. And for what?

I wished for one more chance to stroll the twenty acres of manicured gardens and even beyond to Grey forest. Eva and I often had lessons outdoors. Ah, to sit under the large magnolia tree and read aloud, or watch Lawrence cast our nets where the river emptied into the pond. Then we cooked our day's catch over an open fire.

I was lost in this dream when I heard my name called.

"Myra, won't you be joining us?" Lawrence called again, hurrying up the lane toward me.

It would be him who noticed my withdrawal.

"I would join the wedding breakfast, but my brother's carriage waits. I am summoned, my Lord," I said, bowing with big eyes.

"I outrank him. These gentry today. They think they can call for their sisters whenever the whim inspires them. I would debate the matter on your behalf it would help," he said.

I felt the tears pricking the back of my throat. I was not my own master. I forced a laugh.

"Your interactions with my eldest brother are always amusing, though I doubt either of you could be serious long enough to argue the matter."

"Well then, I may rouse his sense of duty to our friendship. I will simply point out that as his oldest friend I am trustworthy enough to honor him and yourself with the Marquess of Dorset's carriage, livery and all if he will but give leave for you to join the festivities," Lawrence said, smiling and moving to my side.

"You would have your boy dress in livery?"

"Perhaps not, such things are only appropriate in town, but I do have a large carriage at the ready for you, Myra," Lawrence said. He came up to me, and, with such a familiar air, as if it couldn't possibly be inappropriate, he started pinning an orange blossom to my shoulder and said:

"You did not receive your favor."

As he turned to concentrate on the pin, I examined Lawrence, and tried to commit his appearance to memory.

His dark curling hair had started to gray around his temples in his forty-fifth year. His face held a youthful charming quality, that counteracted the gray. His eyes, the color of chestnuts in the fall, crinkled around the corners as if he could laugh at any moment, as if he found everything amusing. His full lips never turned down in anger unless his uncle was around. His very posture held the world in contemplation, and the way he turned further to examine me, his neck muscles strained to see why my tears could not be restrained.

"Come now Myra," he said, "it can't be as bad as that can it? She will come back to us."

"In a way, but in many ways, she never will," I said.

"Can you not defer your leaving at least until she does?" he asked more seriously this time.

"I'm afraid it is not possible. I have put it off these two days already. It is time," I said trying to rein in my tears, but they would not be stemmed.

"Oh Myra! I must hurry to receive my guests, but I cannot leave you in such distress," he said, patting my shoulder to maneuver me toward the path that would lead to the gardens of the hall.

I would lose all my self-respect and beg him to intervene on my behalf if I spent any more time with him. My vulnerable heart could stand no more of this. His consideration, his closeness, the warmth of his breath even now invaded my space.

"Please Sir, I must go," I pleaded. "I must not see our girl. I mourn her childhood. She can only wish to celebrate her future. Please let me go."

"Very well Myra," he said and looked at me with his dark eyes, the eyes that could read me. I could not escape them.

"The walk alone will give me time to recover, Sir. I have already given my good-byes to Eva. She knows of my departure. I have no place in the reception line. I will not be missed," I said.

"I…" Lawrence broke off his exclamation. He looked at me as if for the first time. I could not endure the probe, so I admonished:

"You must leave Hetty alone. She is your housekeeper, do not let her--" I stopped. How could I explain it wasn't fair for him to wrap women in his attention, with no regard to propriety? She already started to watch him when he wasn't looking. Propriety was put in place for a reason. Propriety was safe.

"I was not considering Hetty just now," he said, "I did not consider… where is your home now Myra?"

"I do not know where I will live, but Grey Manor will always be my home Sir," I said bowing and pulling away. I had to leave.

"Myra, you will always have a home," he said. I turned, trying to laugh, but instead the vulnerability I only ever showed him pulled the sorrow and pain up to my face.

"Will you give me a cottage on your property now that I am retired," I said pushing the laugh, "Or would you give me a place in Eva's home?"

"Eva did not offer you a place in her home?"

"I believe she thinks it implied," I said.

"Of course. She does not consider you… she does not understand our arrangement. After her wedding trip and your visit with your brother, we will send for you," he said.

5

"Good-bye Sir," I said bowing. "Send my love to Eva."

"I prefer to say until we meet again Myra," he said.

"I would not censor your word choice for anything Sir," I said, turning away.

"Myra," he called, quickly closing the gap I desperately strove to create. His long firm hands grasped my arms to stop me. I bowed my head praying for the strength to leave and said nothing. His breath invaded my neck.

"Myra, will you not promise to say our goodbyes only until we meet again?"

"I … I cannot. You haven't work for me, and my brother is my true guardian. I cannot say what will be in the next month. I am not my own master; I am not free."

"You are--"

"Lord Hull," Hetty called scurrying toward us, her long body making a strange sashay movement.

"In the country, I am Mr. Grey," Lawrence said looking around to be sure none of the locals heard him giving himself titles, though it was pointless with all the pomp surrounding the day.

"You are required, Sir," she said.

"Myra, this is not over," Lawrence said turning to me.

"No, Sir, I suspect it will never be," I said seeing my opportunity, as Hetty would not be set aside when she felt herself in the right.

I walked quickly away.

"Myra," he called again. I waved over my head not turning. I was the very picture of serene. I practiced until I had it perfected. Who was this man to undo the calm picture I painted of myself to the world?

"I will call for you in a month. Do not doubt that, my dear," he said.

I turned at his affectation, his most devastating breach of decorum. He called me my dear, or lovely lady, churning my stomach and bleeding my heart of every holdout toward safety.

Despite Hetty talking to him, he pointed at me and said, "You raised my child. You will not be left behind! I swear it, Myra."

I had nothing left. I could only dip my head to him. Despite the sentiment, I was a gentleman's daughter. He could only keep me with him in one way. He never thought of any woman to marry, not since his wife died. He had no power to bring me home. Living with an unmarried woman of rank was not a matter of propriety, but a breach of morality, which Lawrence would never consent to. I wondered how long it would take him to realize he could not come to get me.

Chapter 2

I did not cry again until I was alone in the carriage. I gave myself a small window in which to get it out. In my thirty-first year, I expected poise from myself. I was not a young woman in the throes of disappointed passion. I would not behave as such.

My brother's estate was only thirteen miles from Grey Manor. My father, the second son of a Baron, and Lawrence's mother, were distant cousins. The convenient distance between households and the relationship between the two meant my father could impose upon the Marquess of Dorset to transport my brother to school with his son.

My brother, Richard, and Lawrence traveled for days causing mischief in the Hull carriage. They spent more time together during those formative years than apart. The friendship that grew became the most important of my life. I would not meet Lord Lawrence Grey Hull, heir to the Marquess of Dorset, until after his wife died and I was sent to be a governess and companion to his only daughter.

Late afternoon was rounding into the evening when I rode up the gravel drive. Stepping out of the carriage my body ached. I was no longer accustomed to riding in a poorly sprung carriage, and my aching back spasmed, giving me a taste of what the rest of my life was to be like.

The home of my youth, Bolton Lodge, was the fourth home to my grandfather, the Baron. It was called a lodge because grandfather purchased it to go fishing in the Channel, but also stocked the lake on the property to give himself variety. Since it was not entailed to the eldest, my father inherited it.

Though it was nothing to Grey Manor, the lodge was an estate, three stories with two wings, also built in the Jacobethan style. Grey Manor boasted sixty-seven bed chambers alone, Bolton Lodge had half that, but couldn't be considered snug by any sense of the word. The few times I came back in the last eleven years I had to remind myself the great red stone house no longer belonged to my father, but my eldest brother.

I did not know my brother well. He was fifteen years my senior and from what I understand, doted on me as a child the few times he chose to come home from school. Usually, he did not come home, but went on holiday with Lawrence, long before he sent me to be his governess.

By contrast, my father was a cruel, unhappy sort of man who did not breed openness nor friendships among his children, but rather a quiet, solemn silence. The only significant relationship I ever had in the house of my youth was my mother, who died when I was sixteen. My life changed dramatically for the worse after she passed.

I did not thrive when solely under the guardianship of my father. Every time I climbed the steps to the beautiful, heavy oak front door, I missed my mother meeting me in the entryway. Scooting me off to my room before my father could storm in and catch me dirty or ripped dress. I could not approach the door without trembling wearily.

Entering the house, I always heard the echo of my father's fury, so terrible it seeped into the walls of the place. It could not be scrubbed out by mortal hand or holy water. And now I was never to leave again.

"Ah Myra, here you are at last," my sister-in-law, Mary, said greeting me. A servant took my shawl and bonnet.

"Aunt, I am to lead at the dance in a week. Will you do my hair?" Clara, my eldest niece asked.

"Of course, my dear," I said patting the young woman I'd made a pet of over the years. She looked very much like me in my youth. She was not so very thin – because I feared to eat in my father's presence – but in every other respect we looked alike. Her complexion was creamy. Her cheeks naturally flushed. I was always ashen in my youth, but since going to Grey Manor, I could be counted upon now and again to find the lovely blushes that never came upon my cheeks at her age.

In sunlight, our hair glowed the shade of a delicate ripe peach, rosy enough it could not be blonde, but neither could it be termed red enough to be auburn. We both had large, light eyes, brown at the center until they grew green like a tree stump covered in moss. Her eyes shown with the beauty of her youth, and I could not help but think my brother a vigilant custodian of those in his care. This gave me a modicum of hope

"Myra, I would have a word," Richard, my brother, said walking down a large staircase toward me. His eyes squinted, causing a line to appear between them. They pierced me, and I felt the stab as panic in my heart.

I quickly reminded myself Richard only vaguely looked like our father. He was much thinner, as he did not spend years in gluttony and drinking. His coppery hair had dulled considerably, and as he moved closer, staring me down, I could even see a few white hairs cropping up in the sideboards growing down his face. I reminded myself he was Lawrence's best friend. The closer he came, his stare indicated more than just frustration, and without my permission, my feet instinctively stepped toward his wife.

"Richard, do let her have a moment's repose. She has been traveling all day," the lady said. I hated myself for the subconscious retreat I made. Taking a deep breath, I lifted my chin and said, "No, Mary. Do not concern yourself. I am already budding a headache. I may as well hear what he wishes to say."

I stooped to kiss my youngest niece, who escaped from the nursery, and reached her pudgy arms to me in sanctuary. She took my offering, then ran off toward her mother, and away from her nurse. I straightened my dress at the mirror in the entryway. When I felt presentable, I followed my brother into his study at the back of the house.

The study, once dark and dank where my father ruled as master, looked friendlier. Not that my brother replaced the large oak desk or the four busts of barons past set into nooks of oak. The fireplace was still a white stone to match the busts. The mint green wallpaper my father insisted on in every major room of the house faded into a sickly color and was almost worn through in places. Because of my father's excess, my brother could not afford to update anything.

The only change in the place was the light. The huge window on the outside wall was thrown open and allowed a warm August breeze to float in and ruffle the pages of a book sitting on the desk. The slanting sun hit the room and lit the dark corners. The busts of our male ancestors did not scowl with condemnation under the light's influence. It lent a strange stillness to the room that had once moved with shadows and torment.

The room only had a few shelves of books, but many more than when my father stomped around waiting for his next trip to London. My brother added sofas from my father's cramped sitting room to invite his children into the large room. I marveled at how Richard brought the old place to life since our father's death.

"Myra why do you not take off your gloves?" Richard asked after he sat behind his desk. I could see he knew.

"I am cold," I said.

"It is a very warm evening," he said.

"Is it?" I asked as if I didn't notice the sweat trickling down my back and hairline.

"I had a most interesting letter from the Earl of Somerset in March of this year," he said.

"I suppose you did," I said pursing my lips.

"He informed me you were acting in the place of Lady Hull's Abigail," he said.

"It...Lawrence... ur, Lord Hull, sent her to London, alone. Her father insisted she go without title or guardian, with only the Earl of Somerset as protection. He could not even keep her safe against his wife, not to mention his scoundrel of a son and all of London. Did you honestly believe, with my intimate knowledge of that city, and her complete isolation from all things dreadful, that I would not find a way to go with her?"

"Father would..."

I flinched. He let out a deep breath. His tone changed, and he said:

"I suppose I could not, and thankfully no one heard about it. Grandfather was mentioned when you were cited as her companion at her presentation ball in the society columns. Thankfully, there is no harm done. Your reputation only escaped by Lady Claremont Hull's ignorance of your identity."

"Even after she found out, she dreaded a scandal in her own home. I interacted with the lady enough to know it would be so. She never saw me as anything but Eva's maid when she came to Grey Manor, so I knew I could pull off the ruse," I said.

"It was... it is no matter. Your reputation escaped the ordeal, but barely. It is time for that to be at an end. I am asking you to give up the life of a paid servant."

"What other purpose is there for me?" I asked.

"You are young yet, Myra," he said.

"In comparison, I will always be young, as we age at the same rate. I will always be the youngest sister. I am coming upon thirty-one, far past expectations," I said.

"Perhaps not," he said.

"I was asked to sacrifice for our family. I choose my sacrifice," I said unable to tolerate even the thought of another old gouty man coming to court me.

"Myra, Mr. James Evans lost his wife two months ago," Richard said.

"I…I had not heard. How shocking," I said looking away.

"He has three young daughters and a son. They are alone and without a mother," he said.

"I… I suppose his late wife's fortune will allow for him to hire a governess, but you have asked me to leave that life behind," I said.

"You cannot be such a romantic fool," Richard said squinting at me, unfamiliar with my intellect, and trying to determine if I were serious. "He chose prudently, as young men often do. You could not choose him at the time, so what good would have been any sacrifice of his in not marrying?"

"I do not begrudge James his wife," I said looking into my brother's empty fire grate.

"Good. You will be glad to know he is attending church regularly; I suppose you will be in services tomorrow?"

"Because I am a believer, not because I am foolish enough to suppose an extremely handsome man, who could have a young girl in her prime, would show interest in me," I said.

"He must consider his children. He needs a woman to help raise them, not another child he must raise," he said.

"I do not... I have not seen James in twelve years," I said.

"Last year, when I came to the old Marquess' funeral, I thought I detected a preference on your part for my old friend Lawrence. Is that why you resist being set free after your successful time in servitude?"

13

"I... I have done my duty," I said.

"Lawrence was always a kind, loving sort of fellow," Richard said, "I knew many a lady who was certain he maintained an affection for them, due simply to his generous nature."

I said nothing but turned to perusing the titles of books nearest me. I could easily bring to mind the looks Hetty gave him. I had not indulged in such myself but could not deny my brother's observations as they had been my own.

"When will you give up on what you cannot have and take what you can get?" he said with aggravation.

"I paid off father's great debts. Did I not?" I asked, snapping my head up angrily.

"You did," he answered.

"We are free and clear of our troubles?"

"We are thriving because of your sacrifice."

"I have done everything that decorum requires the youngest daughter who did not have the means to marry, have I not?"

"I am not concerned with your duty sister, but your life. I do not deny the sacrifices you made, nor can I be anything but eternally grateful to you for it. With Father's debts paid off, we are producing enough from our industry to do right by you, Myra."

"What is right?"

"I may not be able to give you a marquess, but you would not be so foolish to pass up a life of your own. Perhaps even children that you may raise, and then still have a home once they are grown; that is in your reach."

"Eva will give me a place in her home," I said.

"So, you can continue to watch her live? So, you can have a glimpse of her father now and then when he comes to visit? That is if he remembers you long enough to send for you where you will be confined to the nursery with your lady's children."

I stopped, the tears choking all words at the vision. It was so accurate. I could not be sure my brother had not divined it.

"Myra, you are the daughter of a gentleman. You are not a servant. You are entitled to more of a life than that. Give me a chance to do right by you; let me arrange things for a time."

I closed my eyes, but all I could see was Lawrence, pointing at me, swearing he would come for me. I opened them again, wishing for a reprieve from the longing that sat painfully in my heart. How did one live life when it was simply a human manifestation of unrequited love? I saw my brother's picture of me. It was fair.

What could I do?

As if I asked the question out loud, my brother said, "Be sure to make services tomorrow Myra; it may do you more good than you can know."

"I will go," I said because something had to change.

Chapter 3

The pews in the stone chapel were hard and did not shine like those at Grey church. The stained-glass windows were tall and narrow and let in little light, making the small church gloomy. I arrived early trying to find peace and direction, but nothing came. Instead, I watched as the chapel filled. A little voice trilled, a deep vibration told it to quiet, a soprano joined the throng to soothe the child who started to cry. I listened as I always did, to other people living their lives.

"Miss Bolton, is that you?"

"Good morning Mr. Clarke, how is your congregation?" I asked the rector who had seemed young when I left but somehow reached middle-aged in my absence.

"Very well, we have our struggles as all places do, but it is moving along," he said.

"I am so glad to hear it," I said as the rector moved on toward the pulpit.

"Myra, is that you?"

I looked up to find Mrs. Evans looking down at me, a fine-looking woman for her age, the squint in her poor eyes made her question legitimate. I stood and took her hand.

"Mrs. Evans, how do you do?"

"I am well. Look at you, back to us from the fine house. You're pink and plumped up. I never seen you look so healthy. They must have been good to you," she said.

"Yes, they were very kind to me," I answered.

"Well, that's good to hear. I suppose you heard my James has had a disappointment," she said.

"Yes, I understand he lost his wife. I am so sorry," I said.

"Oh, here he is," she said. "James, look it's Myra, your old childhood friend come to visit us from the fine folks," she said.

I turned to see James. Time had not changed him, and twelve years could have been days. His handsome face shaped like rolling hills with a rounded forehead, his gently curved nose sat perfectly between high cheekbones. Dimples appeared when he smiled, and a perfectly rounded chin made him seem right no matter what he said when he opened his mouth. I took the hand he offered. His perfect azure eyes lit, and his smiling lips said:

"Look at you, Myra. You have grown into a woman."

"I suppose we must still wait for you to age a day Sir," I said in perfect composure, though I remember fluttering quite a bit as a young girl. He laughed.

"Here. Meet my children," he said.

"Sally, come meet my oldest friend," he said.

"Myra, this is Sarah after her mother, but we've always called her Sally. She is ten years, and precocious as anything, Sally this is Miss Bolton," he said.

"How do you do," I said looking at a beautiful little blonde girl with her daddy's blue eyes.

"Fine. Thank you," she bowed, but the action appeared menacing, and her eyes held a loathing which surprised me as I'd done nothing to her. I remembered myself just after my mother died and forgave the poor child everything, though James snapped, "Sally, be polite."

"This is James Junior; we call him Jim. He is eight." The boy who bowed politely could not look further from his father, with his mother's pale pallor, tired grey eyes, and dull hair.

"This is Molly; she is six, and Laura is three," he said. The girls looked like their older sister and I curtsied to them, which made the littlest giggle.

"Your children are lovely," I said. The rector cleared his throat at the pulpit, and it sounded like a reprimand.

"We best sit down, but I am sure my mother meant to invite you to our supper party tomorrow evening," he said.

"Oh," Mrs. Evans said glancing at James uncomfortably.

"It is not—" I started.

"No, it would be my pleasure," the older lady said taking my hand. "You are sweet. I remember your kind heart from your youth."

"We will indeed be able to catch up," he said, offering his arm to his mother.

"Yes, please do come," she said with such warmth.

I could only answer, "I would be delighted, thank you Mrs. Evans."

"My pleasure child, my pleasure," she said, but she looked worried, and I wondered if I made her table uneven, or if she hadn't enough food, as she must have been planning it for some time.

I sat back down in my seat and listened carefully to the preacher, trying to enjoy the sermon. I heard sniffling and chanced to glance over to see James's oldest daughter, Sally, in tears. Her grandmother tried to console her, but she shrugged her arm off and wept even harder in a very showy way. I felt sorry for the child. The sermon was lengthy about pride, and I could have sworn Mr. Clarke had some personal message he meant just for me. The number of times I drew his gaze was high.

After the services ended, James came toward me, but the rector reached me first.

"Miss Bolton, Tuesday morning next we are putting together baskets for missionary service. Can you be counted on to help?" he asked tersely. He appeared angry with me.

"Of course," I said trying to sound cordial while dipping. He nodded and passed me chasing down someone else.

"Ah, I was going to try and warn you to walk quickly as he has committed almost all the congregation to the effort."

"Well at least it will go quickly," I said.

"No, he uses it as an excuse to scrub the pews and dust."

"Surely there is a caretaker for such activity," I said.

"He feels Heaven cannot be gained without hard work and sacrifice."

"I do remember a time when you enjoyed cleaning the pews, as a young boy you often used your best Sunday Breeches to dust," I said.

"Oh, that would vex me," Mrs. Evans said laughing.

"Then should it not be considered. I already had my turn," James said sullenly.

"That is between you and God, Sir," I said dipping my head to the rector. As he walked back by us, he barely acknowledged me. I decided he was busy on his mission, so I forgot about it. I received the time to be at the supper party and moved to my brother and his waiting carriage. Richard smiled and gave me his hand to help me up. He looked a little too smug for my comfort, but neither of us said anything.

Chapter 4

The next evening, I arrived at the home James inherited from his father when he was only seventeen. No one acknowledged his right to it then. When we went for teas and supper parties, we went to Mrs. Evans' lovely stone home. It was three stories, with ivy climbing the walls lending it charm, though half the size of Bolton Lodge. I had always been comfortable in the house when I was a girl.

In the twelve years, I'd been gone the house had undergone extensive renovations. The entryway was made grand by the tearing out one of the bedrooms a level above. Pillars that belonged in a cathedral reached up to the new ceiling. Three short steps elevated gently into a larger entryway that seemed to have no purpose except to exist. The staircase off to one side rose to the next level but vanished abruptly where it met with what remained of the second story of the house. I followed the butler to the end of the entryway. I was announced and let into the drawing-room.

"The place has been… renovated," I said unsurely when Mrs. Evans met me at the door of drawing-room.

"Yes, Sarah did much to… improve it," she said, and we turned to examine the dark, almost creepy blood-red room trimmed in gold that had once been light and comfortable despite its country appearance.

"Miss Bolton, come meet the rest of our party," James called to me. I started to move forward, but Mrs. Evans grabbed my arm, and I turned back to her.

"We have all been through an ordeal, please remember that my dear," she said, a tremor of age ran through her hand.

"Of course," I said looking at her trying to understand what the matter was. A feeling of foreboding came over me as I moved further into the drawing-room that dripped fresh blood from every curtain rod. James was with two other ladies I did not know and a second gentleman.

"Miss Bolton, is that you?"

"Mr. Davies," I said, realizing I knew the man. He'd changed in the dramatic way his friend stayed the same. He grew at least a foot and his straight straw hair receded in the extreme.

"I see you have been well. You are no longer a wisp of a thing," he said, admiring me.

"I am not the only one who grew up. Look at you. I do not imagine Mr. Evans can still manage to get you in a headlock," I said.

"No, he is lucky I sprung up late. As a gentleman, I cannot return the whippings he assuredly deserves."

I laughed.

"Myra, ur… excuse me, Miss Bolton, come here," James said impatiently using the tone he had as a boy to let me know I was holding up his game. "Some ladies are here I wish you to meet."

"Yes," I said moving over to him.

"This is Miss Williams. She is from Meadow Way. Her brother let the Fiddick's property, they moved here in April, so she did not have to spend the summer in London. She is the daughter and heiress of the banking family, Mr. Bartholomew Williams," he said.

The lovely lady graciously bowed to me while James told her who I was. Her hair varied like sand; it streaked lighter then grew darker. Her green eyes were the color of Lawrence's exotic Aloe Vera plant in the conservatory garden and they brightened her face. The dazzling smile arranged on her heart-shaped face made her more than pretty; it made her interesting. She wore the fashion of a few years earlier, though the satin was exceptionally fine. I suspected it acquired for the marriage market when she'd been presented.

"It is nice to meet you," I said, curtsying in return. I observed her with curiosity. She was very pretty, and probably only a few years younger than I. In my experiences, pretty heiresses in fine satin were not unmarried unless there was an exceptionally good reason.

James continued, "Miss Bolton, this is Miss Clarke, she is related to the rector – his oldest brother's daughter," he said. The second lady must have been older than me, and her looks were much plainer than the first. She had dull blonde hair with a flat face and large, round, steel blue eyes that opened wider than necessary, like a fish. She did not dress to her advantage and may have been trying to hide that she was not blessed with a woman's body.

James would not look at me as he introduced the women and I quickly noticed that we were all of the Miss distinction. Though his friend did not appear married, neither of the other women gravitated toward him. He could not compare to the handsome James Evans and his newly renovated home.

"This room is so…um, lovely," Miss Williams said, fanning herself as she looked around at the overly ornate furnishings that belonged in a palace.

"It is considered the finest in the neighborhood," a young voice said from the corner.

"Sally, did you not get your supper in the nursery?"

"Father, I am too old to take supper in the nursery," she said, lifting her nose in the haughtiest of ways.

"I suppose it cannot hurt for you to join us," he said. Surprised at his giving into such nonsense I tried to remember the child lost her mother only a few months previous. He must worry over the young girl to indulge her in such a manner.

"My mother was considered the finest of arrangers, and no room could rival this," Sally said, looking at me as I did not nod in agreement like the other ladies. Instinctively I felt, in this child's case, it might be best for me to give her a real picture.

"The color is too dark for a room this size. It holds the heat in and the light out," I said.

"No, it is perfect, to rival any of the drawing rooms in London," she said.

"Have you been to London?"

She paused, "No, but mother told me," she said.

"Yes, well most homes in London are smaller than this, and except in the large houses, this dark color would be too strong. If she had increased the lighter colors and only accented with the red, it would be a spectacular room. It is gloomy. Do you never draw the shades?"

They all stared at me. I stared at the little blonde girl who did not know she could be wrong.

James cleared his throat, "I think that would be…nice to let some light in."

"As do I," Mrs. Evans said, trying to hide her amusement behind a hand.

"James, do you still ride?" I asked.

"Ride what?" the child asked in a mocking tone.

"Your father was the finest horseman in the county growing up," I said.

"My father's place is in the carriage to protect his family," Sally answered.

"James, surely you have not given up riding?" I asked.

"I… there is very little time for a family man and landowner to ride for pleasure," he said, looking away.

"Even to meet with your Steward?" I asked.

"He comes to the house because Mama could never go out to meet him," Sally said, folding her arms and glaring at me. I stared at the child. Why would her mother need to meet with the steward?

"What happened to Punchy?" I asked James, ignoring the child.

"He was sold, oh, seven years ago, mother," James said, looking to his mother for help.

"He was not replaced?" I asked.

"No, we never got around to it," James said.

"No time like the present. A man is never more honest than on his horse," I encouraged.

"I'd like to take up riding again," James said considering. Thankfully only his mother and I were at such a vantage point to see his daughter cross her arms and shake her head as if her father were living in a ridiculous dream. The child emasculated her father as if her mother possessed her little body. I wished to give him his manhood back, just to spite her.

A much younger man than the butler of our childhood announced dinner.

"Oh, dear. It is excessively warm in this room," Miss William said fanning herself, "I do require your arm, Mr. Evans."

"Of course," he said looking to me apologetically. Miss Clarke surprised me and quickly took Mr. Evans's free arm without invitation. Mr. Davies looked even more surprised, and I realized he must usually escort the plain Miss Clarke to dinner. He stuck out his arm unsurely toward me. I took it and gave him my demure smile hoping James had invited me as a companion for Mr. Davies as he was so pre-occupied.

"I understand you spent the season in London," Mr. Davies said.

"Yes, I saw more Shakespeare than I care for."

"Ah, I enjoy a play here and there. I prefer the more modern shows, but the experience is worth having," he said.

"Yes, it was," I said, "Are you familiar with—"

"Miss Bolton," James called over his shoulder.

"Yes," I said after looking apologetically at Mr. Davies.

"Perhaps you will sing for us after supper. I know you to be quite accomplished."

I stammered. He knew I hated to sing. My father insisted I perfect every womanly talent, so I might be marriageable. I excelled at singing, the pianoforte, dancing, drawing, languages and many other things he deemed a woman should know. Father had gloated over my singing especially, making me hate it. But then again, my disciplined sacrifice to music had guided Eva's natural talent to become much more successful than I could be. Still, I found it peculiar that James would ask me to do what he knew I used to find demoralizing. I answered:

"I have not a piece prepared. The last ten years I have been training my young lady. She sang very successfully in London."

"I delight in singing and would be happy to oblige," Miss Williams said.

"I can sing for you, Papa," Sally said. I had not noticed she walked so near me.

"I do love to hear you sing, Sally," he said turning to grin at her, and I saw another little glimpse of the James I grew up with. His daughter also hinted at childlike innocence in her answering smile. What happened to these people? Could one person turn a household so ill-tempered?

"I intend to go to London when I am older," Sally said looking up at me, "I will attend balls and assemblies. I will go to every museum."

"What particularly interests you?" I asked.

"Going to London," she said confused.

"Yes dear, but what do you want to see in particular?" I asked.

"I do not need to … I will be able to tell people I have been," she said glaring at me.

"Yes, but what will thrill you to see? My young lady was enamored with Shakespeare and could not go to the

Theater Royal enough. What makes you feel alive when you think and talk about it?" I asked.

She stopped and grit her teeth. She looked up at me glaring.

"I will go to balls," she said.

"You love to dance then?" I asked.

"I do not know how yet, but when I learn I will be better at it than anyone, and men will line up to dance with me, just as they did my mother."

"Will that make you happy?" I asked remembering her mother as a sickly, frail sort of woman and tried to picture her dancing.

"Happy?"

"Yes dear, it is an emotion most people strive for, joy, happiness, satisfaction," I said.

"You are not a proper lady," she snapped glaring at me.

"I can see that I am frustrating you, but I am simply asking for your preferences. I am not attacking you," I said, startled at the little person lashing out at me.

"You are unkind to a motherless child and I hate you!"

She stomped.

"What is going on here," James asked running back to us. Seeing his daughter in distress he knelt before Sally.

"She was mean to me, and I hate her. Make her leave," she wailed. Up to this point, I felt startled and amused at such an old child pitching the fit of an infant. However, when James looked to me angrily as if I did something wrong, I met his glare with one of my own.

"Myra, what have you done here?" he asked. As James glared at me, Sally, chin up in self-importance, glowered at me with cruel satisfaction that I would not have supposed one so young even capable of.

"James, can you believe I would do or say anything to hurt this child?" I asked.

"Ah," he stopped and looked at me. I would not argue with him but waited for him to use his reasoning.

"Sally," he asked. "What happened?"

"She said I was not happy and that she hated me," she said with big eyes and watery tears.

"Oh, my angel child, come, I will--" Miss Williams started.

"Do not pander to her," I snapped. They all stopped to look at me. I saw the half a smile James gave me. I often responded to the throngs of ladies who found themselves violently in love with him in this manner when we were growing up.

"Excuse me," Miss Williams started.

"She is lying and if you coddle her, she will believe it is acceptable. Certainly, you do not wish your daughter to be eleven years old and pitching the fits of a two-year-old," I said, staring at the girl who did not seem to know what to say. Miss Williams looked at me intrigued and backed up, proving she would not defend the child further.

"She has grown very haughty of late," Mrs. Evans chimed in.

"I…we must understand, she has lost her mother," James said defending the child, growing heated, "What would you expect from— "

"Sorrow, true sadness, real tears of pain," I said, "allowing her pain to grow into cruelty will not benefit her or you."

"She is not cruel," he said.

"In her true nature, I suspect not. She believes because she lost her mother, she has the right to manipulate you. You cannot seriously think it wise to let the behavior continue," I said.

He glanced at me and I could see the patches crawling up his face, signaling he was embarrassed.

"Sally," he said bending down to her level.

"Yes Papa," she said taking a deep breath and shuddering most expertly.

"Perhaps you ought to go up to the nursery for supper," he said.

"You would prefer her company to mine," she shouted. James stopped and stared at his child.

"You sound exactly like your mother," he said, and he looked at me with terrified eyes.

"Well, someone has to keep order in this house. Grandmother has not a refined bone in her body and you--"

"That is quite enough, young lady. Go to the nursery, now," Mrs. Evans snapped, taking the girl by the shoulder and pulling her away. I could tell by the look on her face she was more terrified of her granddaughter finishing the offense to her son than insulted by what Sally said to her.

James watched the girl go with a wary expression showing clearly on his face.

"What… what can I do?" he asked looking at me.

"She does not need a genie in a bottle, James. She needs a father. Your esteemed father would never put up with such behavior from you or any of your brothers and sisters."

He looked at me and I saw something harden in him as if I'd just insulted him instead of answering the question he posed. He turned from me and gave his arm back to the other ladies. I moved back to Mr. Davies who gave me a sly smile and a well-done head nod. I wondered what happened in this home that had once been my refuge.

Supper turned out to be an uncomfortable affair. James grew haughty towards me. All I could do was sit quietly and notice the china was too fine, the table too big and the outrageously garish portrait of what turned out to be his late wife's parents. To add upon all this, James proved aware of how attractive a suitor he was. He sat at the foot of the table flanked by the other two women. He kept them jumping through hoops while I sat next to Mrs. Evans at the head of the table and across from Mr. Davies.

"How does the child,' I asked under my breath.

"Settled for now, but I do not know how she will ever right, so skewed as she is."

"I have faith you will see her to rights," I said remembering well the child's mother slighting me when she felt threatened by my friendship with James.

"I am not certain she can be righted, and she affects the other kids like a stench in the bog. She torments her brother to a level--"

"Mother," James snapped, "Miss Bolton cannot be interested in our small affairs being so accustomed to the gentility of the titled nobility."

"Human nature affects us all Mr. Evans," I said. "It may even be a little more concentrated among the titled."

"True, and spending so much time with the mighty it would seem you have grown in condescension," he said.

"James, that was unkind," his mother said.

"Mother, I am the master in this home and will not be scolded like a schoolboy."

He turned from us and I looked to Mrs. Evans, hurting for both her and me. She put her hand over mine as she used to do when I came to her in high distress because my father was in his mood. Neither of us said anything. We both sorrowed for James as if he had died because he had grown cruel. Mr. Davies after this showed himself a kind sort of soul and spoke to us of the results of the Ascots. I did not join the conversation enthusiastically because I did not think it would help my situation to tell them that not only had I been there, but I was admitted to the royal box.

29

I left that evening trying to give Mrs. Evans every dutiful daughterly affection, that it might fortitude her against her situation which appeared unpleasant, to say the least.

Chapter 5

The next morning, I took a little extra time to make myself presentable. I did my hair in the latest fashion, so I could be confident, calm, even serene under the scrutiny of James and his misplaced condemnation. I grudgingly climbed in the carriage and went to help with the missionary boxes.

My brother and sister-in-law took their oldest two girls to help with the charity work. Clara was the only one of us who was excited. It was not hard to learn why. After my brother's carriage entered the churchyard, a huge gorgeous carriage drove up behind us. Miss Williams alighted the carriage after a very handsome young man. Clara almost skipped over to the young man, and a few of the other neighborhood girls quickly joined her.

"Who is that?" I asked.

"Mr. Titus Williams," Richard said. "He seems a very well-mannered young man, but I feel he is a touch on the presumptuous side and would make any father uncomfortable. His father spends much of his time in London. We only met the elder once when he dropped off his son from school. The boy's aunt has been his guardian for the summer."

"He seems quite the popular young man," I said watching him closely as we all walked over to the hall. He had a strong jawline, his facial features captured conceit, but I supposed it would be an extraordinary young man with such a following to resist that emotion. He had sandy brown hair and green eyes like his aunt, but his eyes did not glow as hers did, and his smile looked fabricated. He stood at least a foot taller than her.

"We shall keep an eye on the situation, Myra," Richard said.

"Yes, we will," I said with a nod.

"Let her be young," Mary said looking between her husband and myself.

"Of course, just not foolish," I said reassuring her.

"That I cannot argue with," she said laughing. "I feel I have become outnumbered here."

Both Richard and I laughed at the picture she painted, but I could not shrug off my distrustful nature any more than my brother could his.

Miss Williams acknowledged me politely when we caught up to her but walked quickly toward the hall. I couldn't help thinking she was trying to get to James before me. She seemed very intent on being married, and I wondered how her efforts had not yet paid off.

The hall was a large old building built in the same space as the church. It boasted a couple good-sized rooms to be rented out for balls or assemblies. Few in the neighborhood could afford to throw such lavish parties. Public balls were held once a quarter, and since the largest room was often unoccupied, it was donated to Mr. Clarke for his charity work. Most of the room was empty. On the side nearest the main entrance tables held many supplies. Boxes and crates waited to be packed and sent over to India and China for the missionaries.

Mr. Clarke passionately supported the Medical Missionaries. He felt if the natives could be healed, they could come to know Christ. His older brother, Miss Clarke's father, generously supported his efforts. With the girth provided, I started to think James would not be content with a wife only but expected her to come with a decent dowry. I supposed that is why the very plain Miss Clarke was included in his spinster society. His first wife hadn't been a beauty, but her wealth supplemented the deficiency. I never realized how much James must always have valued money.

James and I connected glances, but I looked away quickly. He turned to Miss Williams who approached him.

His previous companion, Miss Clarke, slumped a little until Mr. Davies came with supplies and engaged her in conversation. James moved toward Miss Williams using Mr. Davies as his place holder until he could engage both women. My eyes fell on his daughter Sally who stood next to her younger brother. Among the ebb and flow of noise and voices, I heard catches of her authoritative commands snapping.

"Jim, don't put it there it will be squished…no stop that, not …. I do not see you ever doing well in life if you cannot even pack a box…I cannot believe father means to send you to Harrow in another year…"

When the boy stomped away, she followed him. James was occupied with Miss Williams and Miss Clarke, so I quietly followed the siblings, trying to be discreet. I picked up a stack of blankets to pass out and paused at the children.

"Miss Bolton, I suppose you are here to at least pretend at goodness," Sally said.

"Do not speak to me in that way child," I said, "You will eventually isolate yourself if you are not kinder to people."

"I do not fear becoming an old maid like you. My father can afford to support me," she snapped.

"Does it make you feel better to be cruel? It is not the way to be loved by your brother," I said.

"With my mother gone, someone must show my brother his place," she said.

"It ought not to be you since you mean for his place to be under your boot," I said.

"Better under my boot than in your charge," she hissed, "you will never be my mother."

Then she began to cry.

"What is this, Miss Bolton, what did you say to her?" James asked, scurrying over, his entourage following him, including a few extra onlookers who may as well enjoy the melodrama in progress.

"I did not cause these tears, and I can say your daughter may have a place on the stage. I have rarely seen such a fine act," then turning to Sally, I said kindly, "Be careful, the way you are pushing those sobs out of your throat you may very well end with no voice."

Instantly her sobs quieted to a much softer cry. I glanced at James who saw the immature performance but did nothing to stop it. A few of the onlookers, Mr. Davies most, especially smirked. Miss Williams watched my handling of the child, intrigued. I turned from the scene the child meant to prolong for the sake of the attention it gave her.

I continued with my job of distributing blankets. After a noticeably short time James's son whom they called Jim came and worked by me. When her father grew occupied with his charity cause, Sally came to interfere with Jim. I would not let her at him, and she soon found no pleasure in attacking me, as I would not yield to her temper.

"You are my father's old friend?" Jim asked after a time.

"I am," I said, "I have known him since he was smaller than you."

"Did he…was he always a sad boy?"

"No, never, in fact, he rarely stopped moving. He had more energy than four boys put together. Often he was riding his horse with Mr. Davies there."

The boy looked at me disbelieving.

"Do you ride, Jim?"

"No, I'm not…" He looked down at his trim frame, and I could see he didn't feel equal to the task.

"You would ride fine if you learned; the finest jockeys are smaller framed. Your father ought to teach you," I said. He nodded but said nothing. It seemed a subject which brought the boy some pain and embarrassment, so I did not pursue the matter. After a time, the boy asked:

"Did my father fish?"

"Yes, but he could not bait his hook, he always made me do it."

He laughed. It was something of an unnatural effort, but he did laugh. Then he asked, "Where did he fish?"

"At the lake on my brother's property," I said.

"Father once said he would take me to fish in the Channel," Jim said, "but my mother said it is not something a gentleman does."

"That is not true. I know many gentlemen who fish for the sport of it. The Duke who married my young lady is so fond of fishing he tried to convince her they should go fishing on their honeymoon trip."

"Really?" the boy asked.

"Yes," I said with a nod toward Richard, "I know my brother used to fish often with his oldest son Rick before he left to tour the continent. I have no doubt he would be glad to take you."

"Really?" the boy asked.

"I will have him extend the invitation."

The boy looked up at me astonished.

"My father will never allow him to go," Sally said from right behind us.

"We will see. My brother is an important man," I said looking at her briefly, then turning back to Jim I said, "Can you get me another basket?"

"Yes Ma'am," he said.

"You ought not to give him bad habits, you--"

"Child, what are you supposed to be doing?" I asked.

"I...I am loading—"

"Well, go ahead," I said.

"But you should not be--"

"I am not asking you for permission. I am an adult, and you are a child. I will seek the permission of his father, who is his guardian, before I do anything outlandish. Now go, and when this is over, perhaps I will ask my brother to invite you for a day as well," I said.

"I do not want to spend a day at--"

"Then I will not ask him," I said, turning to the basket Jim brought us.

"Well perhaps, if Jim is to go, I ought to come too. He is not to be trusted to behave as he should," she said.

"He has behaved like a perfect gentleman all this morning," I said, smiling at the boy who looked reluctant to organize the supplies he brought over.

"Sally, Jim, come and work with us," James said calling to his children. Miss Williams and Miss Clarke stood on each side, while another woman I vaguely recognized stood across from him. Mr. Davies waited at the ready should any of the woman need a James place holder.

"I am coming papa," the girl said, skipping over to him. Jim looked longingly at his father who took Sally's hand then he turned back to the women fawning over him. Jim stood waiting to see if his father would insist he come over. When his father forgot him, he sunk a little, then came back to me. We continued to chat through our work. I found him as companionable as his father had once been. We worked well together.

"Myra, it is a wonder all you have done," Richard said joining us after most of the supplies were packed and ready to go.

"I have a very helpful companion," I said. "This young man's name is Jim and he wishes to be taught to fish."

"I will be sure you are of the party next time we go," Richard said nodding to the boy.

"Thank you, Sir," he said.

"Mr. Bolton is my boy in your way over here?" James called, coming up to us.

"No Mr. Evans. The child is a delight and I think my sister is making something of a pet of him. We are going to send for him next time I go fishing," Richard said.

"Fishing is not gentlemanly, is it father?" Sally said. Richard started and looked down at the girl in surprise.

"I do not think she meant to imply you are not a gentleman," James said bowing to my brother. Sally went white and her eyes grew. I doubted even her mother dared insult my brother.

"I do not suppose she did," Richard smiled at Sally to prove he did not take offense, "and as there have been many fly fishing societies opening, and books written on the subject, I cannot see where this opinion can come from. My old friend the Marquess of Dorset enjoys the sport, does he, not Myra?" he asked.

"Indeed, and the Duke of Surry is also rather fond of it," I said, smiling down at Jim.

"Then it is settled. My wife will visit her sister in London in the next few days and while she is gone, young master Jim will come fish with us," Richard said, tilting his head to the young boy.

"Thank you, Sir," Jim said bowing back with a broad grin that startled his father.

"Also, Richard you ought to give James the name of that breeder you were talking about yesterday. This boy is getting old and needs a pony, Mr. Evans," I said. I glanced at Sally, and though she turned a little red, she said nothing.

"He should have been in a saddle a year ago," Richard admonished, pulling out a card and writing the breeder's information on it. "Give him my card as a recommendation. He will take good care of you."

"Thank you, Sir," James said, but smiled almost shyly at me.

"You really ought to get around to replacing Punchy while you're at it," I hinted feeling my face flush. James nodded with a smile that made him look like my old friend and I relished in it.

"Myra, I think we are done here," Richard said nodding to Mr. Clarke who opened the front doors of the Hall, so we might see the church. He then came toward us with a box of cleaning rags.

"Yes," I said and moved to my brother's side.

"Jim, Sally, Mr. Evans, Miss Williams, Miss Clarke, Mr. Davies, Good day," I said bowing. Taking Richard's arm, we walked away.

"Mr. Clarke," Richard said nodding to his wife, who gathered their girls and moved toward the exit. Mr. Clarke looked disappointed, but Richard made an effort not to notice as he smiled at his daughters he doted on.

"Well Myra, I think you made a conquest for the son and forgot the father," Richard said as we walked out of the assembly hall and down the front steps.

"James expects me to stand on two legs and beg like a dog for his affection, and since I will not, he will marry one of those other women who will," I said.

"Well, you may say that, but you did not see the way he stared at you as you brought his boy to life a bit. I never even knew the child had words inside him," Richard said.

"Jim is sweet. He is more like the James I knew in my youth," I said. "His father is changed on the inside, where I always liked him best. What good is an attractive shell if one isn't capable of filling it up with something worthwhile?" I asked.

"Oh for…" he groaned.

"What?" I asked.

"You sound so much like Lawrence I fancy I will soon get tricks played on me in my sleep if I am not careful,"

Richard answered. "You always did pick up the traits of the people you were around."

"Perhaps you ought to send me away to an Abbey that I might become a saint."

"Do not tempt me. Try again with James. His mother is so concerned for him."

"Very well, but if it doesn't work out, I will go live in Eva's nursery rearing her children," I said.

"We shall see, everything may work out better than you can suppose at present."

"I do not know how, but I have agreed to be advised by you, for now. Richard, you must know both Miss Williams and Miss Clarke are well provided for. James is not just looking for unquestioned admiration," I said.

"Myra, I had Henry, and then in his turn Lawrence, hold back some of your wages, so you would have what you needed over the years. Have you saved much of it?" he asked as we drew near the carriage.

"Almost all, I was never allowed to pay for anything, even my dresses. Lawrence wanted every appearance of respectability where it came to Eva's situation. I always appeared the gentlewoman in every respect. I have enough to support myself in a modest way for some time," I said.

"Or in other words, enough to entice Mr. James Evans if the sum were known," he said.

"I doubt it can touch a candle to Miss Williams or Miss Clarke's wealth," I said.

"I am sure it is enough. Even so, it is a relief. I am sorry I could not support you," he said looking down.

"No Richard, Father could not support me. He meant for me to marry wealth, no matter what vile avenue it was to be found. You saved me when you sent me away. I secured exactly what I needed, and I thank you for it," I said.

"Well, I am not done. I will do right by you I swear," he said.

"You have already. The last twelve years of joy will keep me warm for the rest of my life. Besides, I like that I am in a place to financially support myself if I had to," I said. I climbed up into the carriage with my nieces and sister-in-law which effectively stopped the conversation.

"Clara, did you have a lovely morning?" I asked after the carriage started moving.

"She accomplished very little by way of missionary boxes," Mary said looking slyly at her daughter. Clara flushed but said nothing.

I examined her. She looked anxious.

"Clara, the Williams boy. What is he like?" I asked.

"He is very handsome," she said.

"I could see that for myself dear. I mean, what is he like?" I asked.

"He is an excellent horseman, and he prefers coffee to tea," she said.

I squinted and looked at her. She looked out the window and I could see I was distressing her, but I could not tell why.

"Would you call him a happy fellow? He seemed a touch surly to me, but I only saw him from a distance," I said.

"No, I'm sure he is a happy fellow. He is very rich and talks often of the grand house he will inherit," she said.

"I do not know that the two necessarily correlate," her father said, looking concerned.

"And if he has a grand property of his own, why are they renting here?" I asked.

"Oh, I never thought of that. I am not sure," Clara said.

"Well, we know for sure he has a home in London. I mean for you to have a proper season in April. If he wishes to court you, he must wait upon us there and then," Mary said with much less gravity.

"He will leave for school by the end of September and will be gone until the end of March," Clara said as if it weighed heavily upon her young heart.

"My dear, that works out splendidly. His home in London must be very convenient for the season," Richard said looking satisfied that the young man would be leaving the neighborhood in just over a month.

"Come now," Mary said. "You would rather meet him in London in the Spring. Rick will be back from the continent and everything will be properly done, my love. Do not worry so much. If he likes you, he can wait until then."

Clara flushed and nodded as the carriage came to a stop. She descended quickly, and I wondered if she was hiding something. I entered the house meaning to follow her, but the butler who opened the front door for us said, "You have a letter, Miss," and held out an envelope to me on a silver platter.

"Thank you," I said.

"It was sent by messenger. He is in the kitchen eating a warm meal," he said to Richard who stood behind me handing over his hat.

I took the letter and saw it was from Grey Manor. I broke the seal and moved quickly until I entered the chamber of my youth. It had never been given to another member of the family because it was the smallest and furthest removed of all the family rooms, and I was yet unmarried. The pink flowers printed on yellowing curtains my mother had made for me, whipped in a gust of wind upon my entrance.

The maid, who had been with the family for years, always opened my window to air the room in the morning. I had asked her not to close it until the heat of the afternoon stole in. It hadn't grown warm yet, so the window was still open. I quickly closed it, supposing an afternoon shower was probably on the way. Then I tore the letter open.

"Myra, I do not know how to write. Lord Devon has succumbed to death. Our trip is postponed, and we are all in distress. Come to us if you can. I understand from my father there was some confusion about where you are to live. I will not be separated from you. I thought that clear. I am sorry if I did not make it so. I need you, please come soon. Father says he will send a carriage tomorrow to fetch you, so you might be on hand for the funeral. Send word by my father's man when you can be ready. Eva"

I reread it twice before I could even understand the note. Then I set it down and started packing my trunk immediately. A knock sounded at the door.

"Enter," I said.

"Myra, I have learned Grey Manor endured a tragedy," Richard said walking into my room.

"Yes, Duke Garrett's grandfather died. Eva needs me, I must go to her," I said.

"I do not think that is wise," Richard said. I shook my head but did not stop in collecting my things, and asked, "How can I deny her my comfort?"

"Is this not an opportunity for her husband to learn to comfort her?"

I stopped and looked at him. He was serious.

"I…you do not understand. When she lost her Grandfather, she was so despondent. She loved this man as she loved him."

"Yes, I do not doubt her distress is great, but would it not be better for Eva and her new husband to comfort each other?"

I grit my teeth in frustration. He sounded so much like Lawrence I wanted to rage at him.

"You know I am right," he said. "The messenger said the old Lord died on Saturday; it must have been just after you left. If she needed you so badly, why did she not send a horseman to catch the carriage?"

"I…I do not know," I said trying to swallow the tears. It had taken them four days to remember to send for me.

"They take you for granted. They think you should always be available to them whenever they want you. That is not fair to you, Myra."

"You would have me stay here and make a fool of myself for James Evans?"

"He needs your help. Eva will manage her grief with her husband," Richard said.

"James's little girl is--"

"Yes, I met her. She is a very insolent child who needs guidance, or she will plague the neighborhood as her mother did."

"James had three spinsters in his dining room last evening. He is not even courting one lady at a time but bulking up three ladies at once, so he might sort through us," I said.

"I am sure he did not mean to line you up and examine you like the day's catch," Richard said, but he didn't sound confident.

"I understand from our old friend Mr. Davies, James has already eliminated two of the local spinsters. I cannot doubt it is due to a lack of fortune."

"Come now, a man likes to…" Richard didn't know how to defend James. Sitting on a floral print chair next to my bed, he finished lamely, "Explore his options."

"Very well. He can go ahead and explore the whole valley for all I care, but I will not have him around me," I said adding my reticule to the pile on the bed.

"Oh, come now Myra. The two of you are old friends. That has to give you a leg up, hasn't it?"

"No brother, it did not. In fact, knowing his father and how he would not tolerate certain behaviors seemed to aggravate him. I will go to Eva and pretend this whole ordeal did not happen."

"Myra please, please do not make me forbid it. I will not have you go," he said.

"You will not let me go, you mean?" I asked. I turned to him astounded.

"I am sorry Myra. I do not think it is wise. I do not wish to see you put your heart in a situation you cannot recover from. I will take responsibility for your absence. I will write to my friend and apologize, but you are needed here. Not only with James, but I was counting on your assistance when Mary goes to her sister in London."

"Do you really think this for the best?"

"Myra, you must trust me. I know my old friend very well. I assure you I will make everything right."

I turned from him and went to the window. I opened it again and breathed in the thick rich wet air that smelled of muddy paths and spearmint. What could I do? In many ways Eva … what did Eva need?

I had to ask myself a hard question.

Was I only going back to see Lawrence?

If my brother was right, if Jonah and Eva should comfort each other, why was I really in such a rush to go back? Looking out over the meadow behind the house, I watched another gust of wind pull grey clouds ever closer. It looked as though there would only be a few more weeks of summer. Then I would be stuck in this room for all of the long cold winter.

"I admit I cannot see straight," I said turning to look at my brother, "I will allow myself to be guided by you. Please let me add a letter to yours for Eva."

My heart broke at the idea it would not be me that gave her comfort, but Richard was right. This was an opportunity for the couple to grow strong together. I sorely missed finding Lawrence at every meal and interrupting our lessons with his insights. It was better to be away from him than continue to make a fool of myself over him.

I wrote my condolences to Eva and begged her forgiveness as I was detained and could not come. I asked how long she would be bound to put off her wedding trip in favor of mourning and if I could do anything for her from here. I ended with my devoted love for her and tried to pretend it was best for all parties.

I felt so broken, I couldn't be sure any of it was best for me. But then sacrifice and love go hand in hand. Letting her grow up was the only thing I had left to give her.

Chapter 6

The next day I sat in my room watching rain splatter the window, wondering how I would endure the rest of my life when I received Eva's understanding in a letter. She would postpone her wedding trip for the thirty days of deepest mourning, then they would go to Paris. She sent me her ticket to the funeral and hoped I would be able to come as she would not be able to come for me for over two months, and we had never been separated for so long. She understood my brother's desire to keep me for his daughter's companion. She stated there could be no better influence for a young girl, and his wife could safely depend on me when she went to town with her sister.

I sought my brother out in his study that looked sickly green in the gloomy storm showing through the window. I showed him the ticket to the funeral and held my breath. He examined me. Then he examined the ticket. He thought for some time as if he were determining his next chess move. Finally, he said, "I do not think it can hurt to go to the funeral, as long as you are of my party and not the Marquess of Dorset." He reached into his desk. He pulled out a map, "It will be a spectacular sight as the old-fashioned man seems to require a night burial. One rarely gets a chance to see such a thing these days."

"Really," I said hopefully.

"We can ride the train into London with Mary, and stay a night, then take the Western railway into Reading, an easy enough distance to Lord Devon's home."

"Thank you, Richard," I said, surprised.

"Gramdent House is a beautiful place, and I doubt the rains have moved inland yet. I suppose there are worst ways to finish up the summer," he said.

"I have heard it is a Gothic building of some significance. You have been there?" I asked.

"Twice with Lawrence on Holiday. It took a great deal longer to get there in those days."

"Richard," I said watching him trace the route with his finger on a map of the railways.

"Yes Myra," he said.

"You enjoy riding trains?"

"I can be in London in hours," he said with a smile.

"Yes, well I will take advantage of you then and accept your proposal."

I packed my trunk. Clara begged to come with us. She reasoned that her mother was only going to town to prepare for her season next spring, and couldn't she have a say in a few of the gowns? Mary took the young lady's pleas in account, and Richard relented and let her come to the funeral. He made it clear she was not to put herself forward while in London. He left his other girls with their governess. We rode the train the next day and stayed at Mary's sister's home in London.

Mary came from a family of a large fortune, and many daughters. My father would not have permitted the alliance unless it was advantageous. When they married, my brother's situation was much closer to Mary's and the match desirable. Father's spending habits quickly outmatched his income after his heir married respectably. Mary's dowry sustained our family for many years; both my sisters were able to marry respectably from it, but eventually, my father squandered that away as well.

Mary's sister did substantially for better for herself by way of wealthy husbands, and her townhome in London was in a good neighborhood that kept her in the highest of fashion and society. The way Mary and Clara were welcomed warmly by her relations, I suspected they were funding Clara's season in town. Richard, on the other hand, was tolerated, and since I'd been a paid companion, I was barely acknowledged.

Over an extravagant welcome supper, Mary chatted happily to her sister about the preparations to be made for Clara's season. Since I barely knew my sister-in-law, I found intruding on her intimacy with her sister awkward. When we removed to the drawing room, I retreated to a corner, so I did not have to listen to stories of people I'd never seen. The pretty room was done over in good taste using furniture of correct proportions. It did nothing to distinguish itself, but it was safely fashionable.

Not interested in the book I picked up, I surreptitiously watched my relations. Mary's sister seemed to dislike Richard. I always thought it because of our father, but I noticed Mary gravitated toward him when her sister wished to be her only intimacy. Richard and Mary were comfortable together. Mary's sister's husband did not make much of an effort beyond showing us his new fobs. If the conversation veered away from him and his interests, he veered to retrieve it. The couple, though situated in the highest of financial comfort, were uncomfortable and only civil to each other. I could not help but feel despite my father, Mary found herself in a better situation than her sister.

Mary was comfortable with her husband, and often touched Richard's hand when recalling something. Her sister seemed fixated on the touch. A few times the sister even lashed out at Mary, telling her she spent far too much time in the country and did not know London ways. These outbursts usually followed a smile, or a look of adoration Mary received from Richard. It was a silly thing, but I was proud of my brother for being a good husband. He learned that from Lawrence's father. Henry Grey obsessed with defining one's duty. He often said one's duty lay with one's family first and foremost. Everything else came second.

Here my observations became uncomfortable. I understood the sister's frustration. I imagine Lawrence had been such a doting husband, in fact, he still was. He would never consider marrying again. I felt incredibly alone watching Richard and Mary. It was a loneliness that I feared would never be filled because I could see plainly from Mary's sister that a person could marry and still feel lonely. By the end of the evening, I tried to be kind to the woman, who did not seem disposed to even acknowledge me.

Far separated from the people around me, I wanted to sink into a hole. How did I continue so out of place in their company for the rest of my days? I knew my home for a time. I knew and loved its occupants, and I could not be where I was most comfortable. I had only to continue lonely, with no way to go back to my home. I went to bed early but could not sleep. I pretended tolerably when Clara climbed into our bed.

Chapter 7

Knowing Eva was at her London home preparing to go to the funeral, I gave in and wrote to her by the morning's post. I explained we dropped my sister at her sister's home and then would be over to the Earl's funeral. Relief spread across my whole being when Eva came to call, disrupting my solitude in the foreign house.

"What are you doing here?" she asked walking into the drawing-room.

"I am on route to Lord Devon's funeral," I said hugging her and kissing her twice.

"How are you?" I asked, surveying her.

"I am tolerable."

"And Jonah?"

"Lord Devon was failing over the last month and his passing wasn't such a surprise. Jonah is managing his grief, though he likes to hold my hand, even in public."

"Good, the two of you will comfort one another," I said smiling at her. She must have heard something disgruntled in my voice because she asked,

"How are you, Myra?"

"I am tolerable. It is a little strange getting used to people I do not know, but my niece Clara is a dear and needs guidance, so I am finding joy in that. She is out just now calling on a friend with her mother."

"You need not stay here. You have your very own room in this town I believe," she said taking my arm as we walked toward a settee.

"Yes, but my brother and niece haven't."

"Why did you not give them one of the guest rooms?" Eva asked, perplexed.

"Dearest, I am not in a position to invite guests into your father's home."

"Oh posh. Of course you are, or at the least, you could write to me, and I will invite your family," she said. She sat down hard, turning to look at me emphatically. I could see she was starting to understand I was pulling away, and I loved her for fighting it.

"Ah Eva! how nice to see you," Richard said, coming into the room. "My wife's sister was rather overcome when announcing a duchess calling on us."

I did not know he had returned from his ride, and for some reason felt I'd been caught stealing pastries from the window ledge.

"Yes, my father sends his regard. He has business, but extended an invitation to dine this evening," she said.

"We are already engaged," he said.

"May we at least have Myra?" she asked.

"I would rather she stay with us if you will excuse me," he said. He could not even look her in the eyes. When she looked at me, I did try to hide my tears.

"What is happening here?" she asked, standing up.

"Eva, please. My sister is in a position to have a family of her own. You cannot expect her to follow you around now that you are married," Richard said looking at her with pity.

"I have never expected that," Eva said.

"No, I do not believe you have, but you must own she is—"

"She is my family," Eva interrupted folding her arms and taking a step toward him.

"No, she was your companion, while you needed a chaperone. Now that you are married, she is no longer paid by your father to look after you," he said.

"Must I pay you to stay with me, Myra?" Eva asked.

"No dearest, that isn't what he means," I said trying to help her understand. Richard interrupted, "An old friend of Myra's was recently widowed. He is in a position to offer for her as he never was before. He has a young family that needs a mother, just as you once did. It is all within her reach to have a family of her own. You would not deny her a home of her own? You cannot wish for her to live out her life entirely dependent on you?"

Eva said nothing. She looked at me, her young eyes aged in just the glance.

"I want you to be happy, Myra," she said. "I am so happy in love. Would it make you happy to marry this old friend of yours?"

"I do not know, it is only…he has--"

"They are just at the beginning of the thing, but Myra once fancied him, and that attraction will certainly grow into something once more," Richard said.

"I wish you the best then," Eva said to me, tears in her eyes. I went to her and put an arm around her shoulder.

"Oh dearest, I do not know what will happen," I said. Then, turning to my brother, I said, "Richard, certainly, you can make my excuses for tonight?"

"Myra I am sorry, but I think it best if you distance yourself. Eva, do not blame Myra, as her guardian, I am insisting she stay with me," he said.

"I am sure my father will wait upon you very soon," Eva said moving toward the door, "My husband, Duke Garrett, may have something to say about you strong-arming your sister to stay away from us."

Richard stopped her close to the door, his back to me.

"Look at the dilemma from my vantage point. I would keep her at Grey Manor forever, but your father can no longer support her as he has previously," he said. "Can you think of a situation where Myra gets a home and life of her own and stays with you? Is there such an opportunity that you could give her?"

"I…" she faltered watching him.

"Eva, she deserves the best of men. A man who loves her. A man she can truly admire and esteem; do you not agree?" he asked. There must have been something more in his face than what I could detect because she examined him.

"Yes, I do agree," she said slowly.

"I would keep her with you always if I could, but she must have an opportunity at marriage. Can I trust you to find her a marriage?"

"Excuse me," she said.

"Your connections are many, can you think of a man who ought not to walk through life alone, some man who would be desirable for her?"

"Perhaps," she said not hesitating this time.

"What would you do to give her that marriage?" he asked.

"Richard, please do not ask her to do such things." I glared at him, asking Eva to play matchmaker among her acquaintances was humiliating. Eva, for her part, examined my brother. I had taught her so often I could see she was learning something from him, but I could not be sure what. She looked appeased in some way.

"I will do my best to make sure she has everything she deserves," Eva said, bowing to him.

I moved swiftly to her and threw my arms around her. I kissed her face and whispered in her ear, "I love you, dearest, I will always carry our time together as the greatest of treasures upon my heart."

"Oh, we are not to be parted for long. I will have my husband build your husband a house on our land if I must, and then we will dine together every night," Eva said, challenging Richard.

"I do expect to see your father soon," he said challenging her back.

"I will be sure he comes presently," she said. He bent at the waist to her. When she left, Richard turned with the strangest half-smile covering his face. I felt sure he had just played my dearest girl a pawn in some game but couldn't be sure which. And what is more, I couldn't be sure why.

My brother caught me looking at him and he nodded.

"What are you up to?" I asked.

"Ah, you have grown up, Myra. You never used to see."

"What game are you at?" I asked.

"Never you mind, sister. I promised mother I would do right by you and one way or another. I swear I will."

I watched him as he left the room. He bounced like a little girl in her supper dress.

Chapter 8

It was not more than two hours before the bell rang again. I was sent to my room with Clara to help her dress as we were going out for the evening. I knew Lawrence was in the house, and though everything in me yearned to see him, I also could not stand to see him. I almost made it but heard a door slam, then I heard his voice in the hall. I slipped away from Clara peeking around the upstairs corner. I saw the back of his wavy dark hair, his very stance as he walked was rigid, and I knew he was unhappy.

What did Richard say to him to make him look like that? I wished to call out to him. I could not see his eyes drilling into mine, him only seeing a woman he was obligated to, while I saw the man I loved.

That evening we attended an assembly Richard's sister-in-law had much anticipated over. She was warmer toward me after my visit from a duchess, especially as I was acknowledged by many of the nobility I'd met while Eva's companion. There was one nobleman in particular who paid me special attention because he meant for me to marry his second son who could not appear in public due to nerves. I did not divulge this to my brother, who seemed more intent on my marrying than he did his daughter.

By the time we sat down, Mary's sister sat between myself and my niece and just had to have my opinion on everything. After it ended, we went to walk a public garden that was much reputed. Feeling overwhelmed, I offered to accompany Clara when she wished to explore a water fountain in a different direction. She was extremely distracted.

After only a minute of exploring, Clara sat on a white metal bench near a pond of water lilies and said she wished to sit there for a minute or two. She was very content to examine every face that passed and spared little attention to the budding flowers growing near her seat. I stayed near her but was drawn to a grouping of exotic flowers. As I walked by a quiet alcove, I felt my arm yank backward.

"Lawrence," I said, startled. There he stood before me and just by the way he held my arm I felt more at home than I had since I left him.

"Hurry, let's go," he said pulling me further in the brush toward the gate that could be used as an exit.

"What are you doing?" I said, arching my neck until I could see Clara on her bench.

"I am freeing you," he said.

I laughed. He looked confused.

"I can see you are in earnest, but where exactly do you expect to take me?" I asked.

"Home," he said.

"I...oh, Lord Grey Hull, you must see you cannot take me anywhere," I said lowering my voice, so the passersby could not hear us.

"I can. You are my..." he stopped. I watched him waiting, praying for him to define what I was to him. Any glimpse of how he saw me would be such a gift. He mulled it over, his eyes squirming through the gardens, as he pulled at his cravat.

"You are my daughter's companion. I will... I can pay you your wages," he said.

"My brother will not hear of me taking any more wages," I said, unsure how to keep myself from dropping to the ground. He saw me as the companion of his daughter. I doubted I was even a woman to him.

"I will pay you more," Lawrence said.

"I am not to be bought today," I said quietly examining a reputed Chinese climbing flower that shifted from a gold speckled center to an orange, its trumpeted shape snuggled in the shelter of the thick green vine that climbed all around us.

"I did not mean it like that, Myra. I have to see you where you belong," he said.

"Where is that, Sir?"

"It is with us, your family," he said.

"You are the family I would choose for myself, but my brother, he is the family I am born to and therefor I must reside with," I said. "It would be improper for me to--"

"That's it," he said perking up.

"What?"

"I will marry you," he said. My heart stopped. Excitedly he put a hand on my arm and my heart started thrumming out pacing rational thought. I looked down at his fingers grasping me, trying to understand. He explained excitedly, "If we get married, then I will be your guardian."

"You never meant to get married again. You said you would... you said your duty, your very honor required you to keep on the badge of widower until you join your wife in death," I said my face and chest on fire.

"No, I will not marry you. I'll legally marry you, then you can be Eva's companion and your brother can have nothing to do with it."

I stared at him. A cold chill of disappointment drizzled over me as real as if an icy rain had suddenly started. Could a man more clearly define how he saw me? He wished for me to ...he would... I pulled my arm from his grasp and asked,

"And how Sir would that marriage take place? Would it be in a church in front of God?"

Lawrence, cringed realizing his mistake. I asked,

"You would have me deceive my brother and my God, so you can have a companion for your grown daughter?"

"No Myra, I did not mean it like— "

"I would not have thought you, who consider yourself honor-bound to your first wife, could so disgrace the office of marriage, Sir," I said feeling broken.

"Myra, I spoke too quickly," he said.

"No, I understand. It is not even the worst marriage proposal I've had. My father. . . he spent extravagantly, especially after my mother died. Many of his relations tried to stem the tide of his excess, but they never did. He always growled at anyone who tried to interfere. One night in London, he got very drunk and confided in me, his lone companion, that I was the solution to all his problems. A man could only wish to have such an attractive youngest daughter when he fell on hard times and needed a fowl to slaughter. He promised I would be able to recompense his excessive spending, and he expected me to share his joy at my daughterly sacrifice. He told me to prepare myself for marriage so that his finances could be restored. At least you are looking out for Eva and not your own interests," I said, trying to curb the bitterness in my tone.

"Oh, Myra," he said, pity in his eyes. This was not enough. I would sever our relationship here and now. Richard was right. This was no way to live.

"I am reminded of the time Eva had her heart set on Avon, and that man tried to pay the breeder to give him the filly instead. You fought then," I said.

"Yes, I fought for my girl, and I will fight for you," he said watching me, unsure how he had lost his footing.

"And so, I am coming up in the world. Where I was a fowl raised for slaughter to my father, I am the horse Eva wants from you. As her father, are you still obligated to get it for her?" I asked.

"I did not mean that," he said.

"No Sir, you did not mean to say that, but that is how you see me. I could be a favorite trinket or pet for your daughter, and you would fight to give her anything she wanted. Meanwhile, I am heart sore, sick and broken over the whole thing because where you lost a servant, I lost my home," I said.

I turned from him and ran back toward my niece, overcome. I felt certain I would die from the pain of it. He did not love me. I was nothing more than his daughter's plaything. He would do anything to give me back to her, but not for me, for her. He would do nothing for me personally, he only made the effort for his child.

Clara, who still searched the faces of those passing, resisted when I pulled her off her bench. She looked up at me and seeing the tears I restrained, relented. I steered her toward Richard. He saw my face and started. Richard moved to us.

"Myra, please I would speak to you," Lawrence said coming up behind me.

"I am not well just now," I said. My whole world floated, and I thought I might fall over.

"Myra, you look unwell," Richard said taking my arm to steady me.

"I ... I do not think I can manage to--"

I started to sway. Lawrence took my arm from behind and I was on fire. I loved him. He thought of me like an animal he could own. How his father, Henry Grey, would be ashamed. And all to keep me from any other life but Eva's. My brother was right. That wasn't fair.

"Come, Myra, I will see you home," Richard said. "Clara, we are leaving."

"May I stay with mother?" the girl asked.

"Mary?" Richard asked. She nodded. Richard said,

"Lawrence, I'm not sure what happened here, but please old friend, I have already expressed my views on her best interest. My sister is a gentleman's daughter. I cannot have her back into servitude when we are no longer lacking the funds as a family to support her. Please old friend, let me restore my family's honor."

"Myra, I …I did not mean…"

I looked at him, so mottled and confused as to what happened. I begged him with my eyes to fix it. He stared at me, the damage clearly showing on my usually serene face because I had no way to hide it. He stood too long, unsure what to even say. The man who never ran out of words could say nothing to me. How absurd.

"Here, Clara darling, you stay with us," Mary said looking curiously at the marquess addressing me. Her sister looked ready to go into raptures, as she took Clara's arm. Lawrence did not appear concerned we were about to become the prattle of London. He just watched me, his mouth moving, but still, nothing came out.

"Good day Sir," I said bowing my head and moving away with my brother.

"What did he say to you?" Richard asked after we were alone in the carriage.

"He offered to marry me, so he could give me permission to go to live with Eva," I said looking out the drawn window.

"He offered to marry you?" he asked.

"So, he could give me to his daughter like a sweet from the bakers," I said. "He would marry me as a method of payment for obtaining me, so he could then control my life and do with it as he pleased."

I could not continue. I felt my throat grew thick and my heart could not be consoled.

"Are you certain he did not mean to have you as his wife, in his home?" Richard asked.

"He said he would marry me so he could take over my life and send me to live with Eva," I said.

"And you refused him."

"Of course," I said.

"Well, you are a different sort of woman. That is the second titled man who has proposed to you, a marquess no less, and you reject him."

"You did hear the part about him giving me over to his married daughter as if she still needs a plaything, did you not?"

"I did, but when I sent you to live with him, I told him you could stay until he remarried. He swore he never would. I bet him a hundred pounds he would marry again. I am not censuring your action, but rather the loss of my bet. I do wonder Myra, would you accept James Evans if he offered to you?"

"Did you see him at the charity social?" I asked.

"I did, he is courting at least three of those ladies," he said.

"I only saw two," I said.

"Oh yes…that is what I meant," he said looking away.

"It could be ten at this point. He made me…they both made me…I swore to myself some time ago I would never stand for being treated in a way that made me little. I would never let anyone treat me…"

"As father did," Richard finished.

"Yes," I said blinking away my tears.

"Well, neither man is cruel, Myra. They are just misguided. I think they will both come to see your value. Hopefully, one of them can do it before you are put off on the whole idea of marriage and converted to Catholicism to join a convent," he teased.

"Oh, that reminds me. Will you write young Jim Evans to postpone your fishing trip. The poor boy is likely waiting by the door for the post."

"I will. That bossy little girl may need a pair of real London gloves," he returned.

"It is a good thought; it may soften her some." I looked out the window again, thinking I may as well try to help the child since I would never marry. I would love Lawrence for the rest of my days, but he would never be my friend again. My value for his friendship far outweighed his for mine.

Chapter 9

The next morning, I sat like one who was dead. I had not slept but rolled Lawrence around in my head until I wanted to scream. I watched the road as the maid worked to repack my trunk. I did not admit to the rational part of me why I watched the road but was still humiliated that no carriage or even a note came.

I saw the strangest thing out the window. A young man who looked vaguely familiar glanced back and forth nervously while examining the house. Someone came up from the servant's stairs covered in a hot winter woolen cloak, unnecessary even for the morning in August. The cloaked figure crossed the street toward the man and happened to glance up at the house.

It was Clara.

I started and stood up. There was no raising of his hat or bow in greeting. He reached out for her hand and she gave it to the young man. He pulled her inappropriately close as he hooked her arm into his. Then he pulled her forward and disappeared into the brush of the park. I quickly scurried down the stairs and across the road into the park without stopping for my outer things.

The park was not large and had only a few trees and bushes. At the far side of the park was a hired hackney. Only ten yards from the carriage I easily discovered the couple. Huddled behind a bush they discussed something in urgent undertones I could not understand; the young man was insisting, and Clara was trying to refuse him.

"What is this?"

Clara started and looked at me, terrified. The young man moved in front of her, not in protection, but as if he were claiming her.

"How do I know you, Sir?" I said looking at the boy, his sandy brown hair and greens eye seemed so familiar, but I was not able to place him in the bustle of London.

"We are in the same parish," he said looking at Clara.

"What is your name?" I asked.

"This is Mr. Titus Williams. His family is renting Meadow Way for the summer, the fresh air is to do his Aunt good from the London air where they primarily reside," she said.

"If that is so Sir, what are you doing in London?" I asked.

"I am running an errand for my aunt, picking up some of her things from our house here," he said squinting at me, examining me as if to decide how to talk to me.

"Are your father and mother at home? Perhaps we ought to consult with them about clandestine meetings at such an early hour in the park," I replied.

"My mother died in childbirth. My father has gone north for a week. His brother is there."

"Perhaps you are to join him soon and could not stop for even a moment to enter my brother's presence?" I asked. Clara said sadly, "His father is making him go up to see his cousin. A young lady who is a great favorite of theirs. Father says I am not to make a match so young."

"I see," I said, "and yet, I find you here being lured out into the park without a chaperone by this young man?"

"I am not luring …" He cringed at the picture I painted. "We are in correspondence and I learned she is in London, so I came by to--"

"Let us start over," I interrupted. "This time you will not act as though I am a simpleton. Considering you would be in the drawing-room for a visit, or you would have met with us in public last night when my niece expected you. What is really happening here?" I asked.

He seemed to think this over.

"It would be best if you gave me the truth," I said.

Clara started to cry and threw herself into my arms.

"His father is insisting he marry his cousin, and he wishes to marry me. I do not think I am--"

"We love each other," he said. "We must be together before my father can force me to…"

"What?" I asked, choking over the way he said "be together," did not imply marriage was necessary.

"I…" Clara sniffled, "his family is in banking, and we are… with grandfather exploiting our finances and reputation so badly his father will not consent…"

I looked to the man, he looked back and forth from Clara blubbering the whole story to me, and the hired hackney. He was reading me. He was plotting in his head, trying to find the easiest way out of the situation. I could feel his deceit in every innocent word Clara uttered.

"…I swear Aunt, I would not have gone today. I meant to come back and confide in you and my mother," she cried.

I felt horrible. I would have to break Clara for him to come clean. She would never recover if I did not.

"Well dear, all is not lost," I said looking to him.

"How so?" he asked suspiciously. I turned to Clara and said, "He is now honor-bound to marry you. To take a young girl, a gentleman's daughter, away from her home in this way, your father will insist he marry you simply to keep your reputation intact. Come back, dear. It will be uncomfortable at first, but true love will win the day," I said.

"Perhaps we ought to…if she stays with you, this outing is simply a supervised--" Mr. Williams started.

"Not so. I cannot lie, not even for young love. Besides, confessing is the best way to go. Your father, Sir, will have no choice but accept the match when my brother appeals to the law."

"I…I wish to consult my father before we… I owe him an…" he stammered.

"You said we could not explain to our fathers. You, who hate your father, were content to leave without saying good-bye. You spent many days convincing me that we must run away," she said.

"I did not mean to…I cannot…"

"I suppose now, after being exposed, you will not marry without your father's consent," I said.

"I cannot, he will cut me off. His money is not entailed; He has complete control over it."

"But if he condemned the match, surely you already came to terms with being cut off. If you meant to run off today you must have faced your diminished circumstance, or perhaps you have consulted him," I said.

"I…I did not need to consult him…he made it…"

"Then let us post the banns. Surely, he will relent when he sees the respectability of my niece and brother," I said.

"We need not do anything so hasty," Mr. Williams said.

"Sir, my brother is the grandson of Baron Bolton. Our finances were nothing more than what many of the old families have gone through. Your father, in his business life, could not afford to be so quick as to reject Clara's claim to your heart," I said. "Let us appeal to him."

"I will not," he said.

"You choose not to then," I said turning to my niece. "Clara, his father would certainly approve the match considering he is an upstart and we have been of the nobility for centuries."

"I do not understand," Clara said, looking horrified like she did understand. Still, she had to hear it, or she would remain his prey.

"You have not the intention of marrying my niece," I said.

"I...I did not think to..."

"Titus," Clara asked.

"I cannot always..." He flushed red.

"You would have ... you meant to ruin me," Clara said, tears pooling in her wide eyes and stark white face.

"Clara, he did not bring a bag, nor anything that denotes running away. He hired a Hackney when he must have a carriage to run away with you. I understand from his aunt he owns several carriages. Which means he did not wish to be recognized. Why else wouldn't he have sought you out among our equals in the garden when you expected him last night? Again, he feared being recognized or rather implicated if you went missing. It is only a cad who would meet a young lady in such a dishonorable way as this. He has no intention of leaving London. He has admitted his London home empty, but only this week. Where do think he would have taken you?"

"I...I don't... how dare you?" Clara asked reviewing the circumstances until she could only come to my conclusion.

"You can confess, or I will push until the banns are posted," I said.

"You cannot expect me to marry this young," he said.

"You would have ruined me," she said again.

"Don't be so old fashioned," he mocked. "It is nothing. Everyone in London is... out in the country...you are so far behind. My father's house is near here. I would have brought you back before you were even missed." He reached for her hand. "We could have been together. What does it matter if we are married if we love each other?"

Clara pulled away from the young man, her mouth aghast in astonishment.

"I ... I would go home now Aunt," she said.

"Of course, dear," I said. Turning to the young man, I hissed, "If you ever come near her again, I will have the Duke of Surry bury you, your father and his bank, so deeply even royalty could not afford the manpower necessary to unearth it. I have immensely powerful friends. You have only money."

I turned Clara back to toward our lodgings and she curled into me.

"Not yet, Dear. We never let the unworthy see they broke us, never," I said. The way she put her chin forward and her shoulders back made me proud.

We happened upon Richard as we entered the house.

"Clara darling, what happened?"

"We went to stretch our legs in the park before we must sit on the train. She stubbed her toe rather hard," I said.

"Oh dear, shall I send for--"

"Please do not. As soon as we are sitting on the train, I shall be fine," Clara said, running up the stairs. Richard looked at me. He could see something was going unsaid. He patted my arm and said:

"Thank you for looking after my girl."

I bowed and followed her up the stairs. I entered the room we shared to find her face down on the bed. I held the girl in my arms as she wept. I truly could not comprehend how that man could reach so far into the gorge of darkness to tell himself he had the right to use her so abysmally. Seeing her face when she realized what was happening, I could not imagine the horror she would have been in if he'd managed to get her away from the park. Not to mention what she would have to live with inside herself, if he'd gotten away with his scheme, she would have been sent away, confined, never let back into good society. He would have gone back to school. He would have continued his life as if nothing happened. If he never shared her shame, why would he bother sharing her concern?

Lawrence and his father preached that every man doing his duty kept society going. Eva and I disagreed, probably because as women we'd been more vulnerable than they. Yet some people never reach that level of enlightenment and needed consequences to teach them. It should be the Williams boy who was sent away and never again received into good society, not this poor sobbing girl in front of me.

The convent was looking the better alternative for both Clara and me every day.

After her sobs softened, I made her sit up at the dressing table. Fixing my appearance was a ritual I performed after a run-in with my father. I did not know what else to do but help her make the effort to tidy her appearance. I quickly twisted her hair elaborately, even though it would sit under her bonnet. It was something I had to do, so no one would see. Stay quiet, hide the mess under a mask of calm tranquility, and always look presentable. I did not know what else to do. I transferred this to Clara, making her look fine on the outside, no matter what she went through on the inside. She kissed her mother and aunt, thanking both for their efforts on her behalf. Both were distracted by other concerns, and neither noticed Clara was not quite right.

When we reached the train station, I kept my arm linked in hers. The London station was far more enclosed than the country station we left from. Clara stayed close to me, nervous about the throngs of people we encountered in such a small space. The platform was in a shed of sorts and the air was steamed by engines preparing to leave.

We walked out on the platform as a train came in billowing smoke around us. The heat and soot picked up my dress and stole my breath, pitting us in a tornado of turmoil. Clara took my hand as if she would be carried away, and I stood in front of her to ground us while the burning air surrounded us. I did not flinch when the brakes screeched to bring the huge metal creature to a stop before us. When the smoke cleared, Clara unhitched herself from my side and looked about to be sure we had made it through the ordeal together. She dropped my hand and took my arm again.

"That is one moment, dearest. We will make it through the rest. I promise I will see you through this."

She could not reply but set her head on my shoulder.

Eva and his grace Duke Jonah Garrett came upon us. Whether it was the way Clara looked to be choking on the air, as if she may sob at any moment, or the way she clung to me, Eva knew we were distressed. She came up to stand with me, taking my other arm. Jonah examined us.

"I am sorry for your loss," I said to him.

"Thank you, Miss Bolton. By the end, my Grandfather saw it as freedom from this cage, and so we are all striving to see it that way as well," he said.

"Is your mother already at your grandfather's estate?" I asked.

"She is, and she will be most happy to see you. She considers you one of her closest friends," Jonah said bowing to me. I dropped my head, thankful Lady Garrett saw me as a friend.

Lawrence walked out onto the platform. Seeing me, he walked quickly to us. He opened his mouth to say something but stopped. I gave him a sharp look then glanced at my niece. He knew I needed more than our argument from him at this moment. It had always been this way when Eva needed us united. He examined her red blotchy nose, and the rims of her eyes. He said nothing but stood by us in compassion. He did not even take up the argument with Richard, who managed to secure our tickets and came to stand by his daughter. All traces of their battle swept away in the darkness, not fully understood.

We climbed into the same carriage and soon Clara hid in my shawl until she cried herself to sleep. At which point Richard asked, "Is it serious Myra?"

"She will recover. Thank God, I intervened when I did. I assure you, brother, no real damage was done to her, though your neighbors, the Williams, ought not ever to be admitted into your home again."

"I told her the lad was a scoundrel," Richard growled taking my shawl and his sleeping girl from my side and re-situating her into his arm, "Thank you for intervening, Myra," he said kissing her bonnet and pulling her closer into his side.

Chapter 10

We rode the train for over three hours to traverse the forty-one miles. I felt Lawrence watching me often. I knew he felt bad about our argument, but I did not want his apology. It was easier to find fault with him and build up vengeance against him than it was to feel vulnerable in my unrequited love for him. Albeit, after the morning's trauma, I felt my love for him at least worthy. He and I had been a team, perhaps not husband and wife, but an extremely effective team. Was it so unheard of that I would get confused?

He deserved a woman's affection, that much could be acknowledged. Something in me stopped feeling so humiliated for loving him; I talked myself back into it. I should be humiliated. To love without any reassurances in return turned me into a burning hole that grew bigger and emptier every time I saw him. The emotional fight I made within myself to keep from looking at him coupled with the sleepless night and the morning's events exhausted me, and I leaned against my brother's arm that held my niece and slept for the last hour.

I woke and looked up to find Lawrence reaching out to steady me. The train slid, almost as if out of control. Finally, after a screechy lurch, it stopped.

"Thank you, Sir," I said leaning back and pushing against the window frame to steady myself.

In Reading, we alighted. Lawrence climbed down and helped Eva down. Duke Garrett came next and took his wife tenderly in his care. Lawrence relinquished her, but he looked lost doing so. Eva glanced at him, a look of concern swept across her face before she could replace it with a smile. He would be lonely at Grey Manor when Eva left on her wedding trip. In time, he would have to give up always caring for her, but he practiced at it for so long, how was that to be accomplished?

"Come, I will hire a carriage to convey us to the house. Miss Bolton, I hope you and your family will stay with us there," Duke Garrett said.

"We can take a room at this inn," I said looking to my brother.

"It is not necessary. My Uncle gave me many rooms for whomever I meant to invite, and I did not fill half of them," he said.

"We would be honored then," Richard said.

The Inn only had a small carriage, so the gentlemen were given a chance to ride, which Richard and Duke Garrett took. Lawrence passed the opportunity and instead sat across from me in the carriage.

The carriage set off. Clara looked despondently out the window, and shuddered with every breath she took. I wondered if she would appear the most somber of mourners.

"Myra," Lawrence started. I shook my head.

"Never mind what we said to each other. I was too sensitive. You were only trying to be kind," I said, knowing in my heart of hearts I'd already forgiven him.

"I did not think about what I said before I spoke," he said.

"I know you did not mean it; let us just put it behind us," I said.

"I cannot. Will you allow me to apologize?" he said and glanced at Clara, waiting for me to respond. I could see he meant to start her healing, by making her laugh. He would be self-deprecating and show Clara that a true gentleman apologizes when he is in the wrong. It was this kind of a thing that made me think I would never find his equal. And so, I would play along, though it meant I had to let him know

I forgave him to set a good example for Eva and Clara. He knew I would, and this frustrated me even more.

"I suppose," I said slowly, "you could start by admitting that I do not hold the same place as the equine in your household." Clara and Eva looked at me confused.

"He compared me to Eva's horse in importance to his daughter," I said.

"That was ungenerous," Clara said trying to understand. Eva, seeing our mission, as we had used the same tactics to cheer her up many times, joined in, saying, "Surely, he at least put you before the horse in importance,"

"Equal to," I said.

"I did perhaps treat you like Avon, but not out of disrespect toward you," he said.

"But rather respect to the horse," I answered.

"I am not sure one can be compared to a horse without being disrespected," Clara said too seriously.

"Myra, if you have been treated like my horse, you must at least acknowledge Avon is more inappropriately a member of the family. And have you ever been asked to sleep in the stables?" Eva asked, a glint in her eyes.

"Do not let Hetty hear you. She may redo my rooms in hays and troughs."

Clara laughed a little and Eva smiled at our efforts.

"I only meant to make a point," Lawrence continued. "We have been together for many years now, and I feel like I've not only lost my daughter, but my friend."

"You and Eva will always be great friends. Thankfully, Duke Garrett is not a jealous man, so that need not end," I said.

"I meant you. Have we not been great friends Myra?" he asked.

"I thought we had until you equated my value to Avon," I said too seriously, looking out the window.

"I...everything is changing too quickly for me," he said.

"That I can well believe."

"I had hoped Eva would be with me—"

"Forever Sir? You cannot begrudge her happiness," I said.

"I do not, yet, she is to live in Surry of all counties," he said looking at her.

"It is only two counties over, an easy distance with the trains going. I suppose it is fortuitous you do not get an ache in your belly when you travel," I said.

"I already miss you, Myra, and you have not been gone more than seven days," he said. "You cannot come back to Grey Manor to visit me?"

"No Sir, it would not be appropriate," I said sternly looking at his innocent expression like he could not understand the dilemma.

"You and my father are great friends," Clara said.

"Yes, for many years," he said looking at her to find a point.

"You could come to visit us, Sir," she said.

"I...uh..." he looked at Clara, then to me.

"I would like to come to meet this man whom you mean to marry Myra," he said.

"I am not... there is no understanding. I wish you would all stop implying I even wish to marry Mr. James Evans," I said.

"Wait. Is this the same James whom..." Eva trailed off. I had told her of our exploits as children.

"Yes Dearest, but he has changed, and is no longer very..." I stopped and blushed.

"Perhaps on our way to Dover we may –" Eva started.

"Go hundreds of miles out of your way to look at a man?" I asked.

"Or we could sail from—"

"I have my father's fast little clipper sitting in the dock at Weymouth," Lawrence said. "I could convey you over when you are ready to go. It would be faster, and we could go—"

"Lawrence, I know you want to go somewhere in your ship, but on your daughter's wedding trip with her is not advisable," I said.

"Besides Your Grace, you will wish to wait to meet Mr. Evans. Papa says he is a work in progress. He has been through a bad marriage and Aunt is just what he needs to heal," Clara said innocently enough.

"That does not sound fair to Myra," Lawrence said turning to me. Pinning me with his stare, he asked, "Is he kind to you?"

"I have only been in company with him twice since my return," I said.

"You've only been gone seven days and two of those were spent in London," Eva pointed out.

"She has met with him three times if you count church," Clara said.

"What do the neighbors say?" Lawrence asked turning back to Clara, who seemed to forget all her troubles.

"Mrs. Robinson says that he means to court the entire county of spinsters until he finds a woman who will worship him like a Greek God. Excepting the Dodgson's, who have an," Clara paused and glanced at me unsure what to say, "Well, an aging daughter of their own, most everyone else who has been long in the neighborhood hopes he will eventually settle on Aunt Myra and will remember himself when he is with her."

I opened and then closed my mouth. I did not know the whole neighborhood talked about my marrying James.

"Well, I will certainly come for a visit," Lawrence said folding his arms across his chest. Eva looked at me and grinned. I looked back to question her amusement, but she quickly looked out the window.

Chapter 11

Since Lord Devon died at Grey Manor, Lawrence hired an undertaker and sent his manservant with the body to see that everything was done properly. The undertaker put the body of Lord Devon in a lead coffin and insisted, due to rank and position, his remains be embalmed. He hoped the nobleman might be preserved until his funeral could be accomplished.

The man, with every decency available to him, brought the body back, stopping only twice at inns, and covering the room in black cloth. The Undertaker kept Lord Devon's hereditary pennant flying above the hearse and was paid twice for taking such care with the body, once by Lawrence, and another time by Lord Devon's son, who now occupied Lord Devon's home, the Gramdent House, and his titles.

The Great Country House was everything grand and imposing it ought to be. Formed in the Gothic style of a medieval castle, huge stones lay together to create turrets and a spectacular tower overlooking the valley. The courtyard, which was more of a garden square with many trees and a fountain, was full of funeral guests, as the ceremony would take place just after sunset. The gun salute already started, and the animals tromped nervously in anticipation of the next round. Thankfully, Lord Devon was not a royal and his son only insisted the firing go off every hour on the hour instead of every five minutes.

"Do you think knights once defended their lady's honor in this courtyard?" Clara asked sadly, looking as if her knight deflated in her young imagination.

"The building can't be much older than fifty years, dear," I said.

"Despite its reputed fame, it is a poorly executed reproduction, much like certain knights of our day," Eva whispered lifting her eyes at Clara and we all laughed so Clara did not cry. I led the way through the courtyard feeling stiff, trying to stretch out my sore neck. For all I said to defend fast travel, my stomach was queasy.

The entryway, grand and beautiful with imported stone and crystal, could not be appreciated. Lord Devon's stench after seven days, even shielded with turpentine, lavender and chamomile, was pronounced. The dining room was a huge room shaped like a cylinder. Crown molding grew up the walls into medallions on the ceiling, all converging on a huge glorious chandelier the shape of a woman in an old fashion ball gown.

The table that would comfortably seat forty people held the corpse of Lord Devon, pastries, cakes, and wine. We paid our respect. His skin had not taken to the embalming, or the miles of traveling, because it began to slip off his skeleton. The corpse enhanced my nausea, but no one else seemed to notice. They ate and drank to the body, despite the putrid smell.

We were eventually shown to the nicest rooms in the house to freshen up. Duke Garrett being the highest in rank and we being of his party, our rooms were richly decorated and grandly situated, only one floor up from the corpse. The stench followed us. Since there was no escaping it, Clara and I, who chose to share a room since the bed was so large it could fit an entire family, changed quickly and went down. The immediate family all stood in the large entryway greeting guests.

It was interesting to see the way the family treated Duke Garrett. He had only been a Duke for a little over twelve months. Duke Garrett's father had been the second son of the honorable Garrett family, who jealously guarded every title, scrap of land, and wealth for the eldest son. This left Mr. Garrett and his wife, who retained her title from her father, to fall back often on the generosity of Lord Devon.

Being considered a poor relation, they stayed much of the year with Lord Devon who now lay on the dining room table. Most of the family referred to Duke Garrett in his youth as Lord Devon's lackey because he followed his grandfather everywhere.

When the previous Duke Garrett took his two sons to examine their holdings in the West Indies, he meant to leave the second to make his fortune on the property. The last Duke Garrett was warned that even the royal family did not travel together. He was famously quoted as saying even the ocean feared the great Duke of Surry. He tempted the tempest, and the ship was capsized in the middle of the ocean leaving his nephew everything, wealth so concentrated, it tasted far too strong on the current Duke Garrett's lips.

Now all his mother's relations fidgeted around him in respect and wondered what sort of man he grew up to be. They could no longer call him squire and tell him to saddle their horses, and yet, addressing him as Your Grace, seemed to get stuck in their throats.

"Oh Myra, thank you for coming," Lady Garrett greeted me warmly.

"Of course. Are you managing your grief," I asked?

"I am trying," she said, a tear falling.

"Is there any task I can do to lighten your burden?" I asked.

"No, no, everything is taken care of. This grief is an old friend, something I must live through. Thank you for coming," she said, taking the hand I offered. Despite her genuine kindness, she did not linger near me. She seemed to need to interact with her brothers and sister, who could share the full impact of losing their father. Lord Devon's oldest son strutted about the entryway as if to look important and busy, but I could not tell that he did anything. He looked a little lost without his father.

I found it interesting to watch the family unit at work as I'd grown up so much younger than my siblings. Lady Garrett had an arm around her sister while her brother complained to her about something, a third brother kept fidgeting his hands about, and Lady Garrett often appeared to be comforting him. I envied my dear friend her family.

Lady Garrett's children also seemed to gravitate around each other. Duke Garrett had many younger siblings who were all being set to advantage since he'd inherited so much. They also revolved around each other more comfortably together than apart. Duke Garrett's sisters all doted on Eva, and I loved to see her with so much family about. Eventually, Eva called Clara to come to meet the other young people. I encouraged her to go. I kept my face tranquil, so she did not stay back because she could see the loneliness overtaking me as her warmth withdrew.

"What are you thinking Myra?" Lawrence asked coming up behind me.

"I think I missed out on something," I said sighing deeply.

"Nonsense. Many women do not have children, but you could never have been more of a mother to Eva over these years."

"I do feel much satisfaction over her, but I am not speaking in that direction," I said, "I grew up alone with my mother and then she died. Until I came to you I never really..."

I stopped and sighed, unsure of how to say what I was feeling.

"What is it, Myra?" he asked.

"I never had a family like that," I said nodding to the Garretts, "unless you consider...we were a family, were we not?"

81

"Yes, we lived very happily in our little hybrid family. Are you sorry you did not marry when you had the chance?" he asked. I looked at him. He looked sad, or was it guilty?

"Don't take that upon yourself," I said putting a hand on his arm. "I made my own choice. I only had one offer, and I did not consider it a chance, but a prison sentence."

"The Baron you mean?"

"He...he was my father's friend. An old man who had been married many times. All his wives seemed to die in strange ways. The last one hadn't been gone but a few months when he began negotiating with my father."

"Your father would marry you to this man?" Lawrence asked.

"He offered to pay off all the debt we had. My father, he... he died while a settlement was being agreed upon. I was not sorry when my father died. My father was bartering with my life, and he wanted more than I was worth. He had not signed anything yet, because the Baron would not give him enough. In his anger, he drank more than his body could handle, and he... I could not be sorry."

"I am not sorry he died, either," Lawrence said watching me closely while I watched Eva and her new family.

"Richard, after he took over the household, he gave me a chance. He told me something had to be done about the debt, but his old friend had a daughter who needed ... she needed me, Lawrence, it was the first time I was truly needed by another person."

"She did," he answered.

"But she doesn't anymore," I said. "When your father died, she still needed me, but not now. Look at all she has. You and Eva have so much family now, and my family has ended. We will not gather at Christmas or for parties during the season. It all just ended, and I was not prepared for it. I don't know what to do now."

"I understand more than you can know," he said watching Eva laughing with Duke Garretts youngest sister, who was only fifteen.

"Rather you are the only one who can know I suppose," I said.

"Yes," he answered.

"What do we do now Sir?" I asked.

"Perhaps we will dance at your wedding Myra. You are young still, you may have a child of your own," he said.

I turned bright red and nudged him.

"Oh, sorry Myra I always forget I cannot talk to you as I would..."

I looked up at him.

"As you would who Sir?"

"I... just ... oh, never mind it was an odd fancy," he said fidgeting as he watched his feet uncomfortably.

"Thank you for being my family for a time Sir," I said smiling at him so he would stop being self-conscious. I felt this smile and did not keep it contained. Lawrence did not mind the real me. He stopped and stared at me. I could see something in his jaw twitching. His eyes moved back and forth between mine and he looked close to saying something. He opened his mouth, but then shut it.

"Is everything all right?" I asked.

"Come, let us get this poor man into the vault next to his wife," he said giving me his arm. He took me to the dining room. We were pressed to take wine and cake in honor of the deceased.

Lawrence seemed particularly thirsty and though myself, and even Eva eventually tried to moderate him, he appeared out of sorts and drawn to the artificial spirits. I had only seen Lawrence drunk once before. It was a heart-wrenching experience and I could not tolerate such again. Thankfully, my brother took over the care of his friend when we all removed to the courtyard, so the body could be entombed again.

By the time the candles were lit, and the procession called, I could not be near Lawrence. Wine always brought out the tenderness in him. He often professed his love for anyone who stood too close. Lady Garrett insisted her daughters be sent up to their rooms, as she felt it was not a scene for young girls. I asked that Clara go too, but she did not wish to be separated from me, and Jonah asked that I stay close to Eva since her father was incapacitated.

The procession collected in the courtyard, and I took Clara's arm insisting she stay by my side, as some of the bystanders could get a touch rowdy. We put on the scarfs we were offered. The titled men put on their cloaks out of respect for the deceased Earl. The black velvet showed off their family crests. All the other men of the procession, including my brother, wore hatbands and black kid gloves.

There was an awkward moment when Duke Garrett, was given preference as the chief mourner because he outranked his uncle, his black cloak being the longest. Duke Garrett stepped back in favor of his uncle.

"Please Sir," his uncle said, "the College of Arms will be our guide."

"The undertaker is not so rigid," Duke Garrett said looking to the man.

"It is not for me to dictate Sirs," said the Undertaker, clearly intimidated by the status and titles surrounding him. Most in his profession referred to the College of Arms religiously.

"Come, Uncle," Duke Garrett said. "I will walk with my father-in-law."

"I do love the boy immensity," Lawrence slurred, not doing just respect to his robe adorned with the house of Hull's arms, held out by two mutes behind him.

"Yes, perhaps that would be better," The new earl agreed, walking forward to take the prime spot, after being sure his nephew was still in the forefront of the prominent mourners. Arm in arm with Clara and Eva, I walked outside the courtyard to see the front of the procession. Signaling the start of the march, the gun rang. This time I stood close enough to see the flash break the darkness for only a breath, then it was gone, but the ringing in my ears remained.

We were stopped by a soldier in uniform. At first, I thought to scoot around him but noticed he and a few other soldiers were all that separated us from a throng of locals who lined the road to the churchyard to witness the procession.

The house stood on rising ground. Five hundred torches descended along the road. Shadows beneath the torches jostled for position as the firelight wavered in the warm breeze. The procession moved slowly. It began with the Devon family crest waving on over twenty banners flapping above head in a long column. Musicians moaned between them the soft beauty of Handel's "Dead March," from "Saul," soothing all who heard it. The banners beat on the breeze to keep time.

As the prominent mourner, the new Earl proceeded the body of the one who left us.

A single, huge black horse drew the hearse, it clip-clopped to the ebb and flow of the music. The coffin paraded in front of us just as the trumpet sounded triumphally announcing the separation of the shell, the earth-heavy body and the soul which soared lightly home. Shielded by a black canopy, the pall covering the coffin could not be reached by the glow of the silvery moon. Instead, only the unnatural yellow glow from the carriage lanterns showed the gorgeous ornate Prussian blue velvet pall with the heraldic symbols sewn onto it.

As the march drew away, the music dimmed slowly to my ears like the setting sun. As the music diminished, I heard

Clara whisper wishes to God and without giving direction to my mouth, I found it whispering in earnest, "Though I walk through the valley of the shadow of death...."

The words spewed from me, and I remembered Lady Claremont Hull declare to Eva, a spinster could only wish to die young. I thought it cruel but now found the statement fair. I did wish to go to my rest, with no purpose left on this earth to occupy me. No path left to tread. The path moving along the bank of Hull river was closed off to me. Nothing could be left in the sorrow of heartbreak, and the passage of my opportunity.

I looked up just in time to see Lawrence walk by. He turned and looked straight at me. He moved his mouth to say something. A wind with a slight chill reprimanded him by whipping his robes about, keeping my mortal ears from hearing. The night insisted we not focus on our lives, but instead on that of the dead, which ended with no regret.

"Myra," Eva asked in my ear.

"Yes, Dearest," I responded looking at her. She looked beyond me toward the capes that passed us and turned back in the night, showing the different coats of arms in the torchlight, men disappearing in their heraldry.

"If you do not marry, will you come back to me?" she asked, turning to examine me. Did she see the hopelessness oppressing me?

"I will make my brother swear to it. If I try to win James and am not successful, I will make him swear that I may be allowed to come and raise your children with you."

"I do wish for you to marry and have a family of your own, but I do not know how to live life without you."

"Oh Darling," I said, "part of growing up is leaving behind the guidance of your childhood and finding your own way."

"I supposed, but it does make me heart-sore for you to leave me. I wish there were some way I could guarantee we are still often in each other's lives," she said.

"You will invite me for a visit, and I will do everything in my power to come. I will care for you when you have your children. When you need me, I will come," I said.

"Yes, and I suppose Clara does need your guidance more than I do," she said nodding at the girl, whose drawn face shown in the torchlight, her tears glistening. I pulled her warmth back into my side so I could protect her.

This made me stop. The girl did need my help. Though I was a spinster I had helped many people in the last few days. Certainly, James did not want my help, but someone needed to point out his father would not have put up with such things in his own home. Clara also benefited from my presence. Perhaps there were somethings I could still do for the world, though the opportunity of marriage eluded me.

"I love you, dearest," I said pulling Eva close to me against the cooling breeze of the night. She laid her head on my shoulder, and we pulled Clara in, so she did not have to cry alone. After the procession ended a carriage stopped in front of us and we joined Lady Garrett and her sister. Clara almost sat on my lap, but she was such a small thing it did not concern me.

"I do wish we could march," Lady Garrett said to her sister.

"At least we are being admitted into the funeral," Eva said.

"Yes, in the very back; ought not I be able to mourn with my brothers?"

"There are too many of the titled here," her sister said, "if it were just us, you know nothing would be withheld."

"Being admitted into the funeral is a step forward, and even if a small step it, is still better than no step," I said, smiling at my friend.

"That is true," Lady Garrett said.

"Tell me stories of your father," I asked hoping to soothe her wound. I indulged her by listening to stories of growing up with her father, aided by her sister. We arrived in the churchyard laughing and crying together for their father.

A moderate stone church, complete with a steeple, seemed to grow out of the churchyard, the moon shone on it as we moved. We alighted the carriage and an armed guard walked us into the church. I noticed the regiment that guarded the road as we passed had now congregated at the gate to the churchyard.

The crowd behind them, in contrast to the bright torch lights, made vague unknown movements and sounds as if under a black murmuring sheet. It frightened me.

We slipped in the back of the church to the benches under the columns. The organ music already started. We stayed back so that our emotions would not offend.

The Archbishop of Oxford performed the service, and no one seemed in a hurry to put the poor soul to rest. The most reverend archbishop could have preached all night, and no one would have budged. After the service, the casket was moved out a side door to the graves. We slipped out the back.

"We cannot go," Lady Garrett's sister said.

"Take Clara back to the carriage," I whispered to Eva. I would see my friend pay her father his last respects. They climbed into the carriage, while Lady Garrett and I slipped quietly through the field of the dead where we could see the procession enter the tomb.

The old mossy building accepted the coffin into its cold storage.

"It is original, from fifteen hundred. The house burnt down about seventy years ago and was completely rebuilt. The tomb was left untouched," Lady Garrett whispered.

We could not go where Lord Devon was placed inside the large stone tomb of his family by the side of his wife. We stood in the graveyard, lit by the moon, and listened to all that was said echoing from places where the stones came loose. Lady Garrett whispered, "I love you, papa," as we heard the scraping of the sarcophagus closing over his coffin after the archbishop said many beautiful things over the tomb and prayed. Lady Garrett sobbed quietly under the moonlight. I stood with her. And this gave me purpose.

We mourned together, I the loss of my dear girl's childhood, she the loss of he who was the last remnant of hers. I cried with Lady Garrett feeling I was put on this earth to mourn with those who mourn. I would think no more of love I could not have, marriage or diminished prospects. I may be a spinster, but I would certainly not allow it to define me. I would be the person whom other people could lean on. Even if I could not be a surrogate mother to Eva anymore, I would find others who needed me. I could be whole in helping others become whole.

When we heard the procession retreating from the shroud, we stole back over the grass busy with headstones until we made it back to the carriage. This time our carriage led the way. The crowd seemed restless and we heard a few of the guards on horseback yelling at them, as they escorted us back to the Great House.

"I suppose one must hope to find a gentleman one can be buried next to," Clara said, sighing deeply as she looked out the window at the torches.

"I know it is not the fashionable way, but it would be best if you truly get to know the gentleman. Do not allow your fancy to drive the match," I said.

"When I am put up at the marriage market, I will try to remember that," she said leaning back against me, looking tired.

"I will go with you. Together we will figure it out," I said and felt her relax.

"There is but one love of your life, one man who can but satisfy a woman's heart. When you find him, you will be fine, my dear," Lady Garrett said weeping, "I have lost both of mine now, my husband and my father. I feel so alone."

She leaned against her sister. We started at the final firing of the salute: Bang! rang out the shot fired, the coffin closed, and it was over.

We climbed out of the coach and were escorted into the house. I looked over the refreshments, but they had grown stale with the corpse, and the stench had not cleared out yet. Lady Garrett and her sister partook and seemed pleased with the offerings. Something was disarming about the dried-out cakes and warm wine which put Eva, Clara, and I off. After a time, the procession came in singing and rowdy. My mouth dropped.

"Lawrence, what happened to you?" I asked, moving to him with a cloth napkin to catch the blood dripping over his left eye.

"Ah, there you are Myra; did you know your brother has played an awful trick on me?"

"Can someone call his man down here? This needs sewing up," I said holding the napkin to it.

"Are you not curious what trick has been played on me?" Lawrence said, searching my eyes, his soul peering out of his. Capturing me unprepared, he put a hand on my waist and drew me in. I moved back instantly.

"Sir you ought not to expose yourself any longer," I said. Then I panicked.

"Richard, will you see your old friend to bed," I begged.

"No, my Rose, I will not go," Lawrence said. I flinched when he reached out and brushed his fingers across my light hair tinted in peaches, his curved fingers dropped caressing the blush growing deep on my face. I took a step back, but he moved with me. He put his arms around me fitting our bodies together and lay his head on my shoulder. I hesitated only a moment, feeling his curling hair on my cheek. When his lips started to nibble at my neck, I quickly pushed him away. Finally, my brother pulled him back. Lawrence grew irate and shoved Richard.

"You sent her to me, like an angel, to save us. Then you take her back!"

"You are drunk," Richard said pulling him away again.

Lawrence turned to me. Pulling free of Richard, he reached and curled his hand around my neck. He pled with me: "He took you back. He lifted me only to drop me down. Why do you leave me, Rosy? Why do you leave me?" Lawrence reached for me. His man came in and took his arm, pulling him about his shoulder, he heaved him away while his master moaned, "Isn't she beautiful, my perfect Rose?"

"Who is his Rose?" Richard asked.

"I believe that is what he called his late wife," I said trying not to feel the sting. "When he gets drunk, he forgets she is gone."

"He never called her Rose," Eva said. "He only ever called her sweetheart. I did hear him call you a rose once to describe you when you were not around for Squire Gossett to see."

I blushed, glancing at Eva with big eyes, begging her to be quiet on the subject. Eva stared at me as if considering. She could not be ignorant of the peach-colored roses growing in the conservatory at Grey Manor. The year before he died, her grandfather had been attempting to reproduce a French nurseryman's experiment to hybridize a red damask rose and

91

a white Old Bush Chinese rose to grow a pink flower. They had turned out a more rare and appealing peach to apricot color with massive groupings of petals which thrived after Henry Grey died, almost as if leaving the world with a little something of his goodness.

"I think it romantic, Aunt," Clara said to break the awkward silence.

"It is not," I snapped. "Romance is a sober man's game. Drunks are slobbering fools who have lost all sense. Do not trust one of these men until they have sobered up. Now we are for bed and we will be latching our door."

"Thank you, Myra," Richard said seeing the strong hold I had on Clara.

"No," called the new Lord Devon. "We must drink to the newlyweds, and free them from any obligation. I will myself buy your passage to the continent tomorrow, and you will go."

"Sir, we will mourn," Duke Garrett said looking to his mother and Eva in turn.

"No one expects newlyweds to mourn, Jonah," Lady Garrett said. "Your grandfather would not wish it. Take her tomorrow and leave on your wedding trip."

"Eva?" he asked.

"I will stand by your side whatever you decide," she said taking his hand.

"GO, GO, GO," many of the group chanted. Finally, Duke Garrett put up his hands to stop the clattering of voices and said, "We will go and live, by the honor of the one who died. He lived his chance to the fullest, and so will I." He turned, kissing his bride. The group all cheered, and everyone lifted their glasses, and a general chant took the room: "to the bride and groom."

Then many men grappled with each other, talked about kissing the bride.

"Eva, perhaps you should also…" Duke Garrett said looking at the riotous group.

"Shall I share your room tonight, Eva?" I asked looking at the men talking way too loudly.

"Yes, you and Clara both, there is plenty of room, we shall be snug," she said, taking my other arm. We moved to the stairs, Lady Garrett and her sister close on our heels.

Clara and I slept in Eva's large bed sharing the most heavenly goose down mattress. I was content as any mother with two babes in her arms could be, especially with the door securely bolted.

Chapter 12

The next morning, we packed our trunks. I helped Eva's new lady, so she might add all she would need for her trip after she made it to London. Then we gave them over to the servants and went to breakfast. Lawrence stood trying to find something to eat when we entered the room. He would not look at me. It was much like the only other time I'd ever witnessed him drunk. Thankfully, this time he had not kissed me.

Last time Eva had been stuck overnight at a friend's house due to a storm. Lawrence had been mourning his father. He indulged at dinner. A while after we dined, he came into the room where I sewed. Overcome with brandy, he insisted we dance a country jig to his father's memory. We were alone all evening, and it ended with him pulling me most dramatically into his arms and kissing me as only a husband has the right to kiss his wife. I thought he meant it. He did not know himself. What's worse, after he kissed me, I went to my bed-chamber believing he wooed me. That night I finally admitted to myself how much I loved him.

The next day, I dressed with such care. I skipped to breakfast only to find my grumpy master. Upon seeing me, animated in affection for him, that unfortunately, I did nothing to hide, he doused my fervor out like water to a fire before it could grow out of control. He did not directly confess he remembered the previous evening. He gave me to understand what I treasured as gold had been him confusing me for his wife. The whole of that day he spoke often about how a man who has been in love and truly valued his wife cannot have another one, even if the first has been gone for some time. As a duty to his late wife, he would honor her until he may join her.

I could almost hear Lawrence's father in the speech. They both spent their lives studying the human mind. Henry rigidly adhered to what he believed was his duty and any breach in duty equated to his loss of honor. I had not known Lawrence inherited his father's rigidity in the matter.

I learned.

Lawrence was not only a romantic, but prone to tragedies, and would never love another woman out of respect for his first wife.

I could forgive him for his rigidity if I had not entered into his tragedy. I would always feel his lips on mine and didn't think anyone else could ever satisfy me.

That is why this day I moved into the breakfast room quietly. I did not look to him expectantly. I lingered near Richard's paper, so I did not have to draw near him examining the food laid out. I did nothing to excite his concern that I may have thought his lips on my neck meant anything. Eva was not so quiet on the matter.

"Father, you were in a right state last evening. I think you missed the fact that Jonah and I will be going on our wedding trip in two days," she said loudly upon entering the breakfast room. He put a hand to his head and said,

"So soon, will you not—"

"It is not expected for newlyweds to mourn," Lord Devon said entering the room after her.

"Because they respect the severed relationship less?" Lawrence asked setting his empty plate on the table after unsuccessfully finding anything to tempt him.

"No, but rather we honor the deceased wishes for us to move forward with our lives. My father would not have wished them to begin their life together in sorrow," Lord Devon said winking at Eva looking more like his father in the action. Eva grinned and turned to her father. She said:

"I find it rather distracting that you of all people would speak so of disrespect considering your behavior to poor Miss Bolton."

"Yes," Richard said, "You nearly accosted my sister. Sir, what did you mean by it?"

"I…"

I could feel all eyes upon me. I looked at Lawrence. He was all agony. I took up a plate, and pretending to be occupied by the breakfast options. I said, "He does not know himself when he drinks. Richard, please leave him be."

"I…I am sorry if I," Lawrence stammered.

I waved him off, as if it were nothing. As if his lips hadn't seared their shape forever on my neck. Lawrence picked up his plate again, he came in close where I dished my breakfast at the sideboard. He followed me in disarming silence. He filled his plate with everything I choose. I knew he wanted to see my eyes, to see if he hurt me. I kept them moving. I forced myself to disconnect. To find the serenity and calm face I used to protect myself.

After his last drunken escapade, he mended his misstep in friendly albeit uncomfortable attentions to be sure I did not hate him. But he also said much to be sure I knew he would never consider beginning even a flirtation out of respect for the memory of his late wife.

Despite all he said, I could not pretend his behavior toward me wasn't meant to entangle me. He often called me pet names or did me little favors like picking up my favorite treats when he went to town. This only made the matter worse. I did not wish to soften this time. I wished to leave while hating him. That would be easier.

"Myra," he asked trying to get my attention.

"It does not signify," Eva said nudging me out of his way to get a poached egg, "she goes home tomorrow and will be out of reach from you, father. You, who might do her reputation harm, just as she has an opportunity towards a situation of her own."

"We are so far removed, I am sure none of this will reach his ears," Richard said taking a big bite of his beans, watching our interaction from the table.

"I do not think Myra even interested in the young man," Lawrence said trying to move around Eva to direct his next comment to me, "he sounds something like a scoundrel."

"No, he will right himself, father," Eva defended, turning to him squarely while I moved to sit next to my brother at the table, "Mr. Bolton says he is something like Edmund, full of potential. Myra will make him a fine wife, but even more important she will make a fine mother for his orphaned children."

This was not consistent with Eva's sentiments only last evening, wishing for me to come live with her if I did not marry. I looked between my young lady and my brother and I could see in them co-conspirators.

"Besides," the lady continued, "I have made it impossible for the man in question to overlook her. Now that we will leave so soon, I must tell her or risk her not knowing, or worse, explaining all in a letter. I mean to see the joy on her face and receive her gratitude."

I snapped my head up and looked at her.

"What have you done Eva?" Lawrence asked looking warily at his daughter.

"Myra is part of our family, so I have awarded her an income for services rendered to me in my youth," said Eva. "As you know, my husband has been working with parliament, and they all want to grant him these little sorts of favors. He started a letter of patents on Myra's behalf. We hope she will be entitled to a peer for life since she cannot inherit. Myra may be made a Baroness."

"Is that where you two went, leaving your poor father only a cryptic note stating that Mr. Bolton may never let Myra come to us again," Lawrence said, eyeing his daughter. "You went to make her independent."

"My Uncle holds the seat with sufficient heirs. I do not see how you can be successful in the endeavor," Richard said, but he smiled at Eva.

"Perhaps and perhaps not; it is only for life, but it is the practice among the highest of nobility to award those who have sacrificed and served them these little favors. Myra now has access to fifteen thousand pounds. I do not care to call it a dowry, because she need not marry to have it," Eva said.

"What?" Lawrence asked, looking from me to Eva. My mouth agape spoke volumes, as did the smile Eva gave Richard. Suddenly I understood Richard's hints to Eva. They felt I needed a husband. She must have gone out immediately with Jonah to give me money and position, so her father would not see me as his daughter's governess, nor his friend's baby sister any longer. I almost laughed.

They thought they could tempt Lawrence into marrying me.

"For all she has done, it is customary for ladies like Myra, who come from elite homes, but sacrifice for the good of the country, to be honored so. Queen Victoria gave her governess a title," Eva said.

"It is rumored that lady has come between the Queen and her husband. Perhaps one should not have their childhood roaming about when they are trying to be grown up," Lawrence said, holding his head that ached.

My heart dropped.

"You agree Myra should step back and let Eva establish her own home, with her new husband," Richard asked. Lawrence clenched his jaw. I felt anger surge through me. He did not mean to love me, in favor of the tragic love he held for his wife. He did not get to dictate what I did. Instead of answering, he chided,

"Eva, that is too much money. She will be the target of every fortune hunter in the country."

"She wished for a family of her own. Mr. Bolton, I believe you said her admirer cares about wealth?" Eva asked Richard, but glowered at her father.

"Yes, and he already saw her beauty, and kindness without any incentive. I do not think anything will hold him back now," he said bowing to Eva. "Thank you, my Lady."

She turned and bowed, she could not help smiling at Richard, who looked like he might laugh. There it was again. The two of them were almost play-acting, manipulating Lawrence. Forcing him to see me as a conquest, by setting up a rival in a man who had shown little interest in me. The strangest part of the game was that Lawrence didn't seem to see it being played. Usually, he saw everything. Instead of laughing along, proving he would not be manipulated, Lawrence grew heated.

"Eva, do you not see what you have done? Myra will be—"

"Given a chance," Eva said turning on her father. She looked angry. She did not feel his behavior the previous evening should be ignored.

"Please, do not spread this about," Lawrence said.

"I will not, but unfortunately, Aunt Claremont Hull knows. We had to consult Uncle on a few points to prepare the letter in such a hurry. Jonah's man is taking care of it all. It may even be submitted by now. Nothing can be done," she said. I cringed. This did not bode well. Not only would James suddenly make up his mind, but I could not guarantee who I would find at my doorstep. The simple beauty of anonymity in having just enough money to live comfortably without attracting attention was over for me.

"That is what we do, is it not father? Give noble ladies a chance?" she said. We all paused. Lawrence could not respond. Lady Garrett rushed into the room and said:

"We must hurry."

"What is the matter?" I asked, moving to my friend who looked very tired still.

"We must go if we are to catch the train to London. It is the only way Eva and Jonah will catch the South Eastern train tomorrow."

"Are your children ready to go?" I asked.

"They are going to stay another night with their aunt and uncle and meet us in London tomorrow. The trunks have been loaded," she said. I took her hand.

"Perhaps your son may ride with my brother, and I will come with you, Theresa," I said. She looked to Duke Garrett who nodded his assent.

"I would like that, Myra. Thank you," she said.

"We would not want to expose the menfolk to our shows of emotions," I said rolling my eyes.

Lady Garrett laughed despite being on the verge of tears at leaving the house of her childhood, perhaps forever. Now her brother would have to invite her to stay in the room she owned in sentiment, if not in fact.

"We will take the ladies with us, and the gentlemen can have at least another half hour at their breakfast," Lady Garrett said, bowing to them.

"Perfect," Eva said standing.

"Clara, you come with us. Brother, I will meet you at the train station," I said bowing at Richard.

"Of course," he said. Lawrence stood as if to follow us, but Richard put a hand on his shoulder and said:

"We will have a bruising ride without the ladies."

"Sir, you jest," Lawrence said putting his hand to the wound on his head. I did not hear the response, but pulled Clara, eating a sweet roll, away.

Once in the carriage, I said, "Eva, you did not give me such a sum, did you?"

"I did, and I started a letter of patent on your behalf, though I meant to announce it this evening at dinner after we had laid our dear Lord Devon to rest and we were away from the mourning," she said nodding at her mother-in-law.

A hush fell over the carriage out of respect. I put an arm around my friend who again shed tears for her father as she watched her childhood home disappear in the distance.

I could not help but remember the day after I laid my father to his rest, the day I left my own childhood home. I left comparatively calm. I did not have to marry an old man. I lost my mother and James. I had nothing else. The only thing I wanted was a change of scene.

My first few days at Grey Manor I found the abode in a state of true darkness. Lawrence mourned his wife miserably and he was in low spirits while trying to commiserate with Eva. The inhabitants of the place wanted to heal, so after a time, they were ready to be comforted. Unlike my father, who enjoyed his misery and would not relinquish it for anything. Eva, innocent with no trace of bitterness, just sorrow, took to me, and together we healed. Seeing the life come back into Eva, Lawrence and Henry allowed me to soothe them back to life. Then we became a family.

All that was over now. I did not want to marry just for the sake of marriage. I wanted Lawrence, but I knew, as my brother and Eva would learn, he would not re-marry. I was coming to terms with the idea of never being married. It was a relief to stop worrying about it so much. I would instead use my efforts, and now my considerable resources, to care for everyone around me. If I could help it, Clara would marry into a good situation, not just a financially beneficial one, but a happy one.

About a mile from the station, the men on horseback caught up to us. The horses breathed heavily, and I could see they had been ridden hard. Lawrence slowed considerably to stay with the carriage. I noticed him pause twice and then catch back up. I was certain he heaved his breakfast both times. My mother was a firm believer in natural consequences over my father's overly harsh punishments and cruelty. It made me smile that my brother proved the same mold as my mother. Once he gave up his quest to marry me off, we would be great friends.

Chapter 13

The ride to London dragged on and on. Lawrence's enthusiasm for the speed and rocking of the carriage dimmed in his current state and he alighted the train at every stop. Little speech was spared by him as he had to keep everything inside to keep anything inside. I felt exhausted keeping myself together, trying to assuage Lady Garrett, and letting Clara lean against me for the whole ride. During the last half of the trip, Eva and Duke Garrett explained my stipend and gave me the address of his solicitor that I might set up quarterly payments if I wished.

"I cannot believe how generous you have been to me," I said, overwhelmed.

"You deserve it," Jonah said, smiling at me.

"I… I will use it with judgment and economy," I said trying not to cry in my gratitude. Eva waved me off assuring me it was only proper. Lawrence, grave and agitated, jiggled his leg in annoyance.

"Myra, I will not be able to call on you tomorrow as I will leave so early," Eva said ignoring her father.

"It is all right," I said taking her hand as the train slowed, London coming into view.

"We will be leaving tomorrow next anyway," Richard said, "but when you return, please feel free to come to us if you wish. You will always be a particular and close friend of our family."

"Thank you," Eva said. Lawrence started:

"You know Myra if you…you would be welcome to come stay this night in--"

"No thank you Sir," I said with my head bowed and my self-command wavering as the train came to a stop. I began gathering my belongings. I wished to stay this last night with Eva, but she would leave early in the morning by the Southwestern railway, and I would not chance being left alone with her father. It was not fair for him to continue his quest for my good opinion under the guise of his duty to do right by me when it engaged my heart. Did he know what he was doing to me?

We all filed off the train slowly as the climb down was steep. Instead of jumping to Eva's aid, Lawrence allowed Duke Garrett to help her and waited to offer me his hand when it was my turn. I had no choice but to take it.

"I am sorry Myra," he said stepping in close to ensure my skirts did not catch.

"I know Sir," I said but could not help the shudder in my breath.

"Do you...Am I--"

"Come, come, Lawrence," Richard called from the train, trying to help Clara down. I moved up to the platform and out of his way.

"Oh, Myra, I shall miss you," Eva said taking my arm and moving me down the platform.

I took Eva's hand and kissed it.

"You are my dearest girl," I said. "I could not be prouder of you if I were your mother, whom I am sure has watched over my efforts to guide you as only a guardian angel could."

"Do you believe that?" Lawrence asked from directly behind me. It startled me that he had come in close enough to hear us over the noise of the station. He stuck his head between Eva and me, so I said,

"I have often felt..." I blushed, "I have sensed there were certain things her mother would wish for her, especially regarding the way she viewed herself. I even strove by these whispered hints to better myself. As you know, my father did not think it wise for anyone to possess self-worth. I do assure you Eva's mother thought the opposite, and I shall always love her for it."

He smiled at me and moved as if to take my hand, but I turned, unwilling to engage in his touch, and instead gave my attention to Clara, taking her arm and guiding her to the establishment where Duke Garrett left his carriage the day before.

At one time I was amazed how many stopped to look when we rode in the carriage. I spared a glance for a young man who stopped to stare. I turned in my astonishment to look at him again. I could not deny the young man was Mr. Titus Williams, when Clara gasped a little. Then I looked again because I did not believe anyone could be so insolent. He stepped forward as if to speak, but I took her by the arm and pulled her in front of me. I glared at him. I forced her to climb up into the enormous carriage before me. I could not see my brother but heard him say, "Mr. Williams, I did not know you were in town," in an icy tone.

"Yes Sir. I thought perhaps your gracious invitation to your country house might stretch to include our time in the city."

"We have an engagement already and leave in but one day. Perhaps it would be best if you do not return to the country," Richard said.

"I think there has been a misunderstanding," Titus Williams said, bowing but could say no more. Richard climbed into the carriage to cut him off. The horses jumped, and the door closed. Clara, to her credit, did not cry but looked livid.

"The nerve," she whispered to me.

Lawrence craned his neck to see the young man causing us turmoil when I could not hide my wonder. He flinched. I could not turn to see why. Clara leeched to my side, and I could not see what startled Lawrence. What could the boy possibly be about? He meant to ruin Clara, and now for him to approach her father in this way was audacity at its boldest. I could not help thinking him entirely misguided, or the very worst sort of scoundrel.

When we reached my brother's relations house, I stopped to kiss Eva and shook Jonah and Lawrence's hands. Lady Garrett was at such a distance I only waved a kiss to her. Then I climbed down from the carriage and wished the group adieu.

We were met at the entrance by the lady of the house. She wished to speak to me, of all people. Mary came to kiss her husband and eventually translated her sister's overly kind treatment of me.

"Myra, I suppose you are to marry Lord Hull?"

"Excuse me?" I asked.

"The rumor is the Duchess of Surry gave to you extravagantly and is even now petitioning on your behalf for a title, so you can marry her father without scrutiny," she said.

"Oh, Richard, you have created a title wave," I said. He laughed.

"Her Grace did this," Richard said, "I did not--"

"Don't you dare play ignorance in this," I started, "you manipulated her. And now you wish to manipulate your friend into marrying me by rumors and cajoling. Be warned. Lawrence, who only wishes solitude and scholarly pursuits, will not be swayed by public opinion and you know it."

"We shall see," Richard said grinning. I rolled my eyes and took Clara to our room to freshen up, so her aunt and mother could take her shopping.

Exhausted and half-starved, I took soup in my room and slept for hours.

Chapter 14

The next day both Lady Garett and Lawrence called. Both came bearing invitations to our whole group, and instead of being in our power to receive them, we could not even bestow our own to the quiet family dinner. Richard insisted his last evening in town be spent in solitude with his wife, and would if he could, but could not invite his friends into another man's house. Lady Garrett left after a short internment, as her other children were expected at the train station soon.

Lawrence's invitation hurt me to refuse. It meant I would not go back to his home, perhaps ever. He would not be lonely in town; he received invitations every night, but the temptation to stay up all hours and drink would be great. For all I said about his scholarly pursuits, he had not taken them up with enthusiasm since his father died. He needed a project, or else when he finally went home, what would keep him occupied alone in the country?

Lawrence did not keep with civility and stayed much longer throughout the morning than he ought. He and Richard played many games of chess, each winning in his turn. Clara and I went shopping with her mother and Aunt. I had not realized how picky and intrigued with fashion Clara was. I quickly bought all I wanted. When I saw Clara would shop for hours while I was stared at, and whispered about, I went back to the house with a footman.

Lawrence was still there when I entered the drawing-room. He smiled at me as if he'd waited for me to return, and I felt he valued me, even as much as he did Richard. I sat near the men and occupied myself with a book. The outer bell rang once, but I heard the butler say the family was from home, and I was glad of it.

Lawrence did not often engage me in conversation, but I caught him looking at me as if debating something inside himself. This retirement reminded me very much of the days we spent at Grey Manor, and I wondered if his thoughts were occupied by those many happy memories. Clara came in after a while.

"Oh, are you finally done shopping?" I asked.

"No, mother sent me home with the footman. I am not to be allowed to help pick out my dresses anymore," she said, disgruntled.

Considering how picky Clara was, I figured Mary needed a rest from her daughter's exuberance. To appease her, I took her across the room and let her make noise showing me her packages.

I feared for her when she started to say things like:

"Won't I look so pretty in this; don't you think the dark blue is flattering to my light hair?"

"Yes, you will be lovely," I said, looking at her new bonnet, noticing she was wearing my favorite color.

"Then he'll be sorry," she said under her breath, getting a yard of ribbon to make a longer bow.

"Dearest we must leave him behind and try not to think of him. The more you plot revenge, the deeper you will be sucked into his world. Instead, you must rise above it. Do not give him any more of you than he has heartlessly taken. That is the only true way to keep yourself safe."

"Yes, yes, but you must own there is a certain charm in making a man miserable who has disrespected you," she said glancing at Lawrence deep in thought at his game.

"You would not put Lord Hull in the same category as Mr. Williams," I whispered.

She shrugged.

"One is trying desperately to resist me, so he might honor his late wife, and the other would ruin you to satisfy his selfish desires."

Clara answered she had not thought of it like that, but I did not hear. Instead, I examined what I saw in Lawrence's eyes when he called me his rose. Lawrence resisted me. He resisted me to honor his late wife. He glanced at me and instead of trying to avoid his eye, I smiled at him. He glanced up again to smile back. A light went on in him, and in very few moves he took my brother's queen, making sure I watched him and smiled for him when he won.

He loved me, as I did him. We had too much fire between us for it not to be so. Yet, he had an idea of what love should be. And in this picture of love, giving his heart away a second time equated to abandoning his duty, giving up his honor; it equated to clear his conscience, even his soul. To marry me he would have to break with ideals formulated in his youth with his good father.

His grandfather married twice. It tore the family apart. He watched the second wife slash his father's inheritance and his grandfather's honor to shreds. It had caused so many problems in Lawrence's youth as he formed the very core of who he was. He likely could not separate the idea of marrying again from degradation.

I would end a spinster. I could not ask him to give up himself for me. Yet, I could never love anyone else.

Richard could not ask Lawrence to tea, as it was not his place to. The Lady of the house, who would relish the company of a marquess, was still out. Her husband rarely left his club after we came to London.

Lawrence stood to leave as the afternoon grew late. I walked him to the door.

"Are we still friends, Myra?" he asked looking at me in his probing way that I could not stand, now that I understood it. I looked away to watch the doorknob and said:

"We will always be friends, and the truest sort of friends because there can never be offense between us."

"Will you shake my hand as proof of that, dear lady?"

I steeled myself. I commanded every grain of self-possession. I reached my hand to him. He took it, and lifted it halfway to his mouth, he stopped. Lifted it a little closer. He closed his eyes and moved my hand downward. He reached out and put his other hand on top of the first almost as if his other hand would serve as an anchor.

"Are you going back to Grey Manor soon?" I asked, glancing at him self-consciously. I pulled my hand away, to stop him from running his thumbs across each of my knuckles.

"Tomorrow, I ... I have business... I will catch the train with you," he said, agitated, still watching my hand.

"Will you come to visit my brother?" I asked, unable to stop myself. I looked up and was startled to see the intensity in his eyes as he leaned in to read me, to see what I wanted. I felt, except for marrying me, he would do anything for me. I needed to know if he would come. I needed to prepare myself.

"I...I do not know if I ought," he said turning his eyes to watch my hands again, which rested on my stomach, "but I do not think I will be able to stem my curiosity with only an easy ride to satisfy it. Especially since Richard seems predisposed to favor a match that cannot be resisted on the gentlemen's part due to Eva's imprudence. I feel I should... nay, I owe it to you to look out for your best interest."

"I am hardly a girl. Should not a woman who is thirty and one years know how to judge for herself?"

"I do not judge for you, Myra. I must know for myself you are in the happiest situation; with all you deserve." He still looked at my hands, but the melancholy in his face was concentrated. He looked up with great effort and said, "then I will settle into the rest of my days at ease, quiet on the subject."

I looked at him, trying not to feel his words. Didn't he know? He was the only happiness possible for me. Anything else was just settling.

"You do what you think is right, and I assure you, Sir, I will understand," I said.

"Please won't you call me Lawrence again," he asked as if this small concession would make his sacrifice tolerable. "It is how you can prove we are the best of friends."

"Very well, Lawrence, goodbye," I said, but it was too much, it was too close an intimacy. I quickly bowed. I turned and walked away. I heard every creak of the door as he left. I sat in a quiet chair in the corner where my book lay, trying to stem my tears. Knowing he cared for me but resisted the tenderness was worse than believing him indifferent.

Clara worked herself up into such a tizzy redoing her bonnet I finally asked her to go up to lie down. I promised to call her for tea. When my brother and I had the room to ourselves, I sat down next to him.

"He loves me, doesn't he?" I asked.

"Yes," Richard answered, still examining his chess game to see how Lawrence outmaneuvered him.

"How long have you known?" I asked.

"I suspected a few years ago. I was certain at his father's funeral. He managed to function when you were by his side, but when you left him, he looked … lost."

"Why did you not say something? I think you discouraged me from any affection I felt," I said.

He looked up and examined me now.

"Myra, you went to him at nineteen. You were in his employ until very recently. Could you imagine the scandal if the two of you realized and acted upon your affection for one another?"

"I suppose you are right," I said. He nodded like of course he was, then looked back to the chessboard.

The harrowing ache in my heart made me certain I could not have lived with Lawrence, done as I should for Eva and stayed sane if I had known. After Lawrence kissed me, and I admitted how much I loved him, I would have run away if it hadn't been for my dedication to Eva. For weeks I avoided Lawrence until we found a more rigid relationship between Master and Servant. In my thoughts, I referred to him as my master, so I would not get confused again. Four months later when Eva and I left him to go to London I felt relieved, despite the great work load I took on pretending to be her maid. In the last few months before Eva's marriage, Lawrence and I relaxed into a friendship of sorts, our commonality being Eva.

My brother was right about one thing. If Lawrence had returned my adoration that day after he kissed me, if he had thrown caution to the wind and loved me back when I was so animated in affection for him, I would forever be the woman who entrapped the marquess. The servant who did not know her place. I would be the mistress who forced her powerful benefactor to acknowledge her to society. Love, every effort we made to stay honorable – none of that would have mattered. Lawrence would have escaped any blame, Eva would have been pitied as a pawn in my game, but I would have been painted in the ugliest light possible for the rest of my life. The kindest thing Lawrence ever did for me was to pretend he did not remember.

"It is a tragic story, ours," I said.

"It may not be. Your young lady has raised the stakes quite dramatically. You are an heiress and even in consideration for a title. A duchess throwing her resources behind the match goes a long way to legitimize it. There would perhaps still be whispers, but no one, even among the titled, would dare censure you or her."

"I never even saw her gift that way. She is growing up, isn't she," I said. He looked away from his game and said:

"Yes, and you, Myra, what will you do to marry the man you love?"

"I...I do not..."

"Would you open yourself enough to marry, Myra? Are the scars of your youth so deep you would not accept happiness if it came your way?" he asked.

"I... I cannot say about that. I am more open with Lawrence than anyone, simply because he does not stand for anything less. It does not signify what I am capable of regarding romance since I am not capable of forcing him to break his honor to explore the notion," I said.

"It is misplaced," Richard said waving it off as if a trifle.

"It is his, and you wish to break him down until he accepts me. I cannot hurt him like that."

"Oh Myra! There is more joy to be had in a full life, than embracing misplaced honor. I knew Anna. She would not have wished him to live in this manner, throwing himself into his daughter's life so fully that he has nothing left now that she is grown," Richard said.

"I think it goes deeper than that. Henry's stepmother made much trouble. Henry likely instilled into Lawrence this honor in his most delicate stages of youth. Henry swore, he'd never remarry because of his stepmother's antics, Lawrence learned his lessons at his father's hands."

"Which is something from his childhood he should overcome, not cling to, just as you should overcome seeing our father and mother's marriage."

"I am better than I was when I first left for Grey Manor," I said, "and much of that is due to Henry. How could I ask Lawrence to disrespect his father's feelings of duty?"

"I wonder how Henry would feel seeing Lawrence drunk and despondent simply to repress something so healing as love," he said.

"I… no, I don't think he would like that," I admitted.

"I witnessed Henry's marriage firsthand and it made me open and ready for something of the like," Richard said.

"I only knew Henry after his wife died. I can only testify to Henry's unwillingness to remarry because of the trouble a second marriage caused his father, his inheritance, and his peace at home," I said.

"Yes, but Henry had his work, his son and granddaughter, not to mention he was much older when his wife passed. Anna and Lady Grey Hull died within two years of each other. Lawrence will be alone for another twenty or thirty years to add upon the ten he's already endured. That cannot be desirable," Richard said.

"He does need something, but I do not think his honor will give in to another marriage," I said.

"Consider, Myra. Lawrence is the most aware, mindful man I've ever met. He knows what is happening with every person around him. Yet, he does not see what myself, and even his daughter, are about? Are not his calculated efforts to stay ignorant of what we are doing the very acceptance of our prodding?" he asked.

I laughed. I could not deny this. I had also observed this oddity but was unwilling say anything to acknowledge or refute it for fear I may hint at the hope inflating like a soap bubble inside me. Instead, I said, "And we must not forget you have a hundred pounds on the line."

"Yes, I do, and dear sister I must beat him at this. It is required of *my* honor," he said laughing, while moving the chess pieces back into their starting place.

Chapter 15

Just before tea was to be served, Mary came in and
said, "You will never guess who my sister and I ran into."

"No, I cannot," Richard said.

"Bells. Our old friends the Bells, and when you are
gone tomorrow, I will have tea with them."

"Be sure to send my regards," Richard answered.
They sat and spoke in quiet undertones while I read in silence.
It was the best way to recover, sitting still, and listening to the
sounds of London outside the window.

At one time I hated the solitude. My father would go
to the races or out rioting at his club. At times, he took me
with him when the venue seemed appropriate for a lady and
he would show me off to all his friends. More often he would
leave me. I would sit in the townhouse he rented for the
season and read. I would start at every sound out in the city.

Now I found the constant sound of carriages and
people along the street calming. It astounded me how one
person – one toxic, angry man in the house – could break a
household. Was Richard right, would I forever shy away
from marriage because of my father? Or was it more what
Baron Adlay did that made me consider I should never
deserve happiness?

The outer bell rang, and we all looked up.

"He has been refusing visitors all day," Richard
assured his wife.

"That is a relief," Mary said.

Instead of a door opening and closing, there was a
ruckus in the hall. The door to the drawing-room opened and
the butler came in interrupting the solitude.

"I thought perhaps you would change your mind about
visitors when you saw who came to call," he said.

A handsome young man slid around the loyal servant to his mother's cry,

"Ricky Boy," she said rushing to him.

"Father, Mother, I did not know you would be here," he said. "I am so glad I caught you, I thought I would have to impose upon my Aunt and Uncle's generosity."

Richard's oldest son embraced both his parents in a show of affection that was not at all in his character. The boy went by Rick to distinguish him from his father, except his mother who still called him Ricky Boy. A young lad of twenty-one, he looked nothing like his namesake had at that age. Excepting his tawny hair tinted in copper, darker than mine and Clara's, that matched his father's perfectly. His eyes were teal like his mothers. His facial features were not as sharp as Richards and as good as any young man could expect. He was of average height but played in any football match he could at Cambridge, so long as the rules were observed, making him a strong and muscled lad.

The mother and father were too much with their son to welcome the young man he brought with him. The young man was a close acquaintance and from our parish. I had known him as a young boy. Phineas Dodgson had not changed a bit since he was an adorable lad, though perhaps a young gentleman could not desire floppy hair the color of gingerbread that curled at the ends and would not stay put. His adorable, dimpled face had to smile, and one could feel his natural goodness when he did. I liked the lad as a child very much.

"I thought you were taking in the continent," Richard said looking back and forth at the young men who appeared as though they had not bathed in a month; their clothes were filthy.

"We had a fit of bad luck and have barely made it back with our lives," Rick said.

"Oh, darling what happened?" his mother asked.

116

"It shall all be known, but unfortunately, we had to hire ourselves out on a delivery wagon coming from Dover. At first, the owner said we would have to pay him six shillings between us for a ride if we worked for him. We worked like slaves for the man. Now he insists we owe him six crowns apiece for our keep though we slept in his cart to protect his goods and have barely eaten a thing in three days," he said.

"I will go deal with the man. You both stay with Rick," I said.

"Hello, Aunt Myra," Rick said turning to kiss me, seeming to notice me for the first time.

"Hello dear boy. Perhaps your companion, it is Mr. Phineas Dodgson is it not?" The lad nodded

"Will you show me the way," I said to the other boy.

"Oh, Phineas, are you all right?" Mary asked, looking to the young man.

"I am, but the man insists he will get the law if we do not go swiftly," he said.

"Come," I said, allowing him to lead the way. I glanced at Richard and he nodded back at me. Growing up in so close a proximity to our father, we knew the trickery of the criminal mind. Neither of us would be taken by a cad.

I took out six shillings and putting them in my hand, I put my reticule back in my pocket, so the man did not see how much he could take me for. We went out to the curb where a grubby, bewhiskered man stood impatiently. Upon seeing me, he grinned. Surely, he felt his luck dealing with the innocence of a lady of some breeding.

"Ma'am, your boy here told ye he is indebted to me," he said.

"Yes, but I am confused. He said he worked for his ride," I said.

"But not for his keep. They owe twenty crowns to my generosity," he said.

"I was informed six shillings, but perhaps seeing the neighborhood we are situated in, reminded you of some extra expense you were put to on their behalf?"

"I am looking for what is owed me," the man scowled.

"I am just, and with proof will not hesitate. For such a great sum I suppose you have kept a ledger of expenses for rooms, food, and the grand ball you threw for the lads at fifty shillings each," I said.

"I ain't bothered with such rubbish," he said, growing heated.

"Well considering the state of the lads, I doubt they consumed more than they earned working for you."

"I can get the law; we will take it to a--"

"Yes, that would perhaps be the best here. I think the law would assuredly be able to determine how much is owed to an employer who provided no bed and scarcely a bite to his employees."

The man stared at me. He knew the law would be on my side, simply because I was a gentlewoman. Perhaps it wasn't fair, but I would use it to my advantage.

"They asked for a ride. It t'weren't in our agreement to feed the boys, nor house them," he snarled.

"No? And yet you ask me to pay so great a sum as twenty crowns?"

He stopped. He started moving his mouth like he was replaying the conversation we just had, to understand just where he lost his footing.

"Your arrangement was for six shillings. Here they are as promised, and we will leave your robbery at that," I said handing the money over. "You may call the law to this residence if you feel cheated, but you will only have until tomorrow morning at which time we leave our host's generosity for the country where we reside," I said to make it clear he would not be able to torment Richard's sister for more money.

He cursed me, then climbed back onto his wagon and left begrudgingly.

"That was amazing," said Phineas, who had been silent.

"Amazing is my specialty. Now let us go get you cleaned up and some food, shall we?" I asked, taking his arm.

"Yes please," he said, sagging as if days of tension were seeping out of him. Richard and Mary met us in the entrance assuring the boys they would be fed after they bathed as they smelled like a horse's stall. Mary saw to them. I went back into the drawing-room with my brother. Richard looked at me, "Did you see to the man's crowns?"

"It turns out he only required six shillings after all," I said with a grin. He smiled back with a chuckle and considered the matter resolved. He opened the day's paper.

The boys were cleaned up and ready to eat as the tea-things were brought in. Clara joined us and welcomed her brother warmly. Then she exclaimed, "Phineas," and rushed to him. The young man was only confused for a moment but quickly took both her hands and her warm welcome in stride.

"Clara, you are so grown," he said turning red and looking to her sweet eager face.

"It has been almost a year since I saw you last Christmas, and I do feel older," she teased, waiting for him to join her, as they had a comfortable sort of friendship in the past. He did not disappoint. The young man's face grew animated as he said, "Perhaps, but there was that long period between seven and thirteen where you did not look like you aged a day. We all swore some magical creature took you under its care. It must have let you go, however, because I barely know you now," he said.

"I did let the creature go; it was not house trained. I flatter myself the aging is all to my improvement, for I have had many a compliment in the last year. Mrs. Hardy, in only the way she can state, I charge you to imagine her voice telling me every Sunday at church, 'Why Miss Bolton, you have bloomed from a bud to a flower.'"

"You mastered her well, and it is so. Now your brother and I have only to chastise those young men who have been so bold as to pay you compliments before you are out."

"She came out when she turned eighteen, but she will have a turn in town this spring," Rick said. "I am sure I mentioned it."

"You must have," Phineas said, searching the room for something safe to look at.

"And who is there in our neighborhood to pay her compliments but Mr. Frank Hadleigh and the Gibbs boys. They certainly do not harm," Rick said, taking a cup of tea and more than his share of tea sandwiches from Clara.

"No, there is a new family who let Meadow Way after the Fiddicks were unable to retrench, and moved to Devonshire with an aunt," Mary said.

"Who took it?" Rick asked after swallowing a pastry with the help of his scalding tea.

"A banking family named the Williams. They have a boy your age or perhaps a year younger who has shown a marked interest in your sister," Mary said, completely unaware of her daughter's mortified blush.

"Not Titus Williams," Phineas asked, glancing at Clara, setting his teacup down. Rick also put his food down and looked stunned.

"That is the boy's name," Richard said. "Do you know of him?"

"He was at Eton with us," Rick said, "in our very dorm. He is a scoundrel. He claimed his father let a new great house every summer, but never signed more of a six-month lease. Williams bragged of his many conquests. He claimed he had to be removed for a more fertile playing ground after only a short time."

Phineas stopped eating and watched the tense interaction between Clara, her father and myself.

"Richard, if that be true, surely we should warn our neighbors," Mary said. "Though I don't suppose we can give any account aside from hearsay."

"No," Rick said. "Mother, it is not hearsay. I saw myself and even thwarted three schemes in favor of the young ladies. He hates me, and I am most fearful he settled by us on purpose to revenge himself. He is so cold as that."

I felt my heart fall and I could not feel safe about the subject. My eyes did not leave Clara's face.

"He has shown a marked attention toward Clara since the beginning of the summer," Mary said, again looking at her daughter, suddenly appalled.

"Has he… has there been anything inappropriate in his behavior to you?" Rick asked, leaning forward.

"Very much so, but I could not be had by his scheming," said Clara. "Millie, however, should especially be warned, and I can satisfy his character is wretched. Please mama, let Mrs. Fielding know her daughter is in danger," Clara said, looking at the ground.

"Surely, he did not scheme against you my love," Mary said, drilling her eyes into her daughters.

"He tried, but thankfully, Aunt Myra saw what he was about, and saved me from all injury. But he often used Millie to try and make me jealous, and me to her. It was an effective stratagem, that felt more like being bullied than wooed, I am sorry to say. I have been a simpleton--"

"Innocent," I corrected.

"Very well, innocent… but whatever we call it, I have come to no harm. Millie is in danger and should be warned," Clara said, trying to hold back her tears. Ashamed to admit such folly in herself, Clara appeared more concerned with the wellbeing of another.

"I certainly shall," Mary said. "You and I shall be together this evening writing a letter to her mother."

"It would be best if the whole Williams family were to leave the neighborhood," Phineas said, eyeing Clara sadly.

"I believe he has a maiden Aunt who lives with him," I asked, now concerned James would be stuck with another poor choice if he were not careful.

"I believe she has had a few prospects, but Williams gloats he has ruined her as well. Because of his scandals, they leave before she can securely get her hooks in any poor unsuspecting gentleman," Rick said. "He laughed as he said it."

"As much as I feel for the lady, I think it is time they move on," Richard said, scowling. Clara looked near to tears and I gave Richard a quiet nod, that we might drop the subject, but it was Phineas who caught the look and said,

"Clara, do you still play?"

"I do. Aunt Myra has been giving me tips over the last week. I feel improved of late," she said quietly. He offered her his arm, leaving behind his tea and sandwiches, that he might escort her to the large pianoforte in the corner of the room.

She started to play, and the genuinely kind young man attended to her, though he must have been starving.

"Myra, what happened?" Mary asked in a whisper. I told as little as possible to convey what happened but left Clara's folly out of it. When I finished, Rick said:

"I am even more convinced he did this as revenge on me."

"I believe I will write a letter to the boy's father," Richard said. "Perhaps we can run them out of the neighborhood. If I request the father remove from London to check his heir, he will likely take the trouble to quit the house instead."

He discussed the possibility with Mary, while I examined Phineas and Clara. I could see, though Clara only noticed the young man as her brother's friend, Phineas watched her as a man does a woman he favors. I said nothing but thought I might observe this connection for a time and see what became of it. I had, at one time, loved the boy I grew up with, simply because we knew each other best.

If James and I had married when we were young and innocent, untainted by the cruelness of life and belittling characters, we would have been compatible. Everything, except a want of money, would have made the match desirable. What was Phineas' situation, and availability as the oldest son? Though my brother had recovered financially, it could not be supposed he saved much by way of dowries for his many daughters.

I regretted this on Clara's account. The tender way Phineas glanced at her seemed to rehearse a history and write a future for them, that in any other circumstance would grow lovely and bloom fully.

I recollected myself when Rick asked if they could send for some cold meats and cheeses as he was famished, and the dainty little butter sandwiches could not satisfy him. He called to Phineas, who was obligated to move back over to his friend to send their request to the larder.

"We will go to my sister," Mary said. "She will oblige you anything she has; I have no doubt. Then you will tell us how you came to be here in this state, for I am very curious."

Mary said this as she walked out the door before them. Exiting behind her, only I was close enough to hear Phineas say: "Mr. Williams is a blight on society."

"We will take care of him. He will never look at a sister who has a brother to protect her again, I can promise you that," Rick said, and they walked out.

I did not know whether to caution the lad or praise him. I decided it would be best if I pretended not to have heard him, that he might be guided by his conscience. Especially considering Rick had grown into such a strong young man, who played an extremely aggressive game in his pastime. If revenge truly were Mr. Williams' aim, going after Rick head-on certainly wouldn't be his object. Rick could maim him with little effort. Mr. Williams must have believed Rick would be on the continent a little longer.

Chapter 16

The next morning, we caught the train with Lawrence. It was a relief to have so much to discuss with the new subjects Rick and Phineas brought forward. He was curious and sympathetic as the boys explained what happened on the continent. Then when Clara, white and exhausted from pacing our bedroom all night, fell asleep, we broached the subject of Titus Williams. Lawrence, ever intrigued by human behavior, questioned the boys about Mr. Williams' behavior at school. When they finished, I thought him the worst sort of scoundrel.

His exploits reminded me very much of Baron Adlay. I was much admired during my season, but not sought after because of my lack of dowry. The extremely wealthy Baron was my father's old friend. He paid me too much attention and enjoyed all the stares and looks of resentment from the younger men who could not court me. He did not feel he needed to respect me, nor even pretend I could reject his advances because he was wealthy, and I was not. I did not worry much at the time of Baron Adlay's offenses because he was married when he paid them. If I'd known what he was capable of, I would have been terrified.

Lawrence looked at me in concern, and I wondered what my face looked like. I wiped the memory from my head and he said, "I have a dispute between two of my tenants, and cannot come back to Bolton Lodge with you, but I would like to meet Mr. Williams."

"He would not dare show his face now," Phineas whispered, glancing at Clara sleeping. Lawrence looked leery, and said, "He approached the young lady's father outside the train yard. Richard, you told him not to come back to the country?"

"Yes, and I mean to write to his father. I doubt he will come back."

"Yes, but in the train yard, just after you told him not to come back, we were pulling away, I saw a look of smug satisfaction on his face. He looked like he had won, though what he won I could not say. I do not think he has given up his quest," Lawrence said.

"You think he will come back after I have warned him off, written his father, and he finds his schoolfellows, who are completely aware of his exploits, have returned?" Richard asked.

"You look at this from your standpoint," Lawrence said. "To the man without conscience, the chance to bend others to his will only heightens his game. It is a type of sickness. To add upon this, his father does not check him. What does he have to lose? I predict he will push until he is stopped or has seen his revenge on these boys. He means to string them up to see them twist in the wind."

"What should I do if he comes back?" Richard asked, squinting at Lawrence.

We all stopped. What could be done about a wealthy young man who chooses cruelty, and leaves ruined lives in his wake? Nothing. He would come into our lives, impose upon us as he chose, then leave. Didn't I know that better than anyone else could? There was no checking such a man. How would my life have been ruined if my father had lived?

"Can we apply to the law?" Richard asked.

"No," Rick said. "He does not appear anything but amiable when he chooses it. I was never able to prove anything against him. By the end of our schooling, most of the schoolmasters felt I was being cruel to the poor Williams boy because he came from new money."

"Perhaps we catch him in the act and publish his misdeeds in all the society pages so the unsuspecting can be warned. Or at least appeal to his landlord not to renew his lease," Lawrence suggested.

"I should have called him out. I should have slain this dragon at school," Rick said looking at his sleeping sister.

"Perhaps we ought to arm Clara," I said. Upon my uttering her name, my niece stirred and that was the end to the conversation. Shortly after, the train came to a stop. We all alighted. Lawrence came in close and, with a tender hand on my elbow, whispered, "Write to me if the lad comes back. Do not underestimate him. He can pretend at goodness all day long if it serves his purpose. However, if you push him and he snaps, he is capable of any atrocity. I saw it all in the look he gave as we pulled away from him at the train station. Myra, you must understand: he is dangerous. He will hurt you, or anyone he thinks is in his way."

I only nodded. I could not catch my breath as he whispered his adieu, his warmth so near mine.

Chapter 17

We arrived back at Bolton Lodge in the late afternoon and my nieces were so glad to see us; they hovered about looking for sweets and presents. I had, of course, indulged in everything of the sort for them and enjoyed being nearly overrun in their pursuit.

We spent a happy evening playing charades and kissing cheeks in the drawing-room. The drawing-room that had once been silent as the grave after suppers, was loud and full of lovely chaos. It was still papered in the faded minty green my father insisted on, over my mother's objections. Just before he died, my father replaced all the trim in gold leafing and the furniture in the room had been recovered in cream and gold fabric. A perfect dripping chandelier served as a focal point in the center of the room. To him it was a symbol of his wealth and prestige. To me it was more debt for me to recover from an advantageous marriage. All had been done in preparation for his great friend, Baron Adlay, to come for a visit after my season in London.

The room had been marvelous in its prime. Now the gilding sluffed off. The furniture was threadbare and the coloring on the walls faded. Such was the legacy of my father.

The next morning when the post came, Richard opened an invitation.

"Mr. Dodgson, so grateful for the safe deliverance of his son Phineas, wishes for us to join in a supper party he is holding," Richard said.

"I did save him several times," Rick said. "He's too kind-hearted for his own good."

"I suppose we ought to go, though the trouble of including four more to his table will be considerable,"

Richard said, looking at me. I could see he relied on Mary for such decisions.

"He was not on hand to help his son. He must want to do something to recompense. Let him take the trouble. It will make him feel better," I said, glancing at Clara for her opinion to make her feel useful and included.

"That will be lovely," Clara said in a way that sounded too grown up. She seemed to have aged over the few days our trip spanned. The miles we traversed so quickly on the train demanded a toll. Not as they once did on the body, but the soul was forced to give up the same vitality of youth for the number of miles passed, no matter how long it took. To say Clara was a girl could no longer describe her. Now she was a woman of nineteen.

The Dodgson family was in my brother's exact situation. Their home was beautiful, on a grand scale, but the furniture in the extremely large drawing-room was worn and needed replacing. Only little signs like new silk flowers and worked pillows made the room appear fresh. I inquired of Phineas about his siblings and found the large family's children were almost the same ages as my nieces, excepting he had a sister three years his senior.

If their situation weren't so desperately discouraging, it would be diverting to watch Clara start to respond to Phineas' unpracticed romancing. We were waiting for supper with another family when James showed up with Mr. Davies, who helped him escort a few of his lady friends, Miss Williams among them. I watched her, particularly when she noticed Clara. She looked surprised to see her. She glanced at her a few times, perhaps to see if she looked pale and broken.

Phineas was such a pleasant companion; Clara did not allow her spirits to wane. Mr. Dodgson seemed rather nervous about the comradery between the lady and his son. He mentioned another young lady to Phineas several times.

His disconcert, and her quick recovery, only strengthened Clara's claim that she felt more bullied into Mr. Williams's plan than having much affection for him.

Miss William caught my eye and smiled at me. She seemed relieved. Her warmth toward me indicated that her nephew had not come back from London, so she did not know the particulars of his failure.

I longed for Lawrence. He had a knack for guiding people into the natural consequences of their actions. I started to wonder what I could do to separate Miss Williams from James. Not that I thought he deserved it particularly, being somewhat ridiculous with his following. I would not see him trapped for the sake of my friend who cheered me after so many interactions with my father.

How would Lawrence expose the Williams for what they were without appearing to do so? I looked at James and noticed he watched me with curiosity. With a look, he seemed to invite me over to him. I went and sat across from him.

"Are you well?" he asked.

"Tolerably so, and yourself?"

"Yes, I…I wanted to thank you," he said.

"Thank me? I thought you were rather vexed with me."

"No, I… Sally has been petted so long she is sure to be spoiled. My mother and I have taken great pains to correct her in the last week and it is most astounding how she turns around. I …it was almost like she was daring us to give her guidance, and when we did not, she thought her current course acceptable. You were right. My father would never have put up with such nonsense," he said, nodding to me. I smiled.

"Nor mine," Miss Williams chimed in.

"I cannot believe your family would check any indulgence," I said clenching my jaw. She blanched a little and laughed.

"I suppose you mean Titus," she said. "He is much indulged by my brother. Miss Clarke, were you not saying how your mother had a heavier hand than your father?"

Miss Clarke, grateful to be the center of attention even with Miss Williams, and the addition of Phineas' older sister, Miss Dodgson, took up the topic with vigor. Miss Williams glanced at me and I gave her such a look as to understand her respectability was teetering. She looked down at the floor, and I could see the panic in her. I wondered how many chances her nephew ruined for her.

Neither James nor Mr. Davies noticed because they were having a struggle of their own. Mr. Davies seemed to have overstepped his bounds. James used him to engage Miss Clarke when he focused on any of the other women of his acquaintance. When Miss Clarke finished speaking about her mother, Mr. Davies mentioned he found her a treat. He handed her a pouch of hazelnuts. Miss Clarke raved over them, opening the pouch and smelling their musk. They were her favorite. She thanked Mr. Davies warmly and put them in her reticule. That is how none of them noticed Miss Williams panicking or my fiery eyes. James certainly couldn't have Mr. Davies moving in on one of his spinsters. Amid the silent commotion our host came into the room and said, "Ah, let us dine."

We all stood, but I did not move. James went to escort Miss Clarke, but she instinctively reached for Mr. Davies.

"Oh, excuse me," she said taking James's arm. James bowed to Mr. Davies, but he betrayed his annoyance in the action, like his friend should have known it was Miss Clarke's turn to be escorted into dinner by himself. Miss Clarke, a plain young lady, was very considerate and blushed at the interaction, unsure what to do with the two men fighting over her.

"I think you were meant to escort Miss Dodgson in," James said nodding to Phineas' older sister, who was pretty enough with natural curling hair and a fair complexion. A bit shy, at twenty-four, she was teetering at the edge of spinsterhood. With no dowry, she could hardly be on James's radar. Mr. Davies bowed to Miss Clarke but moved to Miss Dodgson. It was a very informal occasion, and since there was no one to escort me to the dining room, I held back. Miss Williams sidled up to me.

"What has he done?" she asked as we lingered in the room away from the group.

"What do you believe he has done?" I asked.

"I… all I know is you left suddenly for London with your niece, and he left by the next train," she said, "I am extremely glad to see she is here and whole."

"Whole is relative. At such a young age, she now must understand that there are men who would try to lure her away under pretenses, and I can see you are not shocked by this news," I said.

"I can do nothing with him. He is his own master, and his father will do nothing to censure him. Please don't say anything, please. My brother's lease is up at the end of September. I will be sure he does not renew."

"My brother has sent yours a letter warning him his son is going to be called out if he continues in this manner," I said.

"My brother will do nothing. He never does. Please, Titus will go back to school in a month and I will be gone."

"I will say nothing if you do not interfere in whatever is dealt him at my brother's hands."

She stopped, surprised. Had no one ever checked the boy?

"Is your brother a vindictive man?" she asked.

132

"No, he is just. The boy will only get what he deserves—no more, no less," I said.

"I will do nothing to interfere. He has done me a most injurious turn. I would have married five years ago if it weren't for Titus. He is not safe with any young woman. I think he may be…wrong in the head. He is so selfish. So incapable of contrition," Miss. Williams whispered looking to the door almost fearfully.

"Thank you for your honesty. I will look out for you when everything falls. Who was this man you lost five years ago?" I asked.

"A soldier. Titus ran away with his youngest sister. Titus took her from her father's home where we all grew up in Norfolk. He took great pains to conceal the young lady by taking her into Scotland. Then, by defrauding a clergyman, he obtained a clandestine marriage," she said.

"He is married?" I asked, taken back.

"No, it was a sham ceremony," she said.

"Still, I'm surprised he bothered. He did not seem inclined to take Clara anywhere to… to ruin her," I said quietly.

"Well, he was still young then, plus, the girl is the daughter of my brother's oldest friend. I do not think his conquest of her could be satisfied in any other way. She would not consent to anything less," Miss Williams said sadly.

"And your beau blamed you?"

"I … I brought Titus with me when I came to spend the evenings. I knew he could not be trusted. We were so young then, I … I should have seen it coming. I just wanted to be with Victor. It was selfish of me. I have paid for my sin. Adelaide is concealed in Scotland. Victor is keeping peace in India, and I am forever consigned to follow Titus around in the summers cleaning up after his indiscretions."

"Her brother, her family, know nothing of her whereabouts?" I asked.

"I do not think they wish to know," she responded. "Victor may, but he was not home when it all happened. He came home a month after the fact and his sister disappeared and was disowned. Titus was sent to a friend's house when she disappeared. Three months after her disappearance, he returned to school as if nothing happened. Victor blamed me as the instigator because I was supposed to be Titus's keeper... anyway, he could not be with me and honor his little sister."

"I see, and he is married now with many children?" I asked.

"Victor?"

"Yes," I said.

"Last I heard he worked his way up to Captain and is stationed in Bombay."

"What of his sister? How did you discover her?"

"When Titus went back to school, I begged... only by swearing to keep her whereabouts a secret, would Titus tell me where she was. She lives by my support in a little fishing village."

"Your brother does nothing," I said.

"He has been applied to several times to check Titus, but cannot remove from town, his obligations are great. Titus's mother died in childbirth. It is left to me."

"Is... is your nephew's foe wife alone now?" I asked wondering if I could somehow help the poor girl.

"About a year after they were married, she had a child. They are established in a fine cottage with two servants. She refused to see her baby sent off, and after her confinement, she stayed in Scotland, where the parish saw her husband and believes she is legally married."

"Your nephew never goes to see her?" I asked.

"No, he lived with her for the first three months instead of going to his friend's house as his father instructed him to do. He left her when school started and has never been back since."

"To which fishing village?" I asked. She told me the name of the village and which shire the young woman resided in. I repeated it in my head a few times trying to commit it to memory since I'd never heard of it before.

"It is a respectable place, and the villagers all think her very amiable. Their clergyman married her, so she is vindicated in their eyes. They see the brute who ran out on her as he deserves to be seen. She is safe and out of the way. Titus threatened… he made it clear she is not to leave Scotland. He is not the sort to have his authority challenged. I have not been able to do so much for his other conquests. Especially those of the lower classes around Eton and Cambridge."

"From the sound of it, my nephew, Rick," I said nodding my head toward him, "spoiled some of his conquests at Eton. We think your nephew may have come here for revenge."

"He said nothing about it to me, but he did choose this parish. He told his father he wished to fish again. His father was pleased he wanted to do something from his youth. I thought it odd, but everything Titus does is odd. Oh, what a monster he is, and what he has made me. I cringe to even think."

"I am sorry for you," I said taking a deep breath.

"I am plenty sorry for myself as well," she said looking upward to control her emotion. "Come, let us go to dinner before we are missed."

"I'll be right there. I need to adjust my lace," I said. She nodded and walked out of the room. I took out a notepad and pencil from my reticule and wrote the name of the parish where Mr. Williams' wife and child resided before I could forget it.

I caught up to her and we walked in silence to the dining room.

"Miss Williams," James called to us once we entered the lively room, "Miss Clarke and I are having an argument you must resolve. Miss Bolton, I would appreciate your solid opinion as well."

"Of course," I said noticing the disgruntled look on Mr. Dodgson's face. He gave this dinner party to put his daughter in James's way. It must have cost him some pride to invite me. Especially after his daughter sat by Mr. Davies at an inconvenience distance across the table from James. Miss Williams gave up her seat next to James in my favor.

Our delay caused even more mischief because the table became uneven. James, to save Miss Williams' place next to him, sat Miss Clarke next to the hostess. Miss Williams and I were forced to sit together. Despite our host's annoyance and his wife's humiliation, I used the positioning to my full advantage throughout the meal.

Miss Williams smiled as much as ever but did not forcefully exert herself into the conversation as she usually did. I listened to the insipid noise James made debating exotic fruit marmalade to berry jelly. I remember having arguments like this when we were children. Perhaps if I had not been educated by one of the most celebrated minds in the country over the last ten years, I would find the debate engaging still.

I indicated a preference for jellies but interjected that personal preference could not be debated because there was no right answer and said nothing else. James would debate it, and Miss Clarke, whom he was most focused on, though she seemed to see it as ridiculous, engaged him, which in turn brought Mr. Davies into the conversation. I glanced at

Richard, who smirked. Had James always been like this? Even when I loved him so much?

A memory of when I was fifteen popped up. My mother was ill. She sent me over to James' house to get me out of the way because my father was in a bad mood. My father called me into his study before I could leave. He grabbed the back of my hair, so I would look him in the eyes. He told me in no uncertain terms if I let James Evans touch me, he'd kill him. I was meant for more than an ill-mannered country family who could not afford to go to London.

He pulled out the chunk of my hair and left. I'd wept the tears of heartbreak. I spent the next few days learning to style my hair creatively, so no one would notice the bald spot. I mourned with the intensity of youthful misery. I once loved James Evans, yet, here he was in front of me debating jellies, and I could not be more indifferent to him.

"I have always wanted to go to India," I said quietly aside to Miss Williams. "Perhaps when this is all over, you, a wealthy heiress, and me, something of the same, could go to India together, thereby making the trip proper."

She glanced at me, startled. She whispered, "He made it clear he would not see me again, and I… I could not tolerate looking at him as things are."

"Many years can do much for a person's sentiments. Besides, I said nothing about your captain, I simply expressed an interest in going to India. I have seen pictures of English ladies up on elephant-back, and I would so desire to try it myself. If we bumped into your Captain, and you, who are so young looking, wore a fine muslin that made you look like a girl, I could not help it," I whispered.

She laughed a little but said nothing. Rick and Richard both glanced at me. I grinned at them, thinking the aunt would be an ally.

As the evening progressed, I learned more about the village that housed Mrs. Williams, as I was determined to call on her, and the child, who would now be over four years. Also, by appearing extremely companionable, I inquired and collected a list of all the parishes Mrs. Williams had lived in the five years since she banished herself and her brother from their home parish. I didn't have any idea what I would do with the information, but Lawrence's first step was always to gather as much information as possible.

James commented, somewhat disgruntled, on Miss Williams and I becoming such friends. I vowed she was a lovely lady; she returned the compliment. As much as he hinted, we ought to fight over him, neither of us did. I couldn't help wondering how much of this folly was his natural person, and how much a result of his degrading marriage, that made him yearn for respect. For the first time since I was a girl, I did not regret losing James Evans. I may never get Lawrence, but at least I found enough sense to love him.

Chapter 18

The next day I woke early and wrote many letters of inquiry to the churches in all the parishes where Miss Williams indicated they had lived. I wrote to the men of the church, certain even if they could not give me particulars, they would be likely to instruct me toward those who could. After doing so I felt grimy and lackluster. I could only hope the country curates were shepherds for their flock and offended enough with the young man to help. When I sealed the last letter, I felt silly.

Why was I doing this? What if Lawrence was wrong? What if the boy stayed in London and we never saw him again? I sincerely hoped Lawrence was wrong and the young man had enough sense to stay away. But then again, Lawrence had yet to be wrong, so I vowed the letters must be mailed, and soon.

In this last crumb of courage, I applied to the very young Mrs. Williams. I was determined the girl should be vindicated because clearly, she did not mean to degrade herself. Not to mention it served my purposes very well if Mr. Williams were married. I wrote:

Dear Mrs. Williams,

I have not the pleasure of an introduction to you but I hope you will forgive me for my impertinence in writing to you. I am writing concerning your husband. He has, as I doubt you can pretend otherwise, been carousing in our neighborhood and I mean to see him recognized for it. He has offered for my niece, and though I cannot be sure he would follow through with a marriage. I must ask you to protect your own. I hate to ask so delicate a question, but can you prove your marriage to Titus Williams?

I am collecting all manner of testimony against him. Though it will greatly pain you I know, please send me whatever you can manage of your own story. You need not vilify, nor aggrandize the young man in question, simply a truth of all that occurred between you. I understand he lived with you for a time. Everyone must face their lapses in this life, and for the safety of my niece, I hope to now force Mr. Williams to be accountable for his.

I know it is a leap, but will you come to us in Dorset Shire? It is my greatest wish for you and your little boy to manage a holiday. We would be most eager to receive you. I will, of course, make all your travel arrangements if you think you can be spared from your daily duties for a month or two, and I can promise you a most extravagant Christmas if you choose to come.

Mr. Williams is in the neighborhood with his Aunt who has talked greatly in your favor. Though I cannot expect you to receive a welcome into their home, I would like very much for you to come to my brother's home. Please at the very least write back. Mr. Williams cannot continue to go unchecked. Surely, for your child's sake, as well as your own.

Yours,

Miss Myra Bolton

I sealed this letter and prayed over it, for the girl that might have been my niece if I hadn't chanced to look out the window.

"Richard," I said, coming into the breakfast room, "Can you frank these for me? This one must be sent post-haste because it must go all the way to Scotland."

He took the stack I handed him and examined them.

"What are you scheming?" he asked, stopping confused at the last letter. I told him all Miss Williams told me and explained that we must get more information.

"What will you do with the information?"

"I do not know yet. I am praying he will stay in London. But Lawrence is rarely wrong when it comes to human nature. I do not wish to be caught unprepared if he comes back. I do not even need Mr. Williams to be here to publish his misdeeds around the neighborhood just in case he tries to somehow manipulate Millie Fielding from London."

"You said the aunt will ensure they do not renew their lease. How much trouble can the young man cause in a month's time if he does come back?" Richard asked.

"That is not all. I want to …" I closed my eyes. How did I explain why I needed to do this? How did I tell him, I was trying to wash my hands of sin so dreadful they could not be cleaned? I took a deep breath and said:

"I hate to just run the young man out of the county to have him terrorize another. I wish to stop him. I am trying to think about what Lawrence would do at this point. He is always gathering information," I said shrugging.

Richard laughed.

"He and I were bunkmates at school. If I think extremely hard, I may be able to put myself in his mindset as well."

"He once said if a person can gather enough information the solution presents itself, but I cannot be certain it will work for me. Considering Titus Williams seems to have an unnatural interest in Clara, we must be prepared if he is insolent enough to come back," I answered.

"We will work together. I haven't had a good lark in years. Since Mary is in town for another three weeks, we may as well see what we can do."

"I agree," I said. We were quiet as I looked over what was set out for breakfast. Unsure of my abilities, I said as nonchalantly as possible,

"I don't suppose… I believe if we applied to Lawrence. Not to have him join us, but perhaps think on the matter and write some direction," I determinedly did not look at my brother.

"I see you have little faith in my scheming abilities," he said.

"Nothing of the kind, but you must acknowledge they are not refined as Lawrence's. Also, I believe you have a scheme against Lawrence himself, and though I cannot approve the scheme as he is behaving in the confines of his honor, this legitimate request can only serve you twice as well."

"Ah, you have grown into a sensible woman, Myra. I will write to him and justly accuse him of converting my sister into a schemer. And because the idea of your marrying a marquess is offensive to you, I will allow you to condemn yourself to Mr. Evans and his condiment debates. However, you must not expect so much from me. Be offended if you must, but I will persist in assisting you to a marquess, as I have a wager on the line," he said, laughing.

"Only if you will not grow offended when I repaper your walls,' I said.

"Excuse me," Richard said, looking around.

"I hate the look of gangrene infection in every room. When Mary returns, the first thing I will do with my money is eradicate this house of father's illness."

"Well, as a proud man I should refuse, but I can see it means something to you. Mary will be delighted, though I must warn you, she has an unhealthy attachment to lilac," he said.

"I do not care what the color, I just cannot tolerate spending all of my years in a house that looks as though the walls are crawling with infection."

"Whatever you like, Myra," he said, smiling to himself as he went from the room.

I could do worse than resigning myself to Bolton Lodge. My brother was a pleasant fellow. I simply couldn't live in the aging carcass of my father's ideals fading year after year. I sat down to breakfast, reading the paper Richard left.

Shortly after this, a letter was brought into me. I did not recognize the writing or the seal, but broke it to read:

He returned, late last night. He is still intent on her. I have never seen him so determined. Take Care. Do not respond to this, he must not suspect me. If you could get a message to Miss Clarke or Mr. Evans to send me an invitation for any space of time in the next few days, I would be most indebted to you. I fear to be alone with him in this state.
Sadie Williams

I handed it to Rick who just entered the room.

"Should we go get her?" he asked.

"Lawrence said to make him pretend he is respectable. Above everything, we cannot make him desperate, if we manage nothing else. He will be gone in a month."

"But if he shows his true colors, we can..."

"Inspire him to run away with one of the local girls? I do not think he would hesitate to use force against a woman," I said remembering how he looked taking hold of Clara, she may as well have been a pheasant pushing away a hound.

"We should help her, somehow," he answered.

"What can we do? The law will not get involved in a family matter, and we cannot prove much if anything against him. We must protect Clara. We either pretend for the next month until he goes back to school, or entrap Mr. Williams in his own net until he runs."

"Even then he will be able to work some somersault to get out," Rick said. I turned to the footman and asked him to go get Richard, then turned back to Rick.

"I believe your father asked the Evans boy to fish. Perhaps we should have James invite Miss. Williams. Mr.

Williams must believe she and I are still rivals, so the invitation must come from that source."

"I'll ride over there this morning with an invitation. I can manage James. He is a bit of a simpleton. Perhaps I will set myself up as his rival. If I seem interested in Miss Williams, and her fortune, I doubt James Evans will allow her out of his sight," Rick said laughing, "In fact, Aunt, I was surprised to find that you had once considered him a beau."

Rick turned to find his father to arrange the day that he might ride over to the neighbors.

"Thank you, dear," I said sarcastically to the back of him.

I wondered that I could have been so enamored with James. He is very handsome, but is that all there was to it?

I spent my few free hours with him riding horses along every path in the county. We played cards or checkers with his mother, so I did not have to go home and spend the little free time I had improving myself at some womanly trait or other. My father would be in rages. My mother would send me to James' home because of the close proximity.

In James' home, his very presence meant I was safe. Safety equated to love for me in those days. I would see him repaid for it. I would be sure he did not enter into a situation that would one day ruin his daughter because Miss Williams would be expected to invite her nephew whenever he chose to come.

The outing was easily arranged. We all agreed upon the roles that should be played. We decided to act unsuspecting of Titus Williams' true nature until we could prove something that would put him out of reach of all women, not just Clara. Richard, upon reading the letter, swallowed his pride, copied the letter and sent it express to Lawrence. Both of us, it would seem, were out of our scheming depth.

Chapter 19

The next morning Clara came into the room closely followed by Rick.

"I do not think I have seen you out of reach of your little sister in the last day," I said.

"I... I like her company," Rick said.

"He is protecting me," she said.

"In her own home?"

"I...I admit the scoundrel whose name will not be mentioned in front of Clara, boasted once of stealing into a women's... into her home while her family was there. He takes what he wants with no regard and claims to have illegitimate children scattered about."

"Even his Aunt thinks there is something wrong with him. She is afraid of him," I said, starting to feel worried.

"Yes, the few of us who knew him at school thought him wrong in the head," Rick said.

"Lord Grey Hull knows all. We wrote to him to let him know Mr. Williams returned to the area. He is most educated in human behavior and can tell us if he thinks the man is sick in the head. Perhaps we can have him committed to a lunatic asylum," I said, thinking that would be an interesting alternative, though a rich young man who could exert his own will would not commit himself. Still, it was a start.

"I think transportation would be a better fate. The petted are often educated to look out only for themselves and would do well in the harsher, untamed climates of Australia," Rick said. I took out a little pencil I kept in my pocket. I wrote perhaps asylum, or have him transported.

"I do not think a young man supported by his wealthy father can be expected to endure either of those fates," Clara said sitting down with her plate next to me.

"We shall see," I said. I had a marquess in my pocket, and though he would not marry me, he would in every other way assist me.

I breakfasted with my kin, wondering if Titus Williams could be proved insane. Perhaps his hatred of Rick could be used against him. My mentor, the late Henry Grey, insisted love and hatred blinded people. Considering the Williams boy did not seem capable of the first emotion, he must live solely by the second. With nothing like love or compassion to counteract the anger, the intensity of negativity would likely blind him even further.

First and foremost, my loyalty demanded that Clara be protected. I started to wonder if it would not be best to send her somewhere at least until we could be certain she was out of reach of the man. The more I thought of it, the more I felt at the very core, there was something very wrong with Titus Williams.

"Clara, how would you feel about taking a trip to India?" I asked.

"Excuse me?" she said, confused.

"Only just thinking out loud," I said.

"Well as the two of you seem so jumpy, I guess it ought to be known, father also felt for my safety," she said, pulling out a small ivory-handled pistol. "I promised father if the man set upon me, even in church, I was to aim for his heart. As you know, brother, I am a better shot than you."

"Not so, I have been improving my aim," he said as she stowed the small pistol back in the pocket of her dress.

"Very well, I suppose that will put my mind at ease, but do be careful not to shoot your leg," I said.

"It sits heavily upon me," Clara said fidgeting.

"The boy is likely to find his way into our outing this morning, and I must communicate something to you, that you may find hard to hear," I said, looking painfully at Clara.

"What more can shock me?"

"Though his aunt insists it was a sham marriage, Mr. Williams has a wife and, what is more, a child to his credit."

Brother and sister were silent.

"He would have engaged me in bigotry," she said.

I said nothing as I never thought he meant to marry her in the first place. The look on my face must have communicated this. Clara nodded, and for the first time, she looked to understand the deceit the man was capable of.

"I do not think he should hurt another woman," Clara said biting her lip.

"No, we will certainly not let him," I said, but could not sound confident. There was no one legally capable of stopping him. In the old days Richard could call him out for a duel, but even that was illegal now. Clara stood and left the room, her breakfast untouched.

When the hour of our outing arrived, we convened in the entryway. The day was warm and lovely for the end of August and though my sleeves were short, I only put on a light shawl and my bonnet. We heard a carriage approaching and all moved to action. Clara came to me, and I helped her on with her bonnet. After that, she held my hand, and with her other, I could see she was steadying the gun in her pocket. We all went to the door.

James drove a lovely little open chaise with no coach box. His two oldest children sat on either side of him as he whipped the horse that was too big for the carriage. Jim watched his father's every movement. Sally gripped his arm terrified. The lovely Miss Williams and Miss Clarke sat on the bench behind him covering their faces from the dust being kicked up.

"Mr. Bolton, we are so excited to fish today," James said when he reached us, "it was kind of you to extend the invitation to the ladies."

"Of course," he said as Miss Williams caught my eye and smiled shyly.

"Is that a new filly pulling your chaise?" Richard asked.

"It is. She's a French-bred Anglo-Arabian. I bought her from your man over in Hampshire. She jumps like a champ and I expect to go fox hunting in a few weeks."

I smiled. James managed to turn the horse's head and the box he drove swung rather violently.

"Miss Bolton," he asked, "can I offer you a ride?"

"I think you are full, I will--"

As I moved Clara to my brother's carriage, a horseman rode up the lane in a billowing cloud of dust; Mr. Titus Williams seemed intent on making a grand entrance. He was a handsome young man on his expensive steed and came to a dramatic stop, prodding up the dust.

"Mr. Bolton, I see you are to have an outing. I hope I may intrude a moment on your time," Titus Williams said, dismounting.

"There are a few things I would say to you," Richard said.

"And they are justified," Mr. Williams said glancing at Clara. I put a shoulder in front of Clara and scowled at him. Rick and Phineas both came forward.

"Ah my schoolmates," he said turning to them. He hit his leg with his whip in a manner that hinted at annoyance. However, he said, with what appeared sincerity, "These boys did me a great many services in school. They checked my folly many times. I was raised alone, without any guidance except to get whatever I wanted. Rick often had to hint at my inappropriate behavior, but now that I have grown, I am mature enough to see the benefit they did me," he said giving his hand to Rick, who did not take it, and then Phineas. Phineas, not only shook but seemed genuinely pleased by this speech and said, "I am glad to see you so improved. There was a time we would not meet with you again because of your folly."

"For myself," Rick said, "I cannot see you have improved and would advise my father to act with great prejudice."

"Yes," Mr. Williams cut in, "your concern would be warranted back then, but I am a reformed man, and owe it to my character to explain myself. You see, I am not come on purpose to see my old school mates. I wish to ask Mr. Bolton permission to court his daughter, Miss Clara Bolton."

Phineas colored, his expression fell, and he stepped back glancing at Clara to see how she took this. Though Phineas watched Clara cross her arms, and glare at the scoundrel, Titus Williams watched Phineas. For only a hint of a glance, Mr. Williams smirked. Was he so quick an assessor of people to see? Or had Phineas' affection for Clara been swelling his heart long enough that he may have spoken of her at school?

"That would have been the proper way to go about the thing many weeks ago," Richard responded coldly to Mr. Williams' request.

"Yes, I understood her to be making her debut in London. I thought I could wait until then to court her, but her charm disarmed me, and I plunged forward. Misguided as I have been, I did not mean to … your sister was mistaken in my intentions. She caught me so unaware, and unfairly pushed me into statements I did not mean. I did not know myself and reverted to my old ways. She accused, without foundation, and I defended without thinking," he said.

"What exactly did I mis-interpret?" I asked as he had all but confessed to me.

"I...I did mean to take Miss Clara Bolton away to Gretna Green and fix things between us before my father could interfere... I would never," he turned to Clara, full of agony, and said, "I would never have hurt you. I did not mean to imply I... I was caught off guard."

I did not mention such a trip to Scotland would be impossible in his hired rig when he had carriages at his disposal, nor did I remind him of his avoiding us so he would not be seen in public courting Clara. I did not wish to make him desperate. Instead, I listened carefully to his words. I waited to hear what he would not openly tell. Henry Grey swore the best liars had some grain of truth to build upon.

"When it came down to it, I panicked," he said, "I was prepared to vex my father and his wishes regarding me, until the truth was so forcefully put before me, and then I could not tolerate vexing him."

"And now?" Richard asked.

"I have thought long on what Miss Bolton said. I believe your sister was right." Here he bowed to me, then carefully continued:

"I believe if I am constant to Miss Clara, it will show my father that I cannot be governed on the constraints of my heart by him. He will see reason. Though I have a cousin he wishes for me to court, your family is of the nobility. Your connections are so good. It will all be righted. I have set all my affection for, and do wish to court, Miss Clara Bolton. I will show my school fellows how much I have changed. My honor, though not adhered to in the past, now requires me to do right by the lady."

He bowed to my brother. Richard bowed back, and said:

"You may be a part of our party. I do not wish you to show attention to my daughter, but rather for today you may be a companion to my son and his friend. I will be guided by my son's previous knowledge of your character until he is convinced you have changed."

"I will by lengths show you I can be trusted," Mr. Williams said bowing first to Richard, then to Rick and finally to me.

And there it was. He just revealed his whole plan. Make my brother trust him, which would transfer to myself and Clara. He meant to take the long route. I could not help thinking he may actually mean to marry Clara. Did he wish to make her miserable through marriage as revenge on Rick? What had Phineas to do with it? Mr. Williams watched Phineas as often as Clara, and more often than Richard and myself, whom he scrutinized.

Would he find another fishing village for Clara, never letting Rick know what happened to his little sister? Perhaps he meant to marry her, take her to London and let the whispers of his dishonor make her and us all horrified every day of our lives? We all lived for years seeing my mother's sad eyes, her broken spirit and at times her unrestrained tears. To see Clara in such a position would be devastating.

"Clara, you will be my companion today," I said sternly. We walked to the coach as I heard Mr. Williams rehearse his speech for what audience I couldn't be sure. He must have needed to say it all to feel the times he practiced it in his head be justified.

"I assure you, sir, I am, by my grandfather well provided for if my father chooses to cast me off…"

I gave Clara a little push into the carriage.

"He seems very sincere does he not?"

"Knowing everything you do about him, that he has a wife and child abandoned, would you still want him?"

"We do not know the situation. He would not be the first to have made such a mistake in his youth. It seems he at least took care of the lady and child. Besides Aunt Myra, if he were already married, he would not address me, or my father so," she said.

I cringed. This was going to be harder than I thought.

"Do you think him capable of securing your happiness?"

"Perhaps not… but running him out of the neighborhood when he is trying to redeem himself seems cruel," she said biting her lip in contemplation. She looked like Eva when, despite her youth and inexperience, she was certain her compassion and understanding should be adhered to before my elderly caution and wisdom. Fortunately, I knew how to counteract such young nobility.

"That is fair enough dear. I will do nothing to him, except to say he will face himself. And if he can do that and find redemption, we will leave him to his fate," I said.

"Thank you, Aunt," she said looking relieved. "Because, right or wrong, I did have an affection for him."

"Yes, and only yesterday morning his aunt was afraid to be alone with him."

"That I had forgotten. It is amazing how quickly he makes one forget," she said.

"It is a curse," I said as the carriage lurched forward.

Chapter 20

"Do me a favor," I said to Clara as we reached the lake.

"Of course."

"Do not take my opinion on this matter. Watch Mr. Williams. Do not get caught up in how he treats you but take notice of how he treats his aunt, Miss Williams, who is his most constant companion, his confidante in every way," I said.

"I will," she said.

Clara and I walked a little path with her sisters and James' ladies. The men went the other direction to little rowboats at the lakes edge. Rick and Phineas kept Mr. Williams from us by making him fish. Sally Evans eventually joined us. She sat next to Clara watching as I showed her how to work beads into her lace.

"May I show you how to embroider?" Miss Clarke asked the girl.

"Can I try making lace?" she asked.

"Of course," I said. "Can you crochet?"

"I can," she said, producing her work of woolen yarn.

"Very good," I said. "Take your crochet needles, and I will give you some finer thread to work with. That will be a good place for you to start. First, you must grow proficient at pairing the yarn over your stitch like this," I said showing her how to find the decrease. She worked at it and was frustrated easily.

"Here dear, let me show you something a little simpler," Miss Clarke started.

"No, I will make lace," she insisted.

"Apologize to Miss Clarke, or I will not help you," I said quietly.

She struggled within herself, then finally said, "Please excuse me."

Miss Clarke nodded kindly and I couldn't help thinking if James married her, Sally would eat her alive. I showed Sally the stitch again.

"This is not working," she complained.

"It is easier to see what you are supposed to do if you look calmly," I said. "Perhaps you should take a little break, then when you are rested, you can try again."

"Or I shall persevere until I get it," she raged, turning red.

"Here, let me get you started, and then you can copy my pattern," I said. I made a few of the necessary holes in her stitches. She tried again, but her angry hands could not manage to make anything of the pattern.

"Miss Clarke, I understand you are under the guardianship of your father," I said ignoring the child as she fumed.

"Yes," she answered, "but I have come to stay with my Uncle Clarke for a time."

"I am sure that is a nice holiday. Has he taken you to the ocean?" I asked.

"No, we stay close to the church," she said.

"Ah, and Miss Williams, is your father still your guardian?" I asked.

"No, he passed on years ago. My mother died last year, my oldest brother is my guardian, and requires me to watch after Titus," she said. She didn't look away from her pattern and clenched her jaw.

"You are not teaching me how to do this," Sally snapped at me.

"You are not patient enough to learn," I said, unstitching her work and showing her again how to find the decrease.

After the sun grew warmer the servants set up a table and put out food. The men rowed in smelling like moss and wet canvas.

"Miss Bolton look at the fish I caught," Jim said, holding up a decent-sized, dark-spotted trout.

"Oh, that is a beauty. Well done," I said smiling at him. James took it with great pride and helped his son wrap it in the paper.

"Well at least you've had some luck. Miss Bolton cannot teach me how to make lace, and I have listened the whole morning to her poor instructions," Sally said.

"Oh, come now," Mr. Titus Williams said. "Miss Bolton has been in the first houses in London. She and Miss Clara are making a beautiful creation."

He smiled his most charming smile at Clara who tucked her head and blushed. He continued, "My aunt does nothing but embroider." He nodded at Miss Williams. I do not know what we will do with one more pillow. You are better off learning from Miss Bolton."

I said nothing. Clara glanced at me. Miss Williams only laughed at his set-down and admitted it true. Then she kept on with her work. When we were called to luncheon, I was ready to end our outing. Only my concern for Miss Williams made me consider staying out after the meal was eaten.

"Miss Bolton, you will not eat cream, will you?" Sally asked. "It is not refined."

"Well, I do prefer the blackberries with cream," I said, putting an extra dollop on, just to make my point.

"I have heard that cream is all the rage this season in London," Mr. Williams said. "In fact, you ought to ask Miss Bolton about Duchess Eva Garrett's ball. I heard rumors that they served bananas in coconut cream."

I looked at him.

"How did you know that?" I asked.

"A friend from university told me," he said, "Viscount Griffiths."

"Ah, I see," I said, but could not be comfortable. He had started to collect information on me and was trying to show me he also had powerful friends. Why would he do that? Not to mention he seemed to think the way to win me over was to diminish his aunt's value in Sally's eyes, thereby winning over James.

"I have never had a banana," Sally admitted looking at me curiously.

"They are very sweet with a smooth texture," I said, putting a roasted potato bathed in rosemary on my plate.

"When I go to London I would very much like to eat a banana," Sally said. "That would be a good reason to go to London."

"Yes, it would," I said smiling at her. "My favorites are the desserts Lord Hull's cook made with lemons, a custard in a pie shell."

"Are lemons very sweet?" she asked.

"No, they tart, until you add sugar, then they become a sweet-savory dish that is very satisfying."

"I would like to have a lemon dessert," the girl said.

"I had cake with lemon zest in it last Christmas," Miss Clarke said.

Sally looked at her interested.

"That would be particularly good. I do like cake," she decided.

"Yes, but Miss Bolton's desert must have been made with fresh lemon juice," Mr. Williams said.

Before the two could say anymore, I walked away with my food. I did not wish for Mr. Williams to help me please James's daughter. How ridiculous, of all things. It did not matter. When I sat down with Clara, Mr. Williams sat with us, primarily addressing Sally, pointing out all my good qualities to the girl. I think he would have acted in my place, flattering James as well if he hadn't been so preoccupied talking to Richard and Jim about the fish his boy caught.

After lunch, Mr. Titus Williams mounted his horse and showed us how well the animal jumped. The two looked in a constant tug a war. Titus William did not hesitate to keep the horse in line with his whip but often pulled the reins too tightly in a conflicting way. I pitied the poor, confused animal. It put joy into my heart when James mounted his new horse, giving Mr. Williams a few pointers. Mr. Williams pretended to appreciate it, but I could see a slight shifting of his eye, indicating annoyance.

James seemed just as proficient as ever on his horse and had more of a rapport with the new animal than Mr. Williams did with his broken beast. James came alive engaged in an activity he spent hours doing in his youth. Mr. Davies joined in showing off his steed. Clara cheered when the three cleared a tall hedge. Phineas grew moody and spilled the last of the cream.

"Is that entirely safe?" Sally whispered to me after her father insisted on jumping a fence in the distance.

"He is a very accomplished rider, and after the horse has been worked your ride home will be much smoother."

"Yes, that would be better," she said conspiratorially. She sat more still after she ate, and I showed her again how to work lace. This time she was able to get an infantile pattern started.

When the afternoon ended, Clara and I rode back in the carriage alone.

"What did you notice?" I asked.

"Mr. Williams seems to be courting you," she said sullenly.

"Yes, he is trying very hard to win me over," I said. "At all costs, it would seem."

"I suppose you mean for me to mention how dismissive, and even cruel he was to his aunt at times," she said.

"Also, he sat near you and only addressed you to see if your food was to your liking," I said.

"He looked at me quite a bit," she said.

"He did. He was looking at you to see if you were pleased with his efforts to win me over. Though he did not try to charm you as much as me," I said.

"No, do you think he is going to woo you next?" she asked, annoyed.

"Oh dear, he thinks he has to get through me to get to you. He will tire of the effort quickly. By the time he decides to refocus on you, he must have lost all his charm to you. You must think him little worth your time."

"I... I do not think I am in danger," she said.

"Until he smothers you with attention. Then it will get harder," I said, not pointing out how she'd already defended him a few times during the day.

"Why are we doing this?" Clara asked. "Why don't we just tell him we know he is a scoundrel and force him to leave?"

I paused. I did not want to frighten the poor girl. I could not tell her she carried the gun because he was dangerous, and we could not push him into hurting her. I said, "Because dear, we need to stop him. Millie is not safe from him. Nor is the next unfortunate parish."

"Very well," Clara said.

"Next time we go out, let's invite Millie Fielding, shall we?" I asked.

"Why?" she asked.

"Because if his affection for you is to be believed, he must throw her off. It would be best for her to feel the sting now than to become his prey later," I said.

"I shall write to her to join us when we go out again in two days."

"That would be nice," I said sitting back. I wondered how long I would be able to tolerate the ridiculous man's behavior.

Chapter 21

That afternoon at tea a letter came into the room and was handed to me on a silver platter. I opened it.

Lawrence received Richard's note and Miss Williams's copied letter. He asked if he should ride out tonight, or if it could wait until morning since his neighbors insisted upon visiting him.

"It seems the young man is pretending at honor. If Lawrence comes so soon, everyone will change with the Marquess in attendance. We must only get through the month until the boy goes back to school. Lawrence must be persuaded to wait a few days at the least," Richard said.

"Did you send my letter, the one that needed to go post?" I asked.

"Not yet. I haven't been to town."

"May I have it back please?"

"Of course," he said.

"I think, if I ask, Lawrence would be pleased for the chance to use the schooner he inherited. He may be a trifle sick of the train," I said, smiling. Rick questioned me with his eyes, but I turned to a side table while the others took their tea and wrote to Lawrence by his messenger.

It was a strange request, but I believed that Mr. Williams' foe wife the key to his undoing. If his marriage could be published in all the major papers, only those willing to fiddle with a married man would be taken in by his deceptions. He could not pretend to be unmarried once everyone considered him to be wed. Especially if he had to face his wife in front of Clara. I wrote:

Dear Lord Grey Hull,

I hope this finds you well. I know you desire to use the schooner you inherited from your father since you commissioned the steam-powered paddlewheel to be fixed to the side. I have the perfect opportunity for you. Enclosed in this letter is a message for the wife of Mr. Titus Williams, yes, the very one so interested in my niece. It must be expediently taken to the coast of Scotland. The exact address of the lady must be discovered. I only know the name of the small fishing village where she resides. I am certain you, with your many powers of discovery, would be the exact person to ascertain her whereabouts. I would not chance to ask so great a request if I did not know you only require a reason to go sailing.

When you find the woman, see if she would be an asset. I cannot help but think being abandoned for five years, would put her in just a state to help us. On our part, assure her we will assist her in improving her situation if she appears willing to testify against her husband. Above all, I do not wish to further injure her. I understand there is a child involved.

This gives me a second inducement for you to go. Can you see if the sickness in the father, presents in the child? Dr. James Prichard would perhaps call this moral insanity, would you agree? I know you and he consulted together several times, and I wonder if the good doctor would consult in this case. Is the illness he describes hereditary or is it a matter of child-rearing? These are the things of most interest to you, and so I do not hesitate to ask, knowing you would enjoy examining them.

Let me know post-haste if you are intent on my course of action or if you have another you think more beneficial.

Yours,

MB

"Aunt, you cannot send that to a marquess," Rick said. I turned to find him reading over my shoulder.

"Oh, we are such informal friends he will find my impertinence not only endearing but a proof of our intimacy," I said grinning at the boy even though he ought to be scolded. He thought the letter all part of the scheme. Rick only saw the two of us together for a short time on the train, and Lawrence had been focused on the tale of Mr. Williams. Rick could not suppose the friendship that existed may require privacy in our correspondence. Rick said:

"If you can speak to him like that, you ought to marry him."

"Here, here," Richard said winking at his son.

"You are a wicked boy," I teased. "Lord Grey Hull does not mean to remarry. Now hand me the wax." I put out my hand. He put it in my hand then sat next to me as I finished. I took the opportunity to ask in a quiet undertone:

"Why does Mr. Williams dislike Phineas so much?"

"I do not know," Rick said, looking at me, surprised I had ascertained as much, as youth often is when discovering the mature mind can have as much merit as their own.

"How were they in school?" I asked.

"Titus always competed with Phineas, but academically Phineas is a wonder. He remembers everything he is taught and for some reason, Titus found that very maddening."

"It is interesting. Phineas must have been well-loved in school," I said.

"Yes, by the students as well as the teachers."

"His being the genuine article of what Mr. Williams pretends at must irk him," I said. "Phineas is such a kind young man. He is the only one who is trying to give Mr. Williams a chance. I wonder if that is more annoying than gratifying to him."

"Phineas always gave him the benefit of the doubt in school as well. I almost think that is why Titus dislikes him so much," Rick said, taking a scone from Clara. I waited until she was out of hearing range and said:

"Has Phineas always felt affectionate toward Clara?" I asked.

"Yes, but he does not admit it."

"Never at school?" I asked.

"He always praised Clara when I brought her up, and… well, he never showed much interest in any other girl." Rick stopped and examined me. He said, "You believe Williams must have figured it out. You think he is here to …"

"I am not sure. He sees he cannot fluster you but seems to enjoy taunting Phineas in his flirtation with Clara."

"I noticed that as well," Rick said, then he smiled a little and said, "which means when we stop Titus Williams for good, perhaps the most fitting lesson for him will be that he never beat Phineas in anything."

I nodded but said nothing. It concerned me the way Rick said he would stop him for good. I could only wonder what Rick planned and prayed it would not impact the rest of his life negatively.

Chapter 22

The next morning, we received a fresh messenger with Lawrence's response.

Dear Myra,

I am so glad to have any occupation on your behalf. You are not wrong. I have been wanting to test out my schooner since making the modifications. Going up the channel seems the perfect opportunity. I will learn all I can. Be careful of the young man. With no conscience, he will employ any level of cunning and manipulation to gain his point. Do not ever let down your guard, no matter how convincing he is. Never be fooled that he is growing sensible. He cannot, though it will be his first goal to make you believe in him. People who cannot be trusted want most for people to believe they can.

The most important thing to know is this, do not make him desperate. As long as he thinks he is fooling you or at least has the chance of fooling you, he will commit to his appearance of respectability. The moment he thinks he has lost his footing, he will not retreat but strike. He thinks he is invincible and will be very reckless. The only concern he will ever have is for his personal safety. After that, nothing is beneath him. Please do not push him past that point until I can get back to you. If you feel him dropping the pretense, protect yourself, Clara, and Rick at all costs. I think he would be more likely to do you or Rick harm because, in his head, you have disrespected him. Be cautious.

I will return with the girl as soon as may be possible. I would feel better taking you and Clara with me. Send word if you will come.

Lawrence

I was astounded that Lawrence could so accurately describe Titus Williams' behavior. He often said very few people ever do anything unpredictable. I thought him very pessimistic but seeing such proof of it before me made me leery. I wrote back that Richard would not be separated from Clara and I had a cot moved into her room.

The next day was the Sabbath. We went to church as we always did. Though he'd never been on previous Sundays, Mr. Williams was there, and he was pious.

"God will punish every man who sins, no matter who the sinner is," Mr. Clarke stormed. Mr. Williams nodded in agreement. He could not be firmer a believer in sin, and the punishment of a person engaged in sin. I remembered the greedy look on his face when he claimed my niece as if she were not a thinking, breathing human being. It was almost as if he set that man aside and pulled out this new one as easily as changing his breeches.

Mr. Clarke spoke of how the rich and mighty would fall in sin the same as a poor man. Mr. Williams had the gall to look over at his aunt and sadly shake his head. She looked at him confused, but his blow struck. James witnessed the action, and when Miss Williams turned her head to James he looked away. She looked up into the rafters, the action she took when she was trying not to cry.

I felt my anger rising. Whatever sin Miss Williams was consigned to, if any, I felt certain they were hoisted upon her shoulders by her nephew. I felt myself a religious person, but often I could not reconcile a hopeless person who sinned out of desperation versus a person who saw sin as a game to be gotten away with, as my father had.

Before he died, Lawrence's father Henry and I discussed it often. We disagreed, him believing any sin, a sin. He lived a very padded life and only knew of his stepmother's indiscretions he was forced to cover up. I did not think he could know desperation leading to sin. Our argument always ended with us agreeing, perhaps, that was the reason only God judged, but it never satisfied me. I needed desperation to excuse sin. It was the only way to assuage my guilt.

When Mr. Clarke spoke of living in the burden of sin, Mr. Williams nodded more vigorously. Rick looked at me from across Clara and I thought the young man may laugh. I gave him a dirty look, but only because he drew the attention of the rector and I did not want Mr. Clarke to think we were laughing at him.

When Mr. Williams bowed his head to pray, he curled into the very posture of a devoted servant of God. I could hardly believe his hypocrisy. Could a man be so devoid of feeling? How could he kneel in such a way before God and not burn up for his blasphemy?

"Aunt, we're praying," Clara nudged me, and I recollected myself.

When we finished, I watched Millie Fielding, the young lady Clara had been so concerned for. She held the posture of one who was despondent. Her mother, however, looked furious. She glared at Clara, until Clara knew she was being glared at. After services, Mr. Williams engaged Millie and her mother in conversation. The widow gushed as if she were being courted. Millie glanced often at Clara, who sent her oldest friend looks of unbridled concern.

For my part, I made sure Mr. Williams knew he was being watched. He did all that was appropriate to remove himself from the Fielding's company. After this, Mrs. Fielding looked devastated, on the brink of tears. She stopped and had a whispered conversation with Richard. Whatever they said, it did not end well. The woman stomped off, yanking her pretty young daughter behind her. Richard watched, looking grim.

"Mrs. Fielding was vexed with you?" I asked as we walked out of the church.

"She heard we took Mr. Williams fishing after we sent her the damning letter about him. She accused us of trying to manipulate her and her daughter to give Clara the advantageous match."

"Oh dear," I said.

"Yes," Richard said. "I do not know what to do for her. The young man has been…"

Richard put a hand to his forehead and closed his eyes.

"What can we do?" he asked.

"Invite Millie to our outings, so at least we may keep an eye on her interactions with Mr. Williams."

"I will write when we get home," he said.

Chapter 23

Our outings resumed the next morning. Millie Fielding, or rather the letter sent in the shaky hand of an older woman, refused the invitation to join us.

Richard, under the guise of determination to teach Jim to fish, invited all the men out on the lake again, forcing Mr. Williams onto the body of water and away from his daughter. James came in his carriage again, but this time Miss Williams was not with him. To keep up the ruse I could not even ask him where she was, because I dared not show any concern for her. Thankfully, Richard asked, "Mr. Williams, where is your Aunt?"

"I do not know. She usually drives with Mr. Evans," he said innocently as if he did not know what he'd done to tarnish his aunt's reputation the day before.

"I had not arranged to pick her up," James said, looking around embarrassed.

"I will send a servant for her," Richard said nodding to his footman. I saw the glint of ire in his eye, and noticed James did not make eye contact with him again.

Miss Williams joined us after the men were out on the lake. She seemed withdrawn, but while her nephew wasn't around, I did my best to cheer her up. Miss Clarke was ever kind to Miss Williams, but her compassion became a little condescending, like she was the shepherd and Miss Williams her lost lamb. I pretended not to notice. Thankfully guided by my civil kindness, Sally and Clara treated her with respect and did not notice the change.

Richard was called away by his steward and promised to return soon with the carriage. He asked us not to wait on the picnic for him. After the picnic meal was eaten, he still wasn't returned. Clara proposed we walk the path home. Mr. Williams agreed, sending his horse with the footman.

Clara was quickly thronged on both sides by Rick and Phineas. Mr. Williams walked next to Phineas.

"I cannot walk all that way in this heat," Miss Clarke said glancing up at James.

"I will take you to your Uncle's house," James said. Avoiding Miss Williams' eye, he continued, "Miss Bolton you will not mind watching over Sally and Jim until I return?"

"Not at all Sir," I said, nodding to the pair who joyfully started up the path toward the orchard. Though kind, Miss Clarke was no fool and saw Miss Williams fall from grace. She used it to her advantage. Strangely her feigned excuse about the heat left me wondering what happened to Mr. Davies. James no doubt felt she was on far too friendly of terms with him, but Miss Clarke had always seemed to value Mr. Davies. She did not notice as of late he was no longer a part of our outings. How easily people were discarded in general.

I sped up the path trying to catch the children but slowed when I reached Miss Williams. I smiled at her, and hoped Richard met us at the house or else she had no way home. When I reached the orchard, I found everyone had stopped to take a rest in the shade.

"Phineas, I heard you received a fellowship," Mr. Williams asked.

"Yes, last year. I will resume after Michaelmas," Phineas answered.

"I had not heard this," I said calling up from behind them. "What was your fellowship in?"

"Mathematics," he said.

Walking up to them and at just the right angle, I saw Mr. Williams' jaw clench in what I supposed was anger.

"What will you do when you graduate?" I asked pushing the subject forward.

"I am studying the mathematics of a physics professor in Munich. He is certain electric engines can be made lighter than steam. I am intrigued by it all."

Clara took up the conversation, asking all about it.

I could not attend what was said after that because Sally wanted my attention. She came to me and asked for a crab apple. I picked one for myself and Sally. She enjoyed the tangy tartness of the fruit and decided she ought to come back with a bucket and make a pie from them if my brother allowed her. Her instinct was so good, I told her she must have a talent for tasting.

"Is that good, my little crab apple?" Mr. Williams asked Sally, making her squirm in delight after she asked him to reach her one of the ripe ones on a high branch.

"Yes, thank you," she said.

I clenched my jaw and said, "We tried to invite Millie Fielding today. She refused our invitation."

"Yes, her mother is keeping a close eye on her," Mr. Williams said too quickly.

"Really," I said, then feigning innocence, I finished, "is this a recent development?"

"I cannot be sure," he said, "I have not seen her since my return from London."

"Except at church yesterday," I reminded.

"Yes, of course at church, but she hardly spoke to me. I think she is rather disappointed I have chosen Clara over her," he said.

"Does she know that?" I asked, confused how and when he would have communicated that to her if he hadn't seen her.

"Yes, I think the whole congregation must know," Mr. Williams, said glancing at me with a squint.

I smiled sardonically with an eyebrow lift to show him I was not buying it. He nodded and walked toward Clara. I followed. I knew it was not wise to draw his fury to myself, but when the facade dropped, and drop it must, I thought it safest for him to blame all his failure on me and not Rick or Clara.

We drew up next to the Victoria Plum trees Richard planted three years previous, after the queen's coronation. The trees were producing for the first time and the beautiful plump amber fruit was full of juice.

Mr. Williams picked one, and took a bite, then spit it out.

"That is awful," he said throwing the rest of the fruit into a nearby tree. Sally looked at me to assess this.

"They are only for preserving at this stage," I said handing her one, "only taste, if you eat too much it will give you a belly ache."

Sally tasted some.

"Those are inedible. The tree must have gone bad. They cannot be used for anything," Mr. Williams said determined to control Sally's opinion.

"I assure you they can be jellied," I said. Sally tasted it again, and I think she found the flavor that could improve to a lovely tartness if sweetened.

"I cannot believe they have any value," he said.

"You do not believe that something which seems bad at first can be reformed to make something good instead?" I asked.

"Certainly not! The tree ought to be chopped and burned," he said, nodding at Sally then winking. She showed her good sense by squinting at him, and I thought her adorable.

Mr. Williams ruffled her hair like she'd agreed with him and moved to catch up to Phineas, Clara, and Rick who were moving along the path toward the house again. Miss Williams glanced at me.

"Such an interesting, and varying opinion he has of reform," I whispered. She closed her eyes and we both giggled quietly.

We caught up to the other group and heard Phineas explaining something about his fellowship and how he felt there were so many other forms of power that were not yet being explored. He swore electric power could be far more useful than steam.

"No, clearly steam is the way into the future," Mr. Williams said, now winking at Clara.

"I cannot agree with you," Phineas said. "I am too well acquainted with the math to think we cannot improve upon other power sources. Steam is too heavy. We will need lighter sources of power eventually."

"Even now the railway is proof that is not true," Mr. Williams argued, but he had no grounds upon which to stand. Phineas simply did not agree with him, because he could prove him wrong. Titus Williams only wanted to be agreed with. Phineas, having a far superior mind to his, could not agree for the sake of agreeing. This bothered Titus Williams. As I had been goading him all day, Mr. Williams turned to lash out at me.

"Miss Myra Bolton, I suppose agrees with you. She spent far too much time with the scholarly Grey family." Turning to Clara to discredit me he said, "but I think you will find there is often a gap between the scholarly and those of us blessed with sound judgement. Perhaps if the scholarly were to join the real world more often they would have a better chance at marriage."

No one answered. He scoffed as if Clara joined him in my censure, when to her credit she did not. He did not notice but looked back at me and waited for me to droop as his aunt had. I laughed, and he flinched.

"Mr. Michael Faraday, a chemist, and friend to the late Henry Grey Hull, is considered one of the greatest scientists in the country. He is a particularly good husband. I met his wife on several occasions. Perhaps their manners are peculiar, but I for one prefer an educated mind and stimulating conversation to the senseless prattle of polite society."

"He must be an exception. Those sorts of men can rarely expect to marry. The ladies of society won't have them. I have heard some resort to marrying their servants, but that really ought to be prohibited by law," he said throwing this accusation my way. He must have heard the rumors about Lawrence and me.

"Marriage is a tricky thing," I said, glaring, "I do not think success or failure can be attributed to education. I suppose you cannot overlook the many cases of uneducated men in unsuccessful marriages. Since none of us here has failed at marriage, none of us has any firsthand experience. It is all supposition, is it not?"

I looked at Mr. Williams shrewdly, giving him half a knowing smile. His eyes grew small, suspicious. Was his mind also strained thinking about the little village where his wife lived in Scotland? I kept his confused glower on me, certain his aunt could not bear scrutiny.

"I believe though," I said with ire, "any relationship, be it marriage, friendship, or even familial, is more likely to fail under the weight of selfishness and cruelty, rather than education. I can only hope none of us here is guilty of that."

Mr. Williams made an exaggerated glance at his aunt, as if I must be talking about her. It was as if he couldn't possibly believe I was talking about him. He pushed the idea of failure away from himself like a snake shedding his skin. I could not have hidden my disgust if I tried. Mr. Williams contorted his eyebrows to return my disgust. He did not like me insisting the skin he slithered out of belonged to him, though it fit him perfectly to size.

I turned from him. Phineas smiled at me for defending him, though I hadn't realized I was. He must have let Mr. Williams's words too close. I decided to do more for him. I took up the subject Mr. Williams could not. I continued to question Phineas about electricity, and Mr. Williams was forced into silence so as not to reveal his ignorance. Being educated, I found Phineas intriguing and knew I had to get him and Lawrence together again.

Clara was interested but could not follow everything Phineas said. Mr. Williams wanted to talk to her in flowery language that made little sense. I thought perhaps I would spend the next morning teaching Clara the basics of what I knew about steam power. Considering she spent most of the afternoon trying to understand Phineas, perhaps that was the best way to keep her safe after all.

Chapter 24

Mr. Williams found a way to walk with us or join our group every day. Rick or Phineas was always at his side, most often Phineas because Clara preferred his company. Mr. Williams appeared in the highest spirits when he stole Clara's attention from Phineas.

Were we playing right into his hands?

I could not see any better way to safeguard Clara's heart than encouraging it in Phineas' direction. In the evenings I explained what Phineas talked about. During the day Clara not only started to understand Phineas but she preferred his kind-hearted company.

Under my tutelage, her quick mind grew even more enlightened by the young man. When she showed her innocent preference for Phineas, I found ways to bring it to Mr. Williams' attention. Usually by letting Phineas know how hard Clara studied to understand him.

I perhaps made two mistakes. First, Phineas began to hope Clara may love him. One day it may cause them both misery if his father meant to force him to marry elsewhere, which he hinted at when he saw the two together at super. Secondly, I taunted Mr. Williams to the point he started to openly show his dislike of me. He criticized me almost as much as his aunt.

Other than that, he was so genuine, Clara in turn, could not help but wonder if Mr. Williams were reforming in some way or another. Aside from his treatment of me, his transformation, or rather his amiable act seemed so complete. Which is why I taunted him, recklessly, though perhaps I should not have. Two weeks after we returned from London, the first of the letters I sent to Essex received a response.

It read:

Miss Bolton,

We have long been looking for the scoundrel who used our parish so cruelly. One young woman, Miss Marigold Black, was irreparably ill-used. He left her to starve to death alone at an inn. She was buried at a crossroads, and her father has long been looking for retribution through the law. He has appealed to the boy's father and was sent money as if money could compensate for the life of his child. I suppose I do not need to tell you, be wary. Lock up your young ladies and keep them away from Mr. Williams at all costs. He is charming right up to the last. He does not appear to have any regret and one would look at him and think he has no soul to feel the torment he should. Find your way free of him. If you can manage some criminal charges against him, do not hesitate to take them. There are three fathers here in this parish who would give testimony.

I showed the letter to Richard.

"Enough," he said slamming the page down on breakfast table, "this man must not be admitted into my home."

"What can we do?" I asked, sickened. "Lawrence said not to make him desperate until we could take some lasting action against him."

"Let us go to the coast for an excursion. We will take the girls," Richard said leaving his breakfast to pace, running his hand through his hair.

"Perhaps we should take Millie Fielding as well. Her mother has been stubborn about letting her come to our outings. I fear he could be somehow manipulating her," I said unsure what to do about the whole thing.

"Mrs. Fielding is being so unreasonable," Richard said.

"Can we trade the widow's daughter, who has no one to protect her, for Clara, whom we can all watch?"

Would I trade Millie for Clara? Take Clara away so his pretense at goodness may drop, and push him into acting against Millie?

"I will have Rick and Phineas ride over and talk to her, handsome young men giving testimony against the scoundrel should help," Richard said. I agreed and was quiet while the footman called for Rick. Rick came in and his father allowed him to read the letter.

"I feel honor-bound to call the man out," Rick said, "he should not be allowed to get away with this."

"Perhaps we could," I stopped.

"We cannot make him desperate," Richard said angrily ticking off his fingers as if they were in his way, "His father will not check him. He is not opposed to climbing through windows, and no officer of the law can arrest him unless he hurts my daughter, which I will never allow."

"Clara must be protected. Innocence so pure would be a sin to destroy in one so young," I said. I felt helpless. I wished Lawrence had come after all.

"We must contrive a reason for Clara to…. No, he followed her to London the first time," Richard said, "I would not have her in the city. There are so many opportunities for harm, even with Mary."

"She and I could go stay at Grey Manor; only the housekeeper is there. She would take care of us, and no one would know where we were," I said.

"But if he found you, you would be alone."

"I am a fair shot, and Clara is better," I said.

"I would rather her here. I will strangle the boy with my bare hands if I must," Richard said.

"What is Phineas' situation?"

"He is the heir to his father. They are squeezing by. His father expects him to make a financially beneficial match," Richard said.

"There is a specific lady, a friend of the family, who will inherit a plantation in India. He is expected to marry her," Rick said.

"I suspected as much, but it is a pity. He is a good sort of boy and he seems smitten with Clara," I said.

"He has always been," Rick said.

"It would be something of a comeuppance if they married and Mr. Williams had to watch," I said.

"His father has made it clear to both Phineas and myself what is expected of him. I cannot have a rift with my neighbors, and I cannot afford to settle upon her nearly enough to satisfy his father," Richard said looking out the window.

I wondered if these were the moments he hated our father most.

Rick left and returned from his call at Fielding's home disappointed. He could not be seen by the ladies of the house. Mrs. Fielding couldn't possibly believe us. Mr. Williams came to the house in the morning and would not leave until evening. Most of the neighbors gossiped about Clara's inevitable union with the young man.

That morning Mr. Williams was again at the door. I had no patience with him. Clara and I stayed up in the sitting room we shared as he visited with Phineas and Rick. I found his presumption overbearing when he sent a letter to Clara containing words of adoration and affection. I read it and then threw it in the fire, worried because she was already starting to soften toward his impeccable manners. If she knew she could not have Phineas, what would stop her from accepting Mr. Williams?

The next day we started early and went for a long drive out to some ruins. I rode with Clara, Miss Williams,

Miss Clarke, and Sally. Mr. Williams rode his horse next to us, competing with James and, after I said a word in Richard's ear, Mr. Davies for some unnamed prize of the finest horseman. We picnicked, poked around the ruins, then drove for a very long time home. When we arrived home, two more letters waited for me in my room. After reading them, I went to the sitting room, knowing Clara was in there.

"Dearest, I..." I looked at Clara, on her settee, sowing in peace. She was lovely and calm, nothing like the images conjured when reading the letters. I did not wish to burden her with the information clutched in my hand. Disgust made me physically ill from reading them.

"What is it Aunt?"

"Do you like him...Mr. Williams I mean? If nothing..."

"Aunt, do you think that you are the only one with good sense," she asked.

"No, I...I did not mean to insult.,."

"Aunt, I would not consider such a man as him. I do not wish to be cruel to him, I try to give him the benefit of the doubt. Having said that, I see him belittle his aunt, and Phineas who has done nothing to him. I am not allowing my fancy to run away with me."

"Yes, I am sorry," I said, realizing how I'd underestimated her. At her age, I choose a life of servitude rather than marriage to a monster.

"You may rest at peace Aunt Myra; I would never consider him for marriage. I have nightmares about the way he would have lured me away from my family under false pretenses. I see what you see, aunt. I am also weary of his company," she said.

"Perhaps you are feeling ill, perhaps a case of the sniffles would give us both a few days reprieve," I asked.

"Yes, I think that would help my nerves," said Clara.

Her cold lasted four days. Mr. Williams sent flowers twice a day.

During those four days, letters poured in, some from fathers, others from rectors. They never contained anything pleasant or redeeming in them. As far as I could tell Mr. Williams had caused much heartache, and yet, he came twice a day with flowers for my niece, pretending to be worthy of her affection. I could not fathom, at times that he was the same person spoken of in the letters.

I waited everyday impatiently for some word from Lawrence. His trip had to be close to an end in such a fast ship. I could not wait for the day Mr. Williams had to face the natural consequences of his actions. Every day I grew wearier of Mr. Williams's presence. He oppressed us in large doses with his conceit, his childish need for constant approval, and the troublesome way his quick eye observed. Especially since every day I frustrated him a little bit more by not believing his façade.

On the third day of Clara's illness, I sat in the drawing-room for a half hour.

"Miss Bolton, how is my dear girl doing?" Mr. Williams asked.

"She is taking a turn for the better I think," I said.

"Well, you really must come out and take the afternoon with us. The weather has held; I have not seen any September so mild."

"Yes, I am devoted to my niece," I said, and just for warning's sake I added, "I have been so concerned for her health I am sleeping in her bed with her."

He forced a smile on his face and said, "How kind of you. I suppose you know I am only in the neighborhood for two more weeks. I am near madness not seeing Miss Clara Bolton every day."

"Well, you may feel some relief knowing she will be in London in only a few short months," I said.

Mr. Williams nodded but he ground his teeth through his forced smile. He hated when I brought this up.

"I do hope she gets better soon," he said trying another approach. "My aunt and Miss Clarke are sweet companions to your old friend, Mr. Evans. Even Miss Dodgson has spent these last two days in his company. I do worry he is likely to give his affection to a … less desirable lady."

Mr. Williams glanced at his aunt talking to Rick. Miss Williams flushed and lost her place in the conversation indicating she heard him. Rick quickly made up the gap by asking,

"Have you lived long by the sea?"

"Most of my life," Miss Williams answered. "My family always has, well, except Titus. He prefers London. As you must have noticed, Titus never had many pursuits in the country. He never learned to fish so he did not always get along with the other boys," she said with an indulgent smile that felt angry despite her simpering look. Mr. Williams laughed a little with a tightly closed mouth and stood.

"Well, we must be going. Give Miss Clara my fondest regards. I hope she can regain our party before the weather turns."

I bowed. Miss Williams forced her smile and bowed to us. I worried about her after they left. She was holding so much in. I suspected only by siphoning some out now and then did she not explode. How would Mr. Titus Williams retaliate?

Chapter 25

Lawrence did not come. I sent a note to Grey Manor
to see if he had sent word there, but Hetty had not heard from
him. We had no choice but to let Clara get better.

Clara's first day back after her illness was a warm
sunny one. We arranged to pick some of the apples in the
orchard for Sally and her pies. Mr. Williams drove up in a
brand new two-seat cabriolet with a hood meant to almost
hide its occupants.

"I brought my new carriage to be sure Miss Clara has
a very smooth ride about the neighborhood," Mr. Williams
said.

We all stood in my brother's drive astounded.

I recovered first.

"Ah my, Lord Grey Hull talked often of trying out
such a carriage, finding it very handsome. I would be very
much obliged for a ride."

Turning to Richard I said, "He was not sure they were
safe with only two wheels like that, but it does look sturdy,
does it not?"

Richard took his cue and said, "I have business and
cannot join you. I would prefer Rick try it out today, and he
may assess how safe a ride it is. Perhaps you may have a ride
tomorrow if the weather holds."

"Of course," Mr. Williams said as Rick jumped into
the carriage.

It was only a short drive down the hedgerow to the
orchard. The orchard was set back on Richard's property
across a lovely field of long grass with a foot path through it.
When the servants came to pick the orchard, they would have
to drive all the way around the property with carts full of fruit.
Who planted the orchard at such an awkward distance from

the road, I could not say. As the trees were established and producing so much, they weren't likely to be disturbed.

"Myra, here let me help you down," James said, giving me his hand as I alighted from my carriage after Clara. Miss Clarke and Miss Dodgson stood behind him. I noticed Miss Williams did not join our group but did not ask after her. I hoped she was at home having a peaceful moment.

"Myra, I think it would be nice to have a game of checkers. It has been years since we played," James said smiling, giving me all of his attention. His sudden devotion to me could only mean he heard of my stipend, as a payment came through the post. Uncomfortable with the amount of awareness James meant to smother on me, I turned to Sally and said:

"Have you made many pies?"

"Three, but I think I can improve. I am going to use lemon zest in my pie. Our cook ordered some," Sally said.

"That will be very good," I said.

"Do you think it will be sweet enough?" she asked.

"You could perhaps add a bit of extra molasses," I said.

"Perhaps I shall try, but its flavor is so strong. What if I can't taste the lemon?" Sally asked.

"You may want to make something dedicated entirely to the lemon zest. I can write to the housekeeper at Grey Manor for a cake recipe if you would like," I said.

"Yes, please," she said, trying to behave in a grown-up way. I could see her grandmother had been giving her lessons on how to be a little lady. I wished to encourage her progress, so we talked quite a bit about spices and pairing flavors while we picked apples.

Rick, who practically lived in trees as a child, offered to get Sally apples from the top of the tree. He climbed up high to fill her basket with the most beautiful yellow-green marbled fruit kissed rosy in places by the sun.

"Phin, come up here. I can see all the way to the edge of your father's property line," Rick called.

Phineas declined. He was occupied by his sister, who had joined us in the place of Miss Williams. Phineas spent much of his time trying to be sure his naturally shy sister felt comfortable. James barely noticed her and Miss Clarke but could not be more interested in reliving the old days with me. So much so he spoke over his daughter trying to tell me her plans. Mr. Davies chose not to come to our outing, having been stopped in his conversation with Miss Clarke at every turn by James. This left Miss Clarke as the odd one out.

"Miss Clarke," I said trying to include her, "have you heard James is contemplating breeding his horse?"

"Oh really," she said, but seemed put out. James must have noticed her naturally mellow feathers were ruffled, because he focused on explaining the process.

Amid the chaos surrounding me, Mr. Williams found this opportunity to fill Clara's basket with the apples from a more exclusive tree. He slipped away from where Miss Clarke was amazed by the price James could charge to sire his horse for the twentieth time. I glanced in their direction noting Clara's very pretty cornflower blue dress could be seen through the trees.

Amid all the distraction, Rick dropped the dried-up, bird-eaten cores down at us. Sally dodged the first and called out, "You missed me."

Rick took this challenge and started to lob apple cores at Jim while Sally complained. We laughed and Sally seemed beautifully child-like as she jumped and dodged the apple cores with her brother. James and Miss Clarke came over to watch. Phineas and his sister kept their distance. They looked to be arguing about something.

Then out of nowhere my heart sank. I turned to find Clara. She wasn't at her tree. I lost her.

She and Mr. Williams were almost to the road where his new carriage waited. We had wandered far into the field, and I could not conceive how I would get to her in time.

Mr. Williams isolated her entirely. The way he tugged at her reminded me very much of the first time I saw him dragging her into the park. Desperate. He had grown desperate. I dropped the basket of apples I was hauling and ran to catch up to them. I pulled my skirt up in a most unlady-like fashion, running along the small path in the tall grass. Their backs were turned to me and before I could intercede, I heard Mr. Williams say loudly, "Come now, Miss Clara, I will take you for a short drive around town. I assure you it will be most refreshing."

"My father asked—"

"You are not a child. Your father does not see you are a woman who ought to go driving with a man such as myself," Mr. Williams insisted. He sounded desperate, like his façade of decency was cracking. Clara paused, and he practically dragged her.

"Clara," I called when only feet from them. I sounded angry and winded. She turned startled, and only then did I notice she had her hand in her pocket where she kept her pistol. Her eyes, near to crying, expressed so much relief to see I had noticed her being dragged away. Winded, I nipped at the girl: "Sick or not darling, you may not disobey your father."

"Yes Aunt," she said lowering her face in shamed obedience. Titus Williams glared at me.

"She is not a child," he snapped pulling her close to his side.

"You will release her. She will not get into that carriage with you," I snarled.

"Do you really think you can stop me," he laughed.

I stopped. What could I do?

No amount of clever could combat brute strength, and if he took her away, she would be lost. Surely his father would pay a reparation, as if that meant anything. Clara would be lost. Why hadn't I called for Rick?

"I am not afraid of a silly spinster like yourself," he said.

"Well, there you are mistaken! Though spinster I may be, I am smarter than you," I said drawing his ire, and attention to myself.

He scoffed, but looked at me, and I blazed, certain my sturdy eyes denoted I believed this. His rage bubbled up, and I smiled. I could blind him, stall him, just as my mentor assured me I could. Just as I was about to go in for another jab, I heard someone running toward us in the tall grass.

"Titus what are you doing? You will lose all the respectability you have worked so hard to gain, taking Clara away in this manner. Not to mention, she deserves her good name," Phineas called, coming into our circle.

"She will grace the drawing rooms of royalty. She will be richer than the queen and she will be such a lady that you, even as an old friend, will not be allowed into her company.

"Her good name, really Phineas!" he said. Then he laughed.

"Come Clara," Phineas said, reaching out for her.

"Please let go of my arm, Titus. You are hurting me," Clara said, looking to Phineas.

Mr. Williams pulled her closer. Watching Phineas, he said, "Oh Clara, you are so soft."

"Let go of her!" Phineas charged at Mr. Williams, who suddenly released her arm as if he had no other choice and pushed her at Phineas. I heard someone else running toward us and suspected Rick must have jumped from his tree.

"Perhaps I can drive you tomorrow," Mr. Williams said with a bow, unwilling to confront Rick. I crossed my arms, allowing a small laugh to escape my lips. He watched my face.

"She is not feeling well. She won't be available tomorrow," I said just to be sure he knew it was I who bested him. His face contorted in anger. He could see I'd never been fooled by him, and never meant to bless his match with my niece. He stomped off, jumped into his carriage, and drove off, way too fast, just as Rick came running up to us.

Clara held to Phineas and he pulled her closer to him protectively.

"What is this?" Rick asked winded.

"Mr. Williams' game is played out," I said.

"Aunt, you have not done anything foolish have you?" Rick asked. Phineas looked at me, fear written in his expression. He kept an arm around Clara as she cried.

"Myra, what is the matter?" James asked, jogging toward us on the path. The rest of the party followed him.

"Clara isn't feeling well. I must take her home," I said.

"Oh, of course. Myra, thank your brother for the apples," he said taking my hand and squeezing it. I nodded and pulled my hand away. I gently coaxed Clara from Phineas, who regretted relinquishing her to me. I helped her to our carriage.

When we were alone, I asked: "What happened?"

"I do not know. He was charming, and we strolled together. Then we somehow, we were closer to his carriage than you, and he insisted I take a ride. Oh, Aunt, he pulled on me so hard! I was frightened."

"It's all right, dear. I think you are going to have a relapse and be unable to go out again until he leaves the neighborhood," I said tucking her in my arm.

As we rode back to my brother's house, I wondered why Mr. Williams would show his true nature now? This worried me more than anything else. I wished Lawrence would come back. Mr. Williams' pretense was at an end. Hopefully, he hated me more even than he hated Rick.

Chapter 26

When the butler received us at the door, I looked to him expectantly.

"Sorry Miss," he said, only handing me another letter from another parish.

Lawrence had been gone too long. He could have accomplished his trip in a week and a half, but it had been closer to three weeks. He had been so worried about leaving us here alone with Titus Williams, and yet, I still had no word as to his whereabouts. Even in the last week, Richard began to question why we had not heard from him.

That evening tea was a simple affair with only the family present. We all, including the children, sat in the drawing-room, singing and reading. The ringing of the bell startled us.

Richard was handed a note. It read:

Millie Fielding has not been seen for several hours. Her mother is beside herself. We interviewed the Williams boy, but he swears he's had nothing to do with it. Please help.

Rev. Silas Clarke

"This is enough," Richard said, "I will go to…"

"Father, he was in a strange mood today," Rick said.

"What?" Richard asked.

"He tried to isolate Clara."

"I do not think he means to keep trying for her in a conventional way," I agreed.

"He could be trying to lure you out of the house," Rick said, "I will go. I will take care of Mr. Williams. Your first duty is to protect Aunt and Clara."

"Here take this," Clara said taking the gun out of her pocket.

"No, you keep it," Richard said. "Come, Rick, I have another."

We followed him toward the door, but the bell rang again. The butler opened the drawing-room door, and barely preceded an impatient man I had never seen before.

"Lieutenant Reginald White a regular in the 95th Regiment of Foot Rifle Brigade insists on an audience with Miss Bolton," he announced.

We all stood and stared at him.

"I am looking for Miss Myra Bolton," he said.

"I am she," I said.

"Can I speak to you about a rather private matter?" he said.

My heart sank. Did something happen to Lawrence? Did his ship sink? Did the lady I sent him to find harbor a grudge and a pistol? He should have sent some word by now. His fast little clipper he could have made the trip already, and I had heard nothing. Richard called for a maid, who took way too long to scoot the children to the nursery.

The man wore a dark green, almost black uniform. Under his arm he held a cone shaped hat with a feather on it. He seemed war-torn, and far too young to look so worn.

"Clara, will you see to it they all go and get ready for bed," Richard said when it was clear she meant to linger, then he whispered, "bolt the door."

"Of course, father," she said, seeing she was not allowed to hear what the strange man said.

After only Richard, Rick and I were left the man, who nervously played with the brim of his hat, was offered a seat. He declined.

"I have come regarding the letter you sent to my Uncle. He's the rector of our parish," he said.

"Oh, yes of course," I said relaxing. He had no news of Lawrence.

"I... I was ...there was a girl I left behind when I went into the regulars. I did not mean for her to ... her mother died when she was young, and well, her father, he didn't do right by her, in protecting her. That scoundrel Williams came into town with his money and his pretending. He made her think he was going whisk her away and marry her. He killed her."

"I'm sorry," I whispered, the man looked near to tears.

"He told her she was no longer fit for me anymore. He left her, destitute three towns over from ours. When her father finally found her, the innkeeper had kicked her out. She was left by the side of the road. She... there weren't nothing he could do for her."

"Oh no," I said realizing he was talking about Miss Marigold Black, the girl from the first letter.

"She was not even given a proper burial," he said.

"That does not seem right," I said.

"No, and what does he get? The next girl along the way. I have come to challenge the man to a duel. I know such a thing isn't proper, but I can't live with myself, knowing I didn't defend her honor."

I stared at the man. What could I do? This was not merely trying to defend Clara and the next girl, but it had turned into so much more.

"Are you a good shot?" Rick asked. Both Richard and I turned, stunned.

"I am a rifleman in Her Majesty's rifle brigade. If he chooses to fence, I am even better."

"I will be your second," Rick said.

"Rick," Both Richard and I said in unison.

"I cannot abide the man pretending, flattering me to escape trouble the way he once did the teachers," Rick said.

"Well, I cannot have you participating in illegal activities," Richard said.

"It is not necessary," Lt. White said. "Her father is in town at the inn. He will be my second."

"Sir, surely there must be another way," I said.

"No, her father and me, well we are stuck. We must see her avenged. Her soul, not even allowed its final rest, must at least be avenged."

"Very well," Richard said. "We will not interfere."

I stammered, "We won't...."

The bell rang again.

This time we all looked at the door confused. The butler opened the door and announced,

"Mr. Bartholomew Williams demands entrance though I told him you were otherwise occupied."

"Well, that's something isn't it. We are being graced an audience with Mr. Titus Williams' father?" Richard asked.

"I couldn't be sure the man actually existed," I said.

"No, he dropped his sister in our parish and hasn't been seen since," Richard said, then turning to his butler he said:

"I have some things to say to that man."

"Please excuse us for a moment, Lieutenant," I said and followed my brother out into the entryway. My mouth dropped open. The man was an exact copy of Mr. Williams, only twenty-five years aged.

"Miss Bolton?" the man asked.

"Yes," I said. From where I stood in the doorway, I could glance from the father of the scoundrel to the soldier standing at attention in the drawing-room.

"I must speak to you in private," Mr. Williams said.

"My sister will not be taken from my presence," Richard said, looking worried.

"Very well, is there a place the three of us can have a private word?"

"My study is open. I will be a moment or two," Richard motioned for the butler to take Mr. Williams Sr. The man nodded but seemed put off we were asking him to wait. He followed the butler and disappeared down the hall.

"Lieutenant," Richard said through the drawing-room door, looking him in the eye, "please remain until we can speak again. My son will stay with you."

"Yes Sir," Lt. White answered, glaring. Richard shut the door on him with a nod.

Once we were alone in the hall, Richard said, "Whatever this man says do not give a firm admittance, or agreement to anything. From all I have heard of him he is capable of ruining people and will not hesitate if you rub him the wrong way."

"Very well," I said, "do we tell him his son is going to be challenged to a duel?"

"That is not any of our business, but the consequences of his son's own...."

The bell rang for the fourth time. The butler scurried from down the hall, passed us and opened it. There stood Lawrence. I did not think, nor even recollect, moving to him, but I had both his hands in mine somehow.

"You are here," I said.

He greeted me just as warmly, though he seemed to lack words at my fervor. He kissed one of my hands then the other. His eyes were bright and his face slightly bewhiskered. I could have looked at him all night. I only remembered myself when I heard the little cough of my brother directly behind me. I let go of Lawrence's hands and looked around him to see two women.

The first was young and strikingly beautiful. I could not help staring at her. Her dark hair, shapely brows, and long curling lashes enhanced huge, curious blue eyes. Her creamy skin set a backdrop for her naturally red lips. Her tall stately figure could not be hidden by the traveling clothes she wore. I couldn't help thinking this woman would satisfy Mr. Williams' pride in the role of wife.

"This," Lawrence said pointing to the beauty, "is Mrs. Adelaide Williams. This is Mrs. MacLochlann, her nursemaid." The lady who bowed her head was about my age, possibly a few years older with flaming red-orange hair that made my hair look dirty blonde. Freckles covered her face from her forehead to chin including her lips. This stout woman held a child that looked so much like a younger version of Mr. Williams it was disarming, but not surprising when the young lad was introduced as Mr. Charles Spencer Williams.

"Myra, they are exhausted and must be given a place to rest," Lawrence said.

"Yes, and we must not leave them standing here. Mr. Williams, the elder, is in the study," I whispered. Lawrence grinned of all things and stepped back to help the lady holding the child into the house.

"Come, master Charley, let us put you to rest," Lawrence said looking to Richard. The incredibly young mother looked at once from me to Richard. Her gorgeous eyes were disarming as they moved with fear and distrust to each of us. The terror in her eyes made her look like a Greek Goddess fallen from the sky and bled of her ichor.

"Get Mrs. May," Richard said to a footman.

"You wish for the housekeeper, and not a maid," I said. She was not the same stern unapproachable lady of my youth and I had not interacted with her enough to know her. He only nodded. We waited a few minutes while Richard inquired about Lawrence's trip, which was not the cause of his delay. Rather, it was waiting for Mrs. Williams to get her affairs in order so that she might leave for a time.

As he answered, Lawrence moved closer to me. He kept a sidelong look on me. When I spoke, he leaned toward me to be sure I heard all he said. When he told us how quickly his trek home was accomplished, I showed my surprise. He reached out and touched my arm a few times to be sure I was still solid.

I was no better. I kept taking in his face, his sparkling dark eyes, his smiling mouth. I would give anything to kiss him, just in welcome so he might know how happy I was to see him. The separation had felt so long.

"Is a guest room ready?" Richard asked the butler who approached us.

"Yes, Sir," he said.

Just then Rick happened to hear our voices and came into the hall.

"Father what is…"

"Rick, do not leave the Lieutenant alone," Richard hissed, "we will explain later."

Rick nodded but did not seem inclined to move, and instead stared at Mrs. Williams until she blushed and looked down. I could not be sure how but in that moment, Rick turned from the silly boy throwing apple cores at us into a man.

"Rick," Richard snapped.

"Yes, sorry Sir," he said moving back into the drawing-room.

"Can your housekeeper be trusted? I would like very much to meet the father," Lawrence whispered to Richard as the housekeeper came down the stairs.

"Ah my darlings, you look so tired. Come, let us get you a hot meal and a warm bed," she said as she took the child from the nursemaid. The kind-hearted woman who had barely spoken two words to me loved children better than adults. The two women followed her warmth without hesitation.

"We cannot leave our guests waiting any longer," Richard said. He led the way to the study. Lawrence stayed by my side taking my arm.

"I am glad to see you," he whispered in my ear.

"And I you," I said leaning against his arm as we walked into the sickly green study behind Richard.

"I am sorry about the delay. We were just receiving my oldest friend. Sir Lawrence Grey, this is Mr. Bartholomew Williams," Richard said as we entered the room.

Mr. Williams assessed Lawrence. Lawrence nodded politely. Mr. Williams flinched a little. He did not seem comfortable with Lawrence's presence. He could see Lawrence was not an unassuming country gentry as his attire and manners would proclaim him to be. Mr. Williams turned to me and said cautiously:

"I have come to ask you, Miss Bolton, to kindly keep out of my son's affairs. It appears you have brought a madman to my door."

"How so Sir?" I asked.

"Titus was sent a letter requesting a duel this evening from the father of a young lady whom, by her own folly, was disappointed by my son. He was young and showed her too much attention. That can hardly be a reason to call him out. How did you even know about Mr. Black and his daughter?"

"Your son was very quick to let slip the many places he has lived. I thought it curious he did not settle in your own country home, or even one of the others, so I wrote to the rectors," I said innocently enough.

"Yes, you must have written a few letters. I am here in the first place because I heard from my good friend, who is the rector at our estate in Norfolk. He wrote to tell me he received a letter asking for particulars on my son's behavior."

"Your son has been courting my daughter and we are not quick to trust strangers around here," Richard said.

"Well, a man ought to be able to make a mistake or two without having to be called upon to explain at every turn," Mr. Williams said. I looked at him. The level of denial he was in would be comical if it were not so sad. Only the one rector had contacted him. It was perhaps foolish of me to contact the rector in his own parish.

"From my understanding, your boy has made more than a mistake or two. Did you know even now a girl is missing?" Richard said.

"The boy was questioned about it. I... he has been awaiting me with his aunt since long before tea and could not possibly have had anything to do with her disappearance," Mr. Williams said.

"Your sister will vouch for him?" I asked. He turned and scanned the room instead of answering.

"Titus told me your boy was his roommate at Eton, and cannot forget a few youthful indiscretions," Mr. Williams said, changing the subject.

"Yes, well I will always protect my daughter against youthful indiscretions," Richard said.

"Do you know how I met your son, Mr. Williams?" I asked.

"No, he did not mention that," he said.

"We were in London and he was trying to convince my niece to run away with him. He also mentioned you were away visiting a cousin he was expected to marry," I said.

"I...I did not..."

"...know your son was in London?" I asked.

"We...we must have just missed each other," he said.

"I wrote to you about it," Richard said.

"My assistant sorts my mail, I will ask him about it," Mr. Williams, in a peevish way, clearly not used to being ganged up on.

"Surely, your son would have told you his interest in my niece as you were so vehemently against the match," I said.

"I...I could be convinced to reconsider," he said looking at the empty fire grate.

"You know nothing of the match," Lawrence said.

"No," he admitted, "but if the lady is reputable and…"

"I do not think he would become an honorable man simply by marrying my niece," I said.

He looked at me for a long time. It was clear he was not used to be spoken to in such a manner, especially by a woman. There was a conflict in him. He seemed as good at reading people as his son was, and I could not be manipulated, nor paid off.

"If she is a good sort of girl, and he truly honored her, perhaps…," he said faltering.

"He cannot change who he fundamentally is through marriage," Lawrence said, stepping toward him, so he did not stare at me so intensely. "There is something wrong with the boy. Something disconnected in his head."

"I do not think that is fair. If he were to settle down, marry a nice girl, gain occupation . . ." his father said.

"Would you have him work with you at the bank your father built?" Lawrence asked.

The father turned white.

"I deal with all sorts of diplomats and it would not be prudent to…"

"Expose them to your son," Lawrence said.

"I did not mean that," Mr. Williams said.

"No father could, and yet it is so. Besides, we know marriage would not help your son because your son is already married to such a lady. He took a girl up to Scotland when he was only sixteen, and married her," Lawrence said.

I flinched. I had promised to protect Miss Williams. Only she and Titus Williams knew where the unfortunate Mrs. Williams lived.

"What a ridiculous claim! The lady disappeared, and we cannot even be sure my son had anything to do with it. How could you know what no one else could learn?" Mr. Williams asked. Despite his firm denial, his eyes darted back and forth in silent confession. He knew his son had been involved.

"Your son often boasted about it to the boys at school," I said quickly.

"That is possible," Mr. Williams faltered. "Boys at school come up with all kinds of prattle. As soon as the girl in question disappeared, Titus was sent away to a friend's house in another parish. If he were responsible, she could not have stayed hidden so well."

Lawrence laughed. Determined to force the man to face his son's real character he started:

"We can ask the girl--"

"I am in correspondence with her," I interrupted glaring at Lawrence. "She believes herself married and abandoned by your son. What's more, I find it interesting you do not think these women can disappear with your son when you are in London and really cannot say where he is."

"How did you find Adelaide?" Mr. Williams asked, fixated on this. "I could not, and I must have more considerable resources then you."

"You do not think I only sent one letter to the one person financially dependent on you in your parish, did you," I said quickly, knowing Miss Williams would be implicated as soon as the man left my brother's house.

"Who told you where she was?" Mr. Williams asked more forcefully stepping closer to me. Richard and Lawrence moved into my sides.

"I think it best to simply say some of your parishioners know more than you think. I will not incriminate anyone, except your son. He often boasts of the parish you own, and how many people are dependent on your generosity," I said.

The father clenched his jaw and muttered something like, "blunderbuss," under his breath.

"I will remove my son from your parish," he finally said.

"I think more assurances are going to be needed. First, we need the missing girl back. You are not so naive to believe your son had nothing to do with it," Lawrence said.

"If she is found in the next few hours, we may be able to hush it up," I said, thankful we left the subject of Mrs. Williams.

"Second, I know of a home, something of a hospital, run by a doctor friend of mine. It is mostly for soldiers, those of the highest breeding, such as your son. Men who need a little extra help assimilating back into society."

"What would my son need with a place like that?" he demanded.

"You cannot be so deluded, man," Richard said sharply, making Mr. Williams step back. "We know your son is in desperate need of help. We did not just write to your home parish. We should have him transported with the witnesses we've collected against him."

"What gave you the right?" Mr. Williams cried.

"He tried to run away with my daughter," Richard bellowed. "When he could not, he came here pretending to be a gentleman trying to win her. What gave him the right?"

"Perhaps he meant to change his--"

"Come, man, you may choose to close your eyes to the situation, but we cannot. Especially when the boy is imposing on my daughter and all her friends," Richard stormed.

"You have not a legal leg to stand on," Mr. Williams said.

"I am the law in this county. I could consign him to transport in the next week," Lawrence said. "Your son has no conscience. He can lie without a single tell, he can wound women with no conscience. This is a sickness."

"Who are you?" Mr. Williams asked.

"Ah yes. Bad news old fellow. Your son happened to impose upon the one family in the area intimately connected to the Marquess of the Marchlands and I have also been in the study of the human mind for many years. Lord Grey Hull," he said bowing.

Mr. Williams analyzed Lawerence for only a moment.

"Dorset still holds a marquess? I understand there was some trouble with that title in years past. I thought it may have gone extinct as ...there was some dispute over who actually possessed it, was there not?"

"My father possessed it," Lawrence said, and his eyes squinted a warning at Mr. Williams. Reading his face, Mr. Williams said more cautiously, "Yes, your father's claim to his titles was challenged by his mother."

"Step-mother," Lawrence said, "it was my grandfather's second wife who caused so much trouble."

"Ah yes I remember now it was his stepmother's claim that her child should hold the titles since your father had not been active in society for ten years?"

"The issue was debated in the House of Lords; my father and grandfather were defended by the aged Sir William Cornwallis, among others. At the time, my family's contributions in defending the channel during the Napoleonic Wars was legendary. Cornwallis said that if the title were not in place, certainly John Bull would have awarded every honor the country had to bestow on Lord Henry Grey Hull and no patriot ought to disagree."

"Your stepmother was…"

"A blight on our family name. Yes," Lawrence said with finality meant to close the subject. I glanced at Richard to be sure he heard the way Lawrence said the word blight. Richard would not meet my eye. But he must know that I could never be the blight in Lawrence's life.

"You can understand my confusion as very little has been heard from the Marquess since," Mr. Williams said.

"Not so, before he died last year my father published as the philosopher Sir Henry Grey."

"Ah yes, duty and all that," Mr. Williams said slowly, realizing his money would get him nowhere if Lawrence was anything like his father. His father who lived for ten years alone after his wife died because he believed second wives were a blight to the family name.

Mr. Williams looked around the room, growing more concerned. He shook his head like he could find no way around the thing.

"What kind of... this hospital is it discreet. If he...would he be allowed back into society after they fixed him?"

"They will bill you as if they are a travel guide. You can tell your friends whatever is necessary. Though I do not think recouping in the country from an extended illness is that bad a story."

"No, I suppose not," he said. "How long would they keep him, a twelve-month?"

We all stopped. Richard and I thought the three months a European tour would take, would be all the father would tolerate. He must have been exhausted by the boy's antics. Lawrence didn't bat an eye when he answered, "At least."

"It might be the best thing for the boy. Heaven knows I've had no success with him, though it breaks my heart, for he is my heir."

"You have another a strapping--" Lawrence started.

"We invited Miss Adelaide Williams to come for Christmas out of concern for my niece" I cut in. "To be drawn into bigotry is an evil we could not tolerate. If she is a tolerant woman, perhaps after your son's confinement is at an end, she would consent to live with him as his wife."

I had no doubt Lawrence was about to announce the man's heir was up the stairs. Titus Williams could legally take Mrs. Williams, and her son. He could do heaven knows what with them.

Lawrence, though kind, could not understand what it was to be a woman. Some magistrates, even in this modern time, allowed for the adage that a man could beat his wife as long as the rod was no thicker than his thumb. Titus Williams had very thick fingers. Didn't I know, firsthand, a wealthy man felt he could do anything he liked to his wife? Not to mention Miss Williams would have no hope of escape. I glared at Lawrence again and he watched me. Unfortunately, Mr. Williams also saw my curious behavior and squinted, trying to understand.

"How is it possible the two entered a legal marriage?" Mr. Williams asked driving forward in search of information.

"It took place in Scotland. From what I understand, it would not take much effort on your part to legitimize it, especially if the lady has a marriage certificate signed by clergy," I said.

"Do you think," he looked at Lawrence still trying to read us, "Do you think if a child resulted from the union, an heir, it would be…ill, do you think he would be prone to the same bouts of selfishness?"

Lawrence looked at me, he could see I did not wish to give away the lady's presence. It would be too suspicious that she was already here. Miss Williams would be the only one who could have given such accurate information as the lady's location.

"I can say with almost perfect assurance the son will be nothing like his father. I am sure he will be much more moldable and, if the lady is the innocent sweetness that Clara is, I have no doubt any son will be properly molded."

Mr. Williams watched us. He nodded as if he suspected such a child existed.

"She was a sweet little thing, quite a beauty," Mr. William's said. "Her father was my oldest friend, her oldest brother my sister's lover. Neither will have anything to do with my family since…"

Here he stopped. Suspicion took over his features.

"Have you become acquainted with my sister, Miss Bolton?" he asked.

"I do not … she is the acquaintance of one of my old friends, Mr. Evans," I said blushing most deeply, and hating that Lawrence saw the blush that made me and Miss William's rivals.

"Oh, I see why you are so desirous of our acquittal of the neighborhood," he said with a laugh. I knew I had to say it. I knew I had to protect her, but I hated that Lawrence would hear it.

"Perhaps, at first, that was my motive, but the more I learned of your son, the more frightened I became for my niece. We are even now fearful for her dear friend Millie Fielding, whom no one has seen in a few hours. It is not safe for your son to be in our neighborhood."

"Is the girl…" Mr. Williams closed his eyes on it all. He was capable of being sorry where his son was not. He finished, "my sister will see to it the girl is found and cared for."

We all looked at him. We waited for more. She was ruined. She was a widow and a gentleman's daughter. That is all he could do.

He examined us and said, "Tomorrow, just after breakfast, I will bring the boy here, perhaps Sir," he said nodding to Lawrence, "you would be so good as to give us direction to the hospital."

"I will take you myself and be sure the boy is given the respect he deserves," Lawrence said. I did not think that level of respect was going to be in the positive but said nothing. Mr. Williams bowed to me, then to Lawrence and my brother.

"If Miss Adelaide Spencer, ur Williams, comes for Christmas—"

"I believe she will," I said.

"Please write to me, that I might be allowed an interview with her. I would legitimize her claim. I did not realize the boy went through with a marriage, ever. If I can legitimize her, I will do it for my old friend's sake as well as hers. I must go see what I can discover from Titus on the matter."

Mr. Williams nodded, suddenly in a hurry to leave. I had no idea how to help Miss Williams but watched in despair as he rushed from the room. When the door closed Richard said: "We best see to the soldier."

"Excuse me?" Lawrence asked. We quickly explained the soldier in the drawing-room and then moved in that direction.

When we opened the door to the drawing-room, the soldier paced, and Rick stood close to the door.

"Did the Scrub offer to pay you for your daughter's honor?" he asked.

"No, in fact, we have convinced him his son needs to be hospitalized. He is going to try and get his son the help he needs," I said.

"That does nothing for my vengeance. It does nothing for Marigold," the soldier said.

"If you wish to speak to the lad, he will be here tomorrow morning, just after the breakfast hour. Then he will be gone," Richard said.

"Richard," I said astonished.

"I do not believe a doctor can help the boy, but a bullet in his wing, that might get his attention," Richard said, and I neglected to realize how angry he had been in his study as Lawrence decided the course of action that must be taken. He must not have felt the boy's incarceration would be enough.

"Richard--" Lawrence started.

"What would you have done if it was your Eva, what if he'd come around your girl, Lawrence?" he asked.

Lawrence said nothing. He watched Richard contemplating.

"Lt. White," I said, unsure what to say to my brother, "Can you give Titus Williams one year? Let us see if he can be reformed. Perhaps after a year if he is not reformed you can visit your duel upon him then?"

"I…how will I know if he has reformed?" the soldier asked.

"I will write to you. I plan on keeping close tabs on the boy," Lawrence said.

"How do I know you would tell me the truth?" the soldier asked.

"I believe in your duty to Marigold. I will not stand in the way of a man's duty," Lawrence said.

"I cannot vouch for Marigold's father. He is not as calm as I am," he said. We all looked at each other. None of us would categorize the soldier as calm.

"Try to reason with him," Lawrence said. The soldier laughed bitterly. Then said, "If his father tries to get him out of this, I will not bother to play by fair rules. Titus Williams never does," he said storming out of the room and slamming the door behind him.

Chapter 27

"I have a very bad feeling about that," I said looking at Richard.

"Come now, he is a soldier. They still have duels among themselves. None of them does more damage than a wound."

"A fatal wound may be the only way to stop such a man," Rick said. Richard stopped, realizing what tender ears heard him. He put a hand on his son's shoulder.

"Please... please son, if it comes down to it, please let me do it. I would not have you, in the prime of your life..."

"Father, in matters of honor like this, I doubt I would be prosecuted," Rick insisted.

"What if you were killed?" Richard asked.

"Then I would die the death of a man," Rick announced standing up to his full height, and staring his father down.

I could not see my brother lose his son. Rick would not waste his potential like so many.

"I have received a few letters that could very well get him transported," I said breaking the tension between father and son.

"Perhaps that would be the safest avenue. I could not control the outcome of a trial," Lawrence said, watching Richard. Richard focused on Rick. I'd never seen my brother this terrified before.

"He would never see the gaol," Rick stormed, glaring at Lawrence.

"You mistake me. I am not so naive to believe any sort of trial would come to pass. His father would squash the thing long before it occurred. But, if you ask me to, I will send for the manpower now. If we get hold of him tomorrow, change his clothes and have him thrown below deck on a transport ship, he would be chained to a gang, building roads in Sydney before his father ever knew what happened to him. The captain, surgeon, and guards would have to be bribed, but I believe I could have him transported," Lawrence said, thinking.

"If you are caught you may lose your title, and be forced to forfeit your land," Richard said.

"You are my oldest friend. Besides God and Eva, who has a greater claim on my duty than your family?" As Lawrence said this, he glanced at me then continued, "Would it not be better for you or I to act before your daughter is destroyed, and your son becomes murderer or murdered?"

Richard put a hand on Lawrence's shoulder and dropped his head.

"Thank you, Lawrence. But as your friend, I could not let you lose all when his father has already agreed to try hospitalization."

"Will that be enough?" Rick asked. He looked as if he wished for the kidnapping and removal of Titus Williams.

"I promise it will not be a holiday for the young man. Considering the harm he could do in the colonies, it may be better for him to be supervised by those who know what he's capable of. Especially since with such sicknesses, the first thing they do is sterilization. Mr. Williams will never have another heir, and may lose interest in women all together," he said.

"That might be fair," I said.

"Very well," Rick said.

Richard, looking very relieved, said, "I am going to check on Clara."

"Myra, will you go check on Mrs. Williams?" Lawrence asked. He took my hand and finished, "She is incredibly young and tired. Just the sort of lady who could benefit from your direction."

"Of course," I said pulling my hand away, frightened by the sensation it caused in my stomach. I walked quickly to exit the room, but still heard Richard say angrily:

"You are my oldest friend, but I must do my duty to my sister. Do you think it fair for you to take her hand and talk to her like that when you have no intention of encouraging the affection it must excite?"

I looked back confused and caught Lawrence's eyes. He watched me, not Richard. I felt my face on fire and quickly turned away. I left the room and almost ran to the steps. I had not fully recovered when I reached the unfortunate Mrs. Williams' room. I stood outside the door until I reclaimed my tears. Finally, I knocked quietly, hoping the lady was asleep and would not need me for the evening.

The lady's nursemaid cracked the door suspiciously.

"Aye," she said.

"We met before. I am Miss Bolton. I hoped to speak to Mrs. Williams," I said. The lady bobbed and opened the door.

Sitting at a table with her hair in long dark ringlets down her back, the very lovely Mrs. Williams watched her child sleeping through the mirror she faced.

"Thank you so much for coming," I said to the lady. She turned to me and nodded.

"I ... from what I understand, my husband is pursuing another wife?" she asked, alarm written in her enormous blue eyes that watched me.

"I suppose you worry about the legitimacy of your marriage?" I asked.

"My little boy is respectable, and my husband the scoundrel. If Titus married again and the people around learn of it, then my boy is..."

"Illegitimate," I said.

"Charley is not. I was married. Titus lived with me for three months, from mid-May until he went back to school at the end of September five years ago… we …he married me the fourteenth of May 1835, the Year of Our Lord," she insisted.

"Mr. Bartholomew Williams, his father, did not know as much. How is that possible?" I asked.

"He…" she blushed, looking down. She admitted, "I thought we both left the protection of our families. After three months passed, Titus left for what was only supposed to be a short week. He did not come back. After two weeks a letter from his father came. It had been rerouted from a friend of Titus's. Confused as to what happened to my husband, I read the letter. It became clear his father knew nothing of our elopement or marriage. He thought Titus spent the summer with his friend. In the letter, his father asked what happened to me. I learned my father disowned me, and his aunt's engagement was broken. He asked that my location at least be known to Sadie that she might provide for me because I was dead to my father. So, you see, Mr. Williams may never admit it, but he knew."

"You wrote to her," I asked, feeling low. What could I do for this woman who had lived such a life?

"She wrote to me before I had to…" she looked down and I could see her pride and shame mingling as if she had to beg for help at every turn and she hated it. "She got my location from Titus. He left… he left me in our little rented house with nothing, and a debt collector knocking the door every other day. I had no way to provide for myself and I was already increasing. I did not even have time to write back before she came to me. Since then, Sadie is the only family I have," she faltered over the word. "I … I pretended to the townspeople that Titus would come back, eventually."

"It was the right thing to do. I have seen Mr. Bartholomew Williams. He is willing to legitimize you and force his son to acknowledge the marriage."

"He will…?" her voice tremored.

"Yes, he means to do right by you," I said.

"Did Titus ask him to?"

"No," I said. She nodded, blinking away her tears.

"Mr. Williams always means to do right," she said looking throw the mirror at her son again, "but he caters to Titus. He will do nothing if Titus spins a story about me in some dark light until I am unfit and deserve to be left behind. Mr. Williams may even try to take Charley if I am not careful."

"He does not know about your child," I said. I could not refute her opinion after interacting with both the father and the son.

"Is Titus still in the neighborhood?" she asked.

"Until tomorrow morning," I said. "His father is taking him to a hospital. Lord Grey Hull believes Titus is unstable and a danger to others. He is not capable of grief or sorrow at his actions."

"I… May I speak to him before he goes?" she asked.

"I do not know how to explain your presence here," I said. "Miss Sadie Williams told me of your whereabouts in confidence. If you are here already, the only way I can explain that is to expose her."

"I do not wish to hurt Sadie, but I … wish to see him," she said.

I thought about this. If Titus were in the presence of his father and all the others, then was transported to the hospital, he could not hurt her, well, physically, anyway.

"Very well, I will arrange it, but do not waste your affection on him. I do not think he is even capable of returning the emotion," I said.

"I know. I have long thought over the three months we spent together. I think he meant to commit to me, but he grew tired of me. I was not enough for him. He was cruel and heartless to me. When he left me, even destitute, I felt I was better off than being with him. Any affection I had for him was a result of the man he pretended to be. Not for the man he truly was," she said.

"Why do you wish to see him then?" I asked.

"I ... my son has the opportunity to apprentice to an apothecary who has taken a liking to ... to him. He intends to send my boy to school, then at thirteen, he will begin apprenticing. I cannot sign the contract required," she said, looking at her sandy-haired angel boy laying on the bed.

"Your son is a gentleman. He will have a proper education," I said, watching the beautiful child sleep.

"How?" she asked. "From the Williams? They have never noticed Charley. Upon his baptism, the Vicar sent a letter to Titus. Only Sadie was there. Her brother did not respond."

"Mr. Williams the senior does not know of your child. His biggest concern in checking his son is the fear he will lose his heir. It would be a gamble, but I believe he would like to know he has a legitimate heir," I said.

"He never made the effort to know," she replied. "Only his sister ever did. Except Sadie, all the Williams' are slippery and unreliable. This apprenticeship is all I can give Charley," she said. "I cannot depend on Titus's family to support him, and I have no family. You must know it is killing me not to do more for him."

"I can imagine," I said.

"If I had been wise, if I had…oh there is no use in regret, what is done is done. But to ask my son to share in the shame of it is not fair."

"No…." A thought hit me hard and fast. I was an heiress. "I will support the lad," I said, surprising even myself.

"What?"

"If Mr. Williams will not support him, I will send him to school and he will find his profession there… I do not think it wise to allow this apothecary such a position of power in your son's life, especially before he is old enough to know himself," I said.

"I do not need your—"

"Consider, I am not doing this for you, but him. This is not charity; I need you here and you have come. I can promise not to push the lad to any profession he might not find appealing. Can you be sure your apothecary friend will do the same?"

She was silent for a moment. Then she said suspiciously:

"Why would you do this?"

"Because I have found myself in something of your position, and thankfully I had a kind-hearted brother who saved me. I am sorry you have no such brother," I said.

"They would have saved me if they could," she said loyally, though if they would help, where were they now?

I finished, "Not to mention you have come here and will save my niece from who knows what treachery that man has in store for her."

"I will, I will do my best for her, and you will help my son," she said.

"Yes, of course, it would be my honor," I said with a bow.

"Thank you," she said looking at her sleeping child, "Do you ... do you think he could wait until he is older to start school?"

"He would not start before he is ten," I said.

"Well, Mr. Jones felt it would be best for him to be sent away in two years," she said.

"At six? I do not think that wise, and I am not sure I would trust your Mr. Jones implicitly," I said.

"I do not, but he is the only one who has ever tried to help me," she said.

"Until now." I said, "You need not be required to sacrifice...any honor to have your son educated."

"Thank you," she whispered.

"Why do you not stay in Dorset Shire and take a holiday for a while?" I asked, worried about her.

"I do not know what to do anymore," she said.

"My brother has young girls that he provides activity and schooling to, it would be a most inviting place for a young boy to be for a time," I said.

"I shall think it over," she asked.

"Of course," I said, "I have imposed upon your time for too long. Did they send up food?"

"More than we could eat," she said.

"Very good. Please have a nice rest. I will have your breakfast sent up as well, so you may recover, and have time to think. We can speak more on the morrow."

"Yes, that would be best," she said.

Chapter 28

After instructing the housekeeper to be sure Mrs. Williams was given anything she desired in her room, I went down to the dining room for supper thinking quietly about all that passed. Richard, Rick, and Lawrence were already seated. As soon as I saw Lawrence, I remembered my brother admonishing him and wished I had taken my supper in my room. He tried to catch my eye, but my brother was quicker.

"Come, Myra, sit and eat," Richard said indicating I sit between him and Rick. I did so willingly.

"How is Mrs. Williams?" Rick asked.

"She is… I do not know. She is surviving, looking out for her child. I do not think she has lived in years, poor woman."

"I only convinced her to come to give evidence of her marriage. She is here to save her child the disgrace of being illegitimate," Lawrence said.

"I gathered that as well," I said. Turning to Richard, I finished, "I invited her to stay for a while. I hope that is acceptable to you?"

"It is your home now, Myra. You may invite whom you like," Richard said, but glanced at Lawrence to see how he took this. Lawrence glared. I rolled my eyes and said:

"It sounds like there is an apothecary who is trying to use her situation to his advantage, and though she is fighting it, she may give in for the sake of her son."

"She must be protected," Rick said angrily. I watched him with interest, sorry the girl was married to a lout who would not claim her, but that she must hold tightly to for the respectability of her son.

When the main course was served, I said, "We may need a plan for tomorrow morning. Mrs. Williams expressed an interest in seeing her husband, not to mention the solider who has our agenda for the morning. I suppose it would serve for Mr. Williams to have to face his victims, but I worry for Miss Sadie Williams to be exposed to her nephew's anger."

"His aunt?" Lawrence asked.

"Yes, even now she is likely implicated. Only she knew how to find Mrs. Adelaide Williams."

"What can we do for her?" Lawrence asked realizing why I'd been so reluctant to tell the man about Mrs. Williams.

"I do not know, besides get her free of her nephew," I said, "which may be harder than we have anticipated. I doubt Titus Williams will submit to this plan."

"I don't think his father is going to be able to take the boy peacefully," Richard said.

"I was also worried about that," Lawrence said, "That is why I sent that letter earlier. I have written my household. We will have at least fifteen armed men to accompany us tomorrow morning."

"What will they do if Titus resists?" Rick asked.

I tried to stay calm, but I could not. I could not endure anymore. I felt my throat clogging with tears and dropping my forehead in my palm I said: "We should have just left him to the soldier. Perhaps he would have aimed for more than his arm."

"Myra!" Lawrence said.

"I can take no more. Someone must protect these girls who have no way to protect themselves."

"Don't worry, we will stop him. We must be vigilant, and we will stop him," Lawrence promised.

Rick started: "Even if he must be taken by---"

We were interrupted by the butler coming in.

"Sir, we have a visitor, and she is in high distress."

We all stood and followed him to the drawing-room. Miss Sadie Williams paced in the room. She turned to us as we entered and I gasped. She looked a mess. Her mouth was bloody, and her hand held the side of her ripped dress that dripped with blood.

"What happened?" I asked, rushing to her.

"Titus knows I betrayed him. His father asked him about Adelaide being his wife. Only I knew. Titus got so angry with me. Barty told him he is to go for a time to a house where they are going to help him. He swears he will not go. He blames me for everything. He stormed at me with a knife, and if my brother had not pulled him off me, I think he would have killed me."

She held more tightly to her side and winced in pain.

"What can we do for you?" I asked.

"You don't understand. I am not here for help. I am come to warn you," she said breathily. "I ran here whilst they wrestled for the knife. Titus swore he would have Clara for wife no matter who tried to claim him. I came to warn you."

"Will his father be able to restrain him?" Lawrence asked.

"No, I... My brother may be injured or... or worse. Titus got away. I heard a horse coming up the lane. I hid. It was Titus. he passed me like the devil was chasing him. I didn't see where he turned... he could be here even now. He is gone crazy, sir I would..."

A loud gunshot rang from the top of the house. Richard ran, with Rick close on his heels. I tried to follow but Lawrence grabbed me around the waist and stopped me. In my ear, he pleaded, "Please stay here. Please do not put yourself in harm's way. Take Miss Williams and lock yourselves in the Study. Please."

I shook like a leaf, but I could not even place my finger on why anymore.

"Please, promise me," he said again.

"I promise. Please go warn Mrs. Adelaide Williams," I said and took Miss Williams by the elbow.

"She is here," Miss Williams whispered.

217

"I miscalculated. She was safer hidden away. I could not…" I stammered, so angry with myself.

"He cannot know. It was part of his condition in letting me go to her. She was never to leave Scotland. He said she would disappear and never be seen again if she did," she said emphatically. "He is obsessed with Miss Clara. It would be extremely dangerous for Adelaide to confront him with any expectations. He may very well try to get rid… Oh! Adelaide and Charley are in danger… they are his. The law would be on his side. He can do whatever he pleases with them. It is why I have done whatever he asks for four years. I did every last horrid thing he asked, just to keep them safe. Oh, what is to be done now?"

"Bring her to me," I said appalled, nodding to Lawrence, who took off at a run toward the stairs. I pulled Miss Williams to the study and bolted the door. The study was filled with shadows in the darkness and all the busts looked angry and condemning. The sickly green wallpaper took on an eerie other-worldly glow when I lit the lamp. I wished we had gone anywhere but the one room in the house that made me feel like a sixteen-year-old girl.

Miss Williams winced and I remembered her injury. I checked my father's old hiding place, a well-concealed opening to the side of the bookshelf and found a bottle of brandy. I soaked my handkerchief and started to clean the sticky mess at Miss Williams' side.

I ripped the ruffle on my petticoat in a long strip and cinched the linen tightly to her side as she winced in pain. I helped her wipe the blood from her hands and gave her the shawl I had been using to help her stave off the chill. Then I cleaned the cut by her mouth. She still looked a mess, but better then she had.

Shortly after this there was a knock at the door and I heard Lawrence say,

"Let us in, Myra."

I opened the door. Lawrence held the young boy and led Mrs. Williams and her maid into the room.

"Adelaide, are you well?" Miss Williams asked rushing to her. She took her hands. The beautiful young woman fell onto Miss Williams and sobbed on her shoulder. Miss Williams struggled to hold her and moved to sit on a sofa at the far end of the room, trying not to show how much pain she was in.

"Lock the door," Lawrence said cradling the child's head into my arm, keeping him asleep as if we'd practiced the action a million times.

"I am going to check on Clara. I didn't see Richard. I swear I will be back before long. Keep vigil, dear friend," he said.

"I will," I said. I wrapped Charley in my brother's morning jacket that was on the back of his chair. The maid looked frantic, so I set the child on the sofa next to his mother. Then I followed Lawrence to the door. He took a long look at me, and then left. I locked the door. I moved back to our small group listening to every small noise. Once we were all settled, I asked in a hushed tone, "Did you see what happened?"

"Titus...he came into my room," Mrs. Williams whispered.

"He shimmied in right through the window," the maid said and I thought she may cry.

"What did he do?" I asked, struck hard in my chest. realizing anything happened to Mrs. Williams it was my fault for bringing her into this situation.

"I do not think he recognized me. I think he was only using the room as access to the house because of the drainpipe near my window," she said.

"He was looking for Clara," I said.

"He must have been. He ran through the room. He glanced from me to Charley in confusion, but it was almost like he could not see anything because he had only one purpose."

"Thank goodness he did not know you. He is not right in the head," I said. "I am only sorry the young man was not stopped before he caused so much trouble."

She nodded in agreement.

"If he is in the house, we must be quiet," I said mostly to the maid who breathed like she may lose consciousness. The others nodded in agreement. We sat in silence for another ten minutes when there was another knock at the door.

"Myra," Richard called.

I rushed to the door and opened it. He held Clara's hand and all the other girls trailed near enough for him to grab them.

"Everyone in," he said. "Lock the door behind us, Myra."

I did so, after glancing out in the hallway. Clara clung to Richard, shaking and crying. Her father sat her in his desk chair and unlocked a bottom drawer. He pulled out a wooden case and retrieved two dueling pistols from it. He whispered so Clara wouldn't hear:

"He is somewhere in the house. If he comes in this room, do not give him a warning shot Myra. Aim for his heart or his head. If you miss, he will show Clara no mercy."

"I have aggravated him much in the hope he will come after me first."

"Myra," Richard breathed out, "aim for his heart. Do not hesitate."

"I will not miss," I said. After he loaded both pistols, he handed me one. He nodded for me to follow and we walked to the door.

"Lawrence and Rick are searching. We've sent for the constable and Lawrence sent an express hoping the servants he sent for are nearer than they can be. I've given permission for the servants to arm themselves. You are well fortified. If he makes it to you, he will not act with mercy. You cannot afford him the consideration," Richard reiterated in an undertone, his eyes drilling into mine. I knew he was right. I felt connected to my brother. We grew up in the same way, if not at the same time. We both knew that the unscrupulous man could talk himself into any atrocity that served his purpose. Because of this connection we shared, my brother trusted me to guard his most precious little family.

I would not let him down.

He unbolted the door, looked out into the hallway and stepped out. I quietly shut the door behind him and bolted it.

"Are you hurt?" I asked Clara.

"No," she cried, and I had to remind her to be quiet. She whispered softer, "I...I shot at him."

"Good. You defended yourself. That is good," I said.

"He caught me so off guard. I had just left the girls to get the pins out of my hair," she said pointing to her sisters, dressed in an assortment of white muslin nightgowns and dressing robes. She still wore her cornflower blue dress, but her warm ginger hair was down her back in waves. Both she and Mrs. Williams were very pretty in such different ways. Clara was saying, "I was alone in my room and he barged in. I pulled out the gun and shot. I... I missed, and he laughed like I'd been playing games with him. He said after we were married, he would teach me better games," she said, shaking.

"What happened next?" I asked.

"He heard Father running toward us and calling out my name. I held the gun steady though it's a single shot. I think he did not come near because he did not know it was a single shot.... He ran out the door, but he promised he would come back for me," she said, shaking.

"He will not get the chance, I assure you. We tried to give him another way. He chose not to take it. I have collected enough evidence against him. He will go to Australia if he does not hang," I said.

Clara flinched at my pronouncement and continued to shiver in her chair, hugging herself. After a few minutes of calming down, she noticed the women at the other end of the room were unknown to her.

"Aunt who are…"

"I need you to be brave, dearest," I said. She nodded, but just by my statement she seemed to understand who they were.

"This is Mr. Williams' wife and child," I said.

"Oh, he is married then," she said.

"Yes," Mrs. Williams said with a bite. Clara leaned back and said, "That is most disturbing. He courts me as if he were entirely free to do so, and he is married to another. What kind of a man he must be?"

She looked away from Mrs. Williams ashamed, as if she'd done something wrong.

"A deeply disturbed one," I said.

"I cannot believe this happened to me," Clara said, wrapping her arms more tightly about herself.

"This did not happen to you," Mrs. Williams said growing agitated.

"Please," I whispered.

"Please indeed, who are these to stand with you, to protect you," she shrieked, startling all of us and waking her child.

We all gawked at her.

"Please, we must be quiet," I said moving to her, but she continued to shriek and sob.

"You are defended. You have a family surrounding you, keeping him from you. This did not happen to you, this happened to me and I have lived with it for five long years."

"Please," I said, "you have every right to your distress, but please do try to keep your voice down."

Her hysterics did not calm down, but instead, she put her son on her lap and sobbed into his sleepy confused form muffling the sound. Miss Williams put an arm around her, trying to soothe her. I moved to the door, listening for any indication we were heard.

The first troublesome noises did not come from the hallway. Instead, a clinking sound came from something hitting the corner of the large window covered by the faded green and golden drapery. We all went silent when a little bit of glass dropped to the ground. I was sure the broken glass came from the corner of the window near the lock.

Chapter 29

Before anyone else could react, I hissed:

"Do not say a word!"

They all looked terrified.

"Stand and move behind the desk," I whispered. The only noises that could be heard were the shifting of dresses, and Mrs. Williams trying to hush her groggy child while moving cumbersomely with him. Clara corralled her sisters under her arms like a mother hen. They all shuffled behind the desk.

I went to the place on the wall with the alcove holding a bust of the first man to be Baron in our family set into oak paneling. I pushed the spot on the wall that served as a release and opened the hidden door meant to be the servant's entrance. My father's escape route from his creditors. I knew the escape route well. Our last few years together my father would pull me through it every few months, and we would end in London.

As more glass fell from the window, Clara yelped a little. I glared at her and she went quiet. She could barely breathe for panicking, but she somehow managed to have all her little sisters in her arms pulling them to the door. Mrs. Williams was ashen and clung to her child. Miss Williams had to push the nursemaid on, and seemed to be my only ally capable of action. I kept my gun aimed at the window where another small fragment of glass fell.

I whispered, "Across the hall and two doors toward the grand entrance is the dining room. All of you together should be able to get the serving table in front of the door. There are no windows, and the door is solid. If the brute tries it, and it does not budge he will think the Butler locked it for the night and move on. You should be safe, as long as you are quiet."

"What about you?" Miss Williams whispered.

"I will aim for his heart," I replied, still focused on the window drapes that now moved as if a masculine hand reached through the broken window grasped for the lock.

"This ought not be your burden," she whispered.

"It was always meant to be. The past comes back upon us when we did wrong the first time. I have been given a second chance. We do not have time to argue. Now go," I commanded.

Miss Williams did not hesitate at my command but shuffled the girls through the door, Clara pulled her sisters in the lead, Mrs. Williams' nursemaid pulled her, half-dazed, through the exit. When they were clear of the door, I closed it again and straightened the area, so it looked undisturbed. Then I moved. Situated as the room was, it would appear as if the women had all left through the main door toward the staircase to the upper floors.

I went to the window and threw back the drape. Mr. Williams' wide eyes met mine, and I held the gun aimed at his head. He successfully knocked out one of the nine sections of glass on the bottom of the window and unlocked the latch. He tried to pull his hand back out, but his cuff was stuck. I grasped the brass handle on the window and threw the bottom pane upward into the top and smashed his wrist into the place where the wood met the other pane.

"Leave, now," I said stepping back and holding the gun on him steady through the open window. He whispered many obscenities at me staying quiet. He did not want to be discovered but wanted me to know he was angry. He appeared immobilized, but then with an effort that twisted his handsome features until he looked villainous, he pulled his hand back through the window and jumped into the house, moving so quickly it was only by some act of providence I didn't fall over my skirts as I backed away from his livid face coming at me. He cradled his hurt wrist into his muscular chest.

"Where is she?" he whispered, holding a knife out at me with his other hand.

I laughed.

I could not help it. I had been threatened in this room so many times. My father was much more imposing than this boy, it was pathetic really. This made him angry, but he still did not raise his voice.

"Where is she? I heard her calling for me. You cannot keep us apart any longer," he hissed, again waving his knife at me and moving away from the open window toward a bookshelf that was too close to the door behind the bust.

What could I do but draw his ire to myself? Hadn't I been hurt in this room so many times? What was one more time? Hoping to distract him long enough to give Miss Williams a chance to get the others to safety, I managed to swallow my fear and give him a curious look.

"Where is she," he said again brandishing his knife. I said:

"To which she do you refer?"

He looked confused.

"The only she that has ever mattered," he said.

"You must understand my confusion. There have been many she's in your life, and to say that there is one that matters over the others would be delusional on your part to assign, and far too optimistic on mine to accept."

"I should cut that mouth right off you," he said, but eyed my gun and did not move toward me. I did not think him capable of putting himself in harm's way, so I aimed the gun carefully and did not flinch. All at once the situation came over me. I gripped the ivory handle of the gun, but the idea of killing a man filled me with dread. Eyeing me he read my hesitation. Titus Williams' posture relaxed, and he said quietly:

"Was that…I seemed to have envisioned a girl from my childhood. Certainly, Adelaide is not here."

I said nothing.

"And the child sleeping in the bed, he is mine, isn't he," he said staring at me.

I nodded. He proclaimed with something near awe,

"You are an enchantress, a haggard old thing who hides behind the form of a spinster. Somehow your powers materialized the girl of my youth. What spell did you cast on my aunt to make her turn on me?"

"I did not do that. You did. You cannot treat someone cruelly and believe they won't turn on you the first chance they get."

"But for Adelaide to be here already. Aunt would have told you about her…"

"Before you were even back from London. Before you came back, she was helping me overcome you," I said.

"She will pay for that, and so will Adelaide for coming."

"You cannot blame your wife. It seems Mrs. Adelaide Williams is rather anxious to legitimize your marriage for the sake of your son," I said.

"If she succeeds, it will simply serve to make me a widower at a very young age. You would do best to deter her from any such action," he said.

"You are not above the law, Sir. Killing your wife—"

"The child is a beautiful boy," he said. "Clara will accept him as my nephew, and we will raise him."

"You mean as your illegitimate son?"

"No, I will be obliged to raise the child for my aunt's sake."

"He is not a baby. The child is four years," I said.

227

"I can simply say I rescued the child from a foundling hospital. Aunt would be just the sort of woman to use such a place to preserve her respectability," he said.

I felt the vomit start at the back of my throat. Of course, he knew where unwed women could leave their babies so that they could go out into the world to find work. He was saying:

"…it will be an apt punishment for her to have an illegitimate child. I believe Mr. James Evans already suspects as much."

He stopped to laugh but quickly continued, as if he wanted me to know the torture his Aunt would endure. He wanted me to know it was my fault.

"I will, of course, take her stipend and she can apply to the workhouse to support the lad. That will be an apt punishment for her."

"You cannot believe your father would let you do that," I said, afraid for Sadie Williams if something happened to Mr. Williams. Had Titus Williams killed his father in their tussle?

"He thinks he can send me away."

"Did you hurt him?" I asked.

"He … it was an unfair fight, he snuck up on me… I should have…"

The way the brute colored I could see his father won their fight. He finished: "It does not signify; he will be dealt with. The boy, my son, will show me the deference, I cannot show my father… he must be four years old. He could be legitimately mine or my aunt's child. No one will be the wiser."

"Except me," I said.

"Yes, you have no idea a women's place. I cannot see how your brother tolerates you, but I'll take care of it for him."

The breath caught in my chest. He was so inconsistent. He meant for me to persuade his wife to go home, but if given the chance he would kill me. I could not reason with his craze. I started backing away toward the door. He saw the shake in the gun I tried to hold aimed at him.

"I don't understand," I said as he looked around at the bookshelf confused. The bloody mess from Miss Williams was still on the desk. He must have heard Clara screech near there because he started to examine the area more clearly.

"Why Clara?" I asked, drawing his eye to myself so he didn't notice the door. "You have had many women before this, including your lovely wife. Why Clara?"

"She is the ideal," he said quietly looking back to the desk.

"She is Phineas' ideal. Is that it? Somewhere deep down you trust his judgment over your own," I said more loudly.

"I do not need that fool's opinion," he hissed. He focused his tight green eyes entirely on me. He looked dangerous again.

"Yet, it must have frustrated you in school when he was right more often than you," I said.

"No, he has nothing to do with it. She is perfect for me, and I will marry her before anyone can stop me. I will shower her with jewels, and she will be the envy of every woman in London."

"You cannot get away with--"

I did not finish my sentence. From the open window, a deep gruff voice said,

"There you es. All I had to do es follow the trail of broken things. Broken horse, broken drainpipe, and now broken glass, and I find you."

The speaker was angled just out of my line of sight. His voice frightened me. This voice was not full of survival at any cost. The deep gruff voice was desperate and full of rage. Mr. Williams chanced a glance at the man and winced in fear. I glanced. The man was ducking through the window, but my focus drew instantly to the gun he held. It was nothing like the beautifully decorated style I held. His looked more like a sawed-off double-barrel rifle, the accurate kind a soldier would use. However, he was not a soldier.

The middle-aged man smelled as though he'd just bathed, this coupled with his strong shoulders and arms indicated he labored hard for his living but had come prepared for an ending of some kind or another. His dark hair shone, and his skin glowed almost ghostly white in the moonlight filtering thought the broken window. As he straightened his large, strong form, he held the firearm steady on Mr. Williams.

Mr. Titus Williams did not disregard him as he had me.

In the glances I spared him I saw the dark, dead eyes of a person who had lost everything. If Mr. Williams' conceit discarded other's lives as playthings, this man, his opposite, was the very image of broken by the loss of a single precious life he valued more than his own.

"What are you doing here, Mr. Black?" Mr. Williams asked. "Ah, the father of Marigold Black."

"You did not answer my request for a duel. It is dishonorable. I expected nothin less, you are the viper, who suns himself in the meadow. You look harmless until you strike, then you run like the coward you are. You may be assured I will follow you, until you are properly dealt with, even if I must learn to slither. If you think I'm letten' you take the next girl, you are very wrong," Mr. Black said.

Titus Williams seemed frozen, then he started to slither in my direction, and I backed up almost to the far wall as he said, "You wrote this madman and told him where I was?" He lowered the volume to a hiss as he spoke. He appeared as if threatening me, but I could see he was striving for stealth and meant to take my gun from me. Mr. Black would not hesitate to shoot.

"You are a bitter old bat who could not marry. Does it not shame you to pry so with a man's business, Miss Bolton?" he asked.

I stopped. I heard an echo of my father's voice condemning me; his threats were always quiet. We mustn't let the servants hear. It was my fault Baron Adlay did not want to pay enough for me. Could I not use my feminine wiles to get him what he needed?

I never defended myself then. I was no longer a scared little girl, and I was not alone anymore. Miss Williams had to be safely tucked away by now. Why was I whispering, reasoning with a mad man? I would not keep his secret. I screeched as loudly as I could at the pestilent little man,

"Who are you to blame me for your folly!"

Titus Williams stepped back surprised. Even louder I screamed, "I will not take responsibility for what you have done. I wrote a letter. I did nothing to the man's daughter. You, on the other hand, you used her ill. You should be transported. You should be hung!"

It felt good to yell. I was trapped in a room with two madmen, and I needed help. Why would I stay quiet when I needed help? Thankfully, someone heard me.

Indistinguishable yelling started down the hallway near the grand entrance, further raising the alarm. Soon, pounding started on the study door. I could hear Lawrence yelling for me to open the door, but I did not dare lower my gun nor turn my back on Mr. Williams. His eyes desperately flew from the window Mr. Black guarded to the door behind me where Lawrence now shouted. His flitting eyes, greedy and anxious, only stopped when he looked at my loaded weapon.

"You had no right to delve into my personal affairs!" Titus Williams bellowed back, edging his way toward me faster now that detection was upon him.

"You imposed upon my niece—you delved into my personal affairs," I screamed back. "If you knew this man was coming for you, why didn't you run? You have Millie stored away somewhere. You had to take Clara, too?"

"She is mine! I'd rather see her dead than married to that … that simpleton," he screamed.

"You will never get to her. I promise you that. What's more, I will do everything in my power to promote her attraction to Phineas. It is now my only goal in life to see them married," I said, holding my pistol steady.

"Spinsters! The whole lot of you have caused me so much trouble."

"I want you to admit you killed my girl," Mr. Black bellowed, joining our screaming match, edging his way toward Mr. Williams. Mr. Williams took another step toward me. If I did not do something soon, he would overpower me in four or five long strides and take my pistol. I raised my gun, steadying my hand. I would not, no I could not let him get to Clara.

Lawrence must have heard, and not recognized Mr. Black because he stopped calling to me and I heard him run down the hall shouting for Richard. Meanwhile, Mr. Williams was trying to reason with Mr. Black while not admitting any fault of his own. Focused on Lawrence yelling behind the door, all I heard was:

"…you can see I didn't kill your daughter. She was foolhardy enough—"

"Don't you talk your filthy mouth about her," Mr. Black bellowed. He raised and fired his gun at Mr. Williams. The explosion deafened me. Mr. Williams flinched, but my shoulder stung. I looked down to find blood seeping through my gown.

"You shot a gentlewoman. You will be hung now," Mr. Williams shouted, goading Mr. Black. The yelling behind the door became more desperate and was joined by pounding.

"Give me your gun," Mr. Williams commanded holding out his bloody hand to me.

"You are out of your faculties," I laughed crazily, edging toward the door, trying to put pressure on my shoulder and not drop the gun. I didn't flinch pointing it at him—instead, I told myself if he came one more step toward me, I had to shoot him.

"This doesn't have to end with you bleeding to death. Give me the gun," Titus Williams shouted at me.

"I will not bleed to death from this," I said. I knew pain; this wasn't so bad. He wanted to control me through fear. I wouldn't cry for him, so I laughed again. My forced laugh seemed to set him off. He lunged toward me.

I ran for the door. I dropped the gun, but my numb fingers could not manage the rim lock fast enough. Another gunshot rang out. I felt a sting in my lower back and glanced over my shoulder. Titus Williams fell face-first into me. Something snagged the back of my dress as he dropped. He lay limp and heavy on the hem of my gown. His extremely sharp knife had been stretched out toward me. It caught and then ripped the bottom of my dress as he fell. I pulled away from him and sagged against the door. Mr. Black just stared at the body, like he couldn't figure out why blood would spurt from the base of Titus Williams' skull, just under his ear. Then he looked at me in terror.

"I… Look what I done," he whispered.

"He would have killed me," I said, feeling the slight cut on my back, the thrust of the knife through the layers of my clothes had been hampered only by Mr. Black's bullet.

"I hit you, too," he said.

233

"You saved my life. I... I don't know if I could have shot him."

"They'll hang me for shooten' a lady," he said.

"Myra," another voice shouted through the door. Lawrence shouted, "Richard – the key."

"Go," I said looking at the desperate man.

"I died when she did. It doesn't matter much what happens to me now. I'm just sorry for hittin' you," he said. "Now it will end."

Chapter 30

The lock turned, and I stepped away so as not to be hit by the door. The door opened only so far, wedged in by the body on the ground.

"Myra," Lawrence said and slipped through the door. He grabbed me around the waist pulling me away. He tried to find the source of the blood. Richard shoved the door harder by pushing Titus Williams's body further. He wedged past us and held his gun on Mr. Black as he was the only other person standing. Mr. Black dropped his gun and raised his hands in surrender. Richard searched the room, barely registering Titus Williams bleeding on the ground.

"Where is Clara?" Richard asked panicked.

"She is safe. She is in the dining room with her sisters," I said.

It did not register. His wild eyes couldn't make sense of anything.

"Richard," I yelled. He looked at me. I shook like I may never be warm again. I said, "She is not in here. I sent her to the dining room. The girls are safe."

He nodded like he heard me this time. He lowered his gun.

"Thank God for that," he said.

"Titus," A voice shouted, and we all turned toward the door. "I swear boy I am going to bind you and--"

The boy's father pressed hard on the door and pushed into the room. He looked around the room and he reared back when he found his son, losing his life's blood on the ground. He turned white and fell to his knees in front of his boy's corpse. Rick entered the room next and his eyes fixated on the body. I could not read his expression, but rather thought he did not know how to feel about it.

"What happened?" Mr. Williams asked, turning the body over and moving his son, so the door didn't continue to contort his body.

"He... he killed—" Mr. Black started, but I quickly interrupted.

"He lunged at me with a knife. Mr. Black was forced to put him down to save my life."

"Put him down," Mr. Williams balked at my choice of words. Though Rick shot me a disapproving look, I did not take it back.

"He... he ruined—" Mr. Black started again, so I cut him off again, this time with a glare to keep him quiet.

"He ruined any chance we gave him at redemption. Mr. Black fired a warning shot which unfortunately hit my shoulder. Titus lunged at me anyway," I said slurring a little at the end, and feeling woozy. Mr. Black nodded and turned from the quickly cooling body.

"I clipped her; it was an accident. He lined up with her from where I stood," Mr. Black said, admitting his crime.

"Myra, you've been hit," Richard said like he couldn't string the words together to make sense out of them. Lawrence picked me up in his arms.

"I am capable of standing," I said, hooking my good arm around his neck.

"She needs a surgeon," Lawrence called, setting me down on the sofa and putting his cravat on my wound though it was barely bleeding anymore.

"I will call for one... and, I," Richard stammered still looking around the room like he might find his daughter.

"I must... the constable has not yet arrived," Richard said as if he were coming back to himself.

"Miss Williams was cut by his knife. Her wound would not stop bleeding when I cleaned it. I wrapped it as tightly as I could, but she will need the surgeon, and soon. She lost a considerable amount of blood and is in danger of infection. Especially after the exertion it took her to run here and warn us."

"Yes, my sister, she is... He wounded her. He would have... If I hadn't stopped him, he would have..." Mr. Williams stammered, still looking at his son. They looked so alike. Over the years the elder kept his youthful appearance and they could have been brothers. Except such a look of sorrow likely never crossed the youngster's face, in all of his life.

"Oh, my boy! What have you done!" the father cried. Tears spilled from his vibrant green eyes. He had his son's hand to his chest. Richard and Rick crossed the room to where Lawrence and I sat so Mr. Williams did not have to hear us discuss the crimes of his son and what was to be done. Richard, Rick, Lawrence and I huddled in a circle while Mr. Black edged his way toward Mr. Williams. Regret was written on his face.

"Where is Miss Williams – if she has been attacked, we must determine how severely," Richard whispered.

"She is with Clara and the others. I... Mr. Williams came through the window. He only broke the corner out at first. He could not unlatch it right away, so I sent them all into the dining room through the false panel and told them to push the table up against the door," I said.

"Why did you not go with them?" Lawrence asked.

"I ... I knew if I did not stop him here, he would follow them. He was so determined to get to Clara, he said he'd rather her dead than married to...anyone else. He wanted his aunt and Mrs. Williams dead as well. I was the only one who had a chance of stopping him," I said.

"You stayed here and aggravated him, so he'd attack you," Lawrence accused.

"Come now, Lawrence, you know a spinster can only hope to die young."

Rick laughed, surprised at my sardonic turn.
Lawrence cradled me and said, "That is not funny, Myra. You should have gone with them."

"I... I couldn't. I couldn't let him hurt anyone else," I said, standing and moving out of his grasp. I did not deserve his honorable arms around me.

"It wasn't your responsibility," Lawrence snapped, following me.

At his words, something broke free inside me and I felt gripped by a hysterical madness.

I wailed, "It was my responsibility. I couldn't let him... I couldn't let it happen again...I killed a woman once. Did you know that? You allowed your daughter to be raised by a murderer. I could never do it again."

"Myra, that was not your fault," Richard said. He watched me pace the floor and tear at my hair.

"I don't follow," Lawrence said, trying to stop my pacing.

"I... Baron Adlay was married when I first met him. Did you know that?"

"What happened?" Lawrence asked, the look on his face petrified as if he might know.

"My father, he... he told me if I did not gain the Baron's favor he would... he threatened me... so I was very kind to the Baron. I made him very aware of my..." I retched a little. I could not think of the dress I wore showing off my femineity in a way that would have horrified my mother if she lived. Baron Adlay, a married man, held me often and I encouraged his antics.

"My behavior to a married man was not... I thought it a whim of my fathers, to please his old friend, so I acquiesced... only days later Baron Adlay's young healthy wife died in a tragic accident. An accident that Baron Adlay himself accounted for. Nothing happened, not even an inquest. She was killed because I was a flirt."

"You didn't do that," Lawrence said taking my face in his hands and forcing my wild eyes to look at him, "You didn't do that!"

"I was detestable in my desire for self-preservation. I all but propositioned the woman's husband only to avoid Father's horsewhip on my back, I … Where was my duty? How can I live with myself if I…"?

"Myra," Richard started but seemed unable to continue. He watched me, horrified. I suppose for all he had endured at our father's hand did not compare to what I endured. I would confess all. The infection would be siphoned out of me. Given to those whom I trusted to be my judges.

"After she died, Baron Adlay courted me. I hate myself. I … I encouraged him. Father could not whip me, because he did not want my future husband to see lash marks and bruises on my back."

I started to sob. Lawrence pulled me into his chest, and I wept saying:

"I should have been brave enough to save her. What a human being I am, my father's truest heir, black hearted and selfish."

"You could not have known he would do her harm," Lawrence soothed.

"Myra please consider, Clara, and Miss Williams, the widowed bride; you saved them. That is who you are, that is fundamentally who you are," Richard insisted. He must also have examined the core of his soul, to be sure he did not find our father there.

I turned and looked up at Richard, "I did. I wish I'd been brave enough then, but I was brave enough to stand in his way today."

"That is who you are. You take care of the people around you. Father only used them. You must let him go, take his shackle from your neck and let him die," Richard said forcefully.

Lawrence compelled my face back to his chest and held me tightly. He needed me there. He still loved me. He would block out the horror of what I confessed.

Rick, was the reason that brought us all back.

"Father, we must contain this situation. We still have not sent for the surgeon. You go get Clara and take the ladies to the drawing-room to be sure they are not harmed. I shall send a runner to find the surgeon and another to hurry the parish constable. It will be hard for Frank to leave off the search for Millie."

"Is not the constable already coming?" I asked.

"He is out looking for Millie. She is his cousin. I think we will have to get a runner if we wish to see him tonight," Rick said.

"Is there a magistrate we can send for?" Lawrence asked.

Richard answered: "Mr. Frank Hadleigh is best. He often is acting magistrate for his older brother and the Justice of the Peace. His family has been doing it for generations. Frank is a barrister by education, but cannot apprentice because he is obligated to keep performing the role his family has always done for the parish. Lawrence, you could perform the duty if you wish."

Lawrence examined me, then he squinted at Mr. Black.

"I do not think I would be impartial," he said.

"Well, Frank's father abused the position abominably, he increased their lands and holdings substantially. I don't suppose you would be any worse," Rick said. Lawrence seemed to think this over.

"Myra, this is no place for you. Why don't you come with me?" Richard said tenderly. He still fought the pooling in his eyes.

"I must stay with Mr. Black and give testimony," I said.

"He shot you," Lawrence whispered.

"He saved me," I insisted, "I will not abandon him after all he has been through. Please brother, we will join you after this grim business is put to right. Go, let Clara know she is safe. Please."

"You do not leave her side," Richard said drilling into Lawrence.

"I never will again," Lawrence assured under his breath with fire in his eyes.

Richard nodded, and he and Rick left. I felt my body sag into Lawrence. He did not hate me, even after seeing what I hid behind my mask of serenity. Lawrence felt me sinking and took me back to sit down on the sofa.

We fell into a tense quiet, unsure what would happen next. Mr. Black stared out the window. Mr. Williams wept. Finally, after a particularly loud sob from Mr. Williams, Mr. Black moved over to him. He put a hand on his shoulder and said:

"I am sorry you have to feel such sorrow. No man should have to die before 'is young'uns."

"He had to be put down," Mr. Williams echoed me. Then I felt bad for using the term.

"I should not have... I am sorry I said it like that," I said. Even the father of such a boy deserved my compassion in this moment.

"What did you say that was not correct," Mr. Williams said looking at the corpse. "It didn't matter how hard I tried for him. I could do nothing. I left him in my sister's care because I could do nothing for him and it broke my heart. I left him, long before he left me."

This started a strange one-sided conversation of confession between the men as if the eerie green room squeezed the darkness out of each of us. Each man stared into the vacant eyes of Titus Williams giving away theirs.

"I understand your misery, Sir. My wife left me with a girl child. I had no idea what to do for Marigold. I did not teach her how to guard herself. I did not ground her," Mr. Black admitted.

"No more did I," Mr. Williams said. "What if I had gotten Titus to your hospital years ago? What if they could have done something for him before he ... I pretended nothing was wrong. A young man and his pursuits, what could be done? I am to blame here, sir, you simply ended this. I let it continue."

"He took my girl," Mr. Black cried, "he made her believe he was going to give her the life of the masters, and she went with him. If I'd been the kind of father she could talk to, she may have confessed to me. When her soldier went away, she was so lonely, and I was not patient enough to be her companion."

"My boy could sense the need in a person," continued Mr. Williams. "I can, too. I can tell who will make it, and who is a liability. I use this ability to gain business. Every day I try my hardest to allow those who can succeed a chance, as my father did before me. This makes me successful. I would never use raw human need to hurt someone. Titus, he saw their need, he could tell who would be left defenseless and took everything from them. It filled me with shame."

"He found my lonely unprotect' girl," Mr. Black said. "I don't know what 'appened to her. Marigold ended up on the roadside. I found her, barely a breath. She mumbled and couldn't see her old papa when I found her. I don't even know what happened to her."

"He would have been hung," Mr. Williams said. "Two years ago I had to pay off a man who accused my son of such brutality he would have been hung. The man didn't want justice he wanted money. I ... I was thankful the man could be bought off. What of the scandal? I should have let my son face his actions many years ago. I killed your daughter."

"Come now, stop this," Lawrence finally said.

"He was a boy, but a boy," the father wailed.

"No Sir, he turned the course of many lives as a man, and he suffered the consequences of his actions as every man must," I said.

"As a lad, I took him to church every Sunday ...I ... I made him pray ...what happened, where did I go so wrong?" Mr. Williams asked me.

"This is a kind of madness of the head," Lawrence said. "He could not see right from wrong. He had a gift of sight, but only used it to get what he wanted. There is nothing you could have done."

Lawrence examined the lifeless body as if he wished for answers, knowing someone someday would be able to understand. He hated it wasn't him. Finally, he said, "Parenting is hard. We do everything we can to protect our children. We see the best in them, and not always the truth. Eventually we let our children grow up then release them into the world and pray God they make it to a place of happiness and peace.

"Usually, they find turmoil and hardship, just as we did. Mr. Williams, no matter the guidance you gave him, your son was not right in the head. What could you do? Mr. Black, nothing would have stopped the young man from exploiting your daughter because he had no sense of right and wrong. Neither of you could change that. Sad as it may be, neither of you can now change this outcome. Blame and regret will do no good. We all must simply move forward and find a way to heal."

This ended the confessions. Lawrence was right. What could we do but move forward in our lives, and away from the dark? I could feel something real and palatable fall across me. Nothing changed, but it felt as if sunlight warmed my insides. The cold penetrating dark spirit in the room died. The shadows lost their power. What could I do now to break free of the ground and progress to something beautiful?

The lily grows best when planted in well-rotted manure.

Chapter 31

A maid came in and tied up my arm. Then she gave me a shawl to keep me warm, the fall night coming through the open window grew even chillier. After another bout of waiting in silence, a knock sounded at the door. Rick came in with the parish constable, a much younger man then I had been expecting, though I must have known him as a child because I vaguely recognized him. Lawrence helped me sit up. We were forced to retell the story, while he examined the broken window and the blood upon the latch. Mr. Black let me speak and Mr. Williams gave witness against his son. The constable wrote impatiently and then, when he finished, he asked, "We still have a girl missing. Do either of you have any idea where she could be?"

We all stopped. I had forgotten about Millie. The constable, who was the Widow Fielding's nephew, seemed distracted and more worried about his cousin than the corpse on the ground. Mr. Williams thought, then said, "My sister may know."

Rick nodded and went to fetch her. We watched the young man pace. He looked over the room as if nothing could escape his notice even agitated. He walked to the bust with the door behind it, and easily found the latch to open it. I couldn't help thinking the young man and his family must have a gift for observation that led the people to trust them with law enforcement considering how long they'd been doing it.

Miss Williams came in. She looked at Titus Williams' body and her mouth moved, but nothing came out. She put a hand on her brother's shoulder. The constable did not allow her time to digest the scene, even.

"Millie Fielding. Where is she?"

Miss Williams took a deep breath and said,

"When Titus came home yesterday, I told him I'd just received an express from his father. He was coming to bring him back to London. I told him we would likely not be coming back to the house after so he must gather all his belongings."

"Naturally, he starts to gather all the neighborhood's daughters," the constable said.

"He left this morning, like normal anyway. He went to see Miss Clara who was finally well enough to leave the house. He told me to stay home and pack. He insisted he would give excuses for my absence. He was gone for hours. I did not know he still ... I thought he would only go to Miss Clara Bolton, whom I knew to be protected at every angle," Miss Williams said holding her side. I could see the blood had soaked through my strip of petticoat. I whispered to the footman to go get more bandages, and if he could find my father's Irish Whiskey, it would be needed. He left, and the constable then continued, "You did not know he still courted Millie."

"No," Miss Williams said, "I thought he had to give her up to keep courting Miss Clara."

"My aunt said he has been to see Millie many times in the last few days," Frank said. I closed my eyes. I made Clara pretend to be sick and he had nothing else to do.

"Millie will most likely be at an inn. He often rents a carriage. Then he can only be traced to the inn he took it from," Miss Williams said.

"He drove a cabriolet. He claimed it was new," I said.

"No, he's not bought a carriage. It likely belongs to the inn where Millie is. He changes carriages along the way so as not to be recognized. She will be north of here, somewhere nice enough to have luxurious carriage rentals. He... he was set to go back to London, then school at Michaelmas. He would have put her on the road."

"He left us after the noonday meal," I said.

"He was home by four in the evening to receive his father," Miss Williams said.

"My Aunt last saw him at two. She'll be within an hour's ride," the constable said, thinking hard.

"It could only be an hour at the most," Miss Williams confirmed, unable to look away from the body. "He was back before his father came, and was in time to receive Mr. Black's note to duel."

"He knew he was going to back to London, perhaps tomorrow morning," The constable said.

"In my letter, I indicated we would leave this evening and stay near the town of Dorchester," Mr. Williams informed.

"Yes, he would take her to an inn on the way there. I am sure he intended to establish her in London … she will be no more than two or three towns northwest," Miss Williams said.

"There are only two inns between here and Dorchester. Only one within an hour's ride with such a carriage to rent," the constable said.

"He… he has a pattern of… had…he had a pattern…he is… I am sure she will be in one of them. She will be in a private parlor, confused as to what happened and growing frightened that she has been away too long. He … I do not think she is entirely lost to…" Miss Williams said, looking down at her nephew's body. She could not hide her look of disgust. Whether the look was for the gore of his body or his life, I could not say.

"Miss Williams 'es how I found my Marigold, she 'ell help you find your girl too," Mr. Black said. The constable blushed and focused too hard on the footman who came back with a maid to patch Miss Williams up. More curtly than necessary he said:

"Miss Myra Bolton, do you mean to arrange for a citizen's arrest against this hero who has saved us all and rid the earth of a monster?"

"No Sir," I said doubting he would have arrested Mr. Black even if I'd said yes.

"Very well Sir, you may go on your way."

"Mr. Black," I said standing. "Would you take a warm meal?"

"No ma'am. The boy who loved my Marigold will be looking for me—I must return this," he said retrieving the firearm from the ground. I'll go find him, if ets alright," he said.

"Good day to you sir," the constable said. I noticed he did not even write down Mr. Black's address, nor did he inquire after his first name. We all fidgeted. The constable wrote in his notebook as he narrated so we all knew the story if ever questioned.

"I find a case of home invasion, under common law Mr. Black had the right to defend Miss Myra Bolton from the crime being committed against her by Mr. Titus Williams. In turn, Miss Bolton waives her right at a citizen's arrest when she was injured by Mr. Black in his attempt at stopping Mr. Titus Williams from harming her. The surgeon will be here as soon as possible. He will give me his report."

He flipped the book shut and then said, "I must go. It is an easy ride to the inn described. I think we may have located Millie."

"When you find her do tell her we hope she enjoyed her little holiday with your mother. Now is always such a nice time to get away to take tea at a lovely establishment. Especially when there is much drama going on in the neighborhood," I said. He looked at me uncertainly.

"I am sure Millie would not have left so irresponsibly. No doubt she took your mother to the inn as a chaperone. Your mother will no doubt testify to such when you return to your aunt's house with Millie, so the rector may know his mistake," I said.

The constable clenched and unclenched his jaw a few times.

"Thank you." He bowed.

"Frank, can I do anything?" Rick asked, walking him to the door. Frank glared at Rick for a moment then reconsidered.

"Ride out to the house and tell Mr. Clarke and my aunt there has been a misunderstanding and not to ask for anybody else's help. I think...if I can find her before... I will bring her home tonight, I'm sure she's with my mother," the man said, glancing at me. I nodded.

"Of course," Rick said, nodding at the well-worn footman to saddle his horse.

"Come, Miss Williams, let me escort you back to the other ladies so you may be more comfortable near a fire where your wound can be tended to again," Rick said.

She drew near her brother, but he said, "Go, Sadie. Get taken care of."

They left. I could not force myself to move but watched the door where they left as if I could still see the shadow of them.

Mr. Black came in close to me. He fidgeted like he was finally ready to leave.

"I am sorry I hurt you," he said nodding to my arm.

"You saved my life. I will not hear another word you were at fault," I said.

He was not satisfied.

"Would I 'ave shot him, even if he hadn't charged you?"

"You hesitated, as I did. We both of us recoiled against taking human life. Mr. Williams did not hesitate. He would have stabbed me in the back if you hadn't shot him."

I stood and turned to show him as I had shown the constable where the bloody knife had pierced my dress and the torn trail down my skirt.

"He launched himself at me, but if he hadn't, I think you would have held him captive until the law came," I said.

Startling me, Mr. Black abruptly fell to his knees and I assumed he prayed. I thought I heard him say something like:

"Thank you, God, for making it righteous…Thank you for letting me save her and turnin' darkness ento the light that es her life."

Then it hit me. I almost died. Titus Williams was aiming for my heart. Obsessed with fixing a mistake I made at nineteen, I did nothing to save myself. My chest stopped, and I could not fill my lungs with air. Lawrence tried to sit me down. Like a statue encased, I stood in front of the man praying at my feet. I could not move. Tears dripped down my face.

"I didn't do anything. I didn't shoot," I whispered.

"You screamed. You let me know you were in trouble. The whole house knew you were in trouble. We came to your aid. Mr. Black came to your aid," Lawrence said.

I looked around the room of my nightmares, the room where my father terrorized me. I stopped panicking. The darkness that dwelt here died, only somehow, I knew if I tried, I could revive it. I could revisit the room until it had just as much power over me as ever. Why would I do that?

I lived: the darkness was dead. I stood up for myself. What's more, in that most desperate moment, I know not where Mr. Black came from, but he came, and I lived. Maybe God heard my prayers all those years ago and hesitated the hand that whipped me, hesitated it for ten years. He sent me to a place where I would love and be loved in return. A place where I would learn to stand up for myself.

Then he brought me back to this room, and, to kill the threat, sent me the loving father I'd always wanted. Mr. Black was not given the advantages in life my father had, wealth, consequence, a seat at every grand table, and yet he was a father worth having. He was the man I preferred. He could not save his own daughter, but he saved me. He answered my constant prayer, the prayer I prayed every moment since my mother died.

I dropped my head and joined Mr. Black's prayer of thanks. I would forever be connected to the father I knew only for a couple of hours. Mr. Williams joined in and Lawrence too. All thanking God for my life. I don't know how long we stayed that way, but I felt heavy and my arm started to throb.

At some point Mr. Black slipped back out the window he had come in. I would never see him in the flesh again. Yet, I would see him now and then when I closed my eyes. Every time the mad man came at me with his horsewhip or knife, Mr. Black, the great defending father, would make the gun ring out, and the crazed man would fall. I had a second chance. This time, I saved my niece. I stood up to the monster, and I lived.

Chapter 32

"Myra, there is tea in the drawing-room, and it grows drafty in here. Perhaps we can have my man take care of the body," Richard said, entering the study. His man had entered the room with him.

"Come," I said, leaning against Lawrence who really may have meant what he said about never leaving my side again, "Mr. Williams, come."

He looked up at me like nothing would induce him to leave his son's side. I moved to him and put a hand on his shoulder. He took my hand and the comfort I offered. His impeccable appearance changed. His hair was messy, and he must have left his coat behind in his rush. He looked up at me with his sister's aloe green eyes and said, "You are a strong lady. I respect you greatly."

"And I respect you," I said. "So much so, I will tell you. "Your daughter-in-law, Mrs. Adelaide Williams, and grandson, are in the Drawing Room."

He looked up at me surprised.

"Then there is a child," he said, nodding.

"A beautiful young lad, who is healthy and good-natured," Lawrence said.

"He is… is not stubborn and selfish?" Mr. Williams whispered.

"Not so. He is moldable and easily manages his disappointments," Lawrence said.

"There is nothing so comforting in death as a budding young life," I said.

"There is a child," Mr. Williams stammered. He turned his head and kissed my hand. Lawrence tightened his grip on my arm.

Mr. Williams, who had only moments ago looked unmovable, stood and allowed me to turn him. The front of him was covered in his son's blood. Richard's man took him to clean up and promised to return him to the drawing-room when he wouldn't scare the little lad. Lawrence turned me toward the back of the house and walked close to my uninjured side until we reached the washroom. He stopped and said nothing. He knew I needed a minute to clean myself and straighten my appearance the best I could. I asked the footman to bring me a different shawl. I gave him the bloody one, and the new long one brought to me covered most of the blood splattered on my back. The stiff, crusty stain at the bottom of my skirt was dried and did not leave a trail when I walked.

I still looked tattered, but could not spare more time. I needed to speak to Mrs. Adelaide Williams. We walked in silence to the drawing-room.

We entered the room and Clara rushed to me and kissed my face.

"Are you okay, Aunt?, I thought you would die for me. I could not bear you to take responsibility for my being a nincompoop."

I did everything I could to comfort her. I would have appreciated her affection more if it did not jostle my arm, increasing the throb. Lawrence put a shoulder in the way of my hurt arm, but Clara did not seem deterred by his presence. Finally, sounding as if he spoke to Eva, he said, "Let your aunt be. She must communicate urgently with Mrs. Williams," and he put his arm around Clara, taking her back to a settee.

I grinned at him. Not the slight smile I used when oppressed, but a grin. He stopped and examined me. I did not have time for him to explore my changed face. I moved quickly toward Miss Williams who, now clean of blood, rejoined her niece. Her pallor was ashen as she struggled to comfort Mrs. Williams and her child. I did not know how much time I had, so I did not mince words.

"Mrs. Williams, we have told Mr. Williams you are here. He is heartbroken over his son and wishes to meet his heir," I said.

"His heir," Mrs. Williams said, looking at me suspiciously.

"Yes, his son's wife and child, legitimate and whole, are here, and he wishes to see you. Is that acceptable to you?" I gave her an encouraging nod to take up her opportunity where she found it.

"Legitimate," she whispered as she looked around the room.

"Of course, you are legitimate. I saw the child baptized myself," Miss Williams said, quickly seeing my mission. The young widow nodded, blinking back the tears. How long and hard she must have worked to keep her son respectable. Now, if I could help it, her father-in-law would make it ironclad.

"He knew nothing. Please do not blame him, Adelaide," Miss Williams said quietly at the girl's side.

"Adelaide," Mr. Williams echoed coming into the room. Mrs. Williams stood, and I could feel her shaking next to me as she grasped for my hand. He finished saying, "you've... you are a woman now."

"Hello, Sir," she said ducking her head to him in the very posture of shame.

"Your father has been sick to know what happened to you."

"She has been a married woman in Scotland this whole time," I said.

"I will write to him. Upon opening the letter, he will learn everything was done properly. Oh, what joy this brings us," Mr. Williams said.

"I..." Mrs. Williams flushed, "you will..."

She bit her lip.

"Oh, dear girl! Do permit me to know your son. I suppose you heard mine is no more?"

"Yes," she said quietly.

"We will bury him proper and you will be mentioned in the papers as his grieving widow. You'll not have to worry one bit. There is a widow's jointure set up for you. My mother passed last year and is no longer in need of it. I will personally see to it your son is given every honor as the young gentleman he is." He smiled fondly at the child.

Mrs. Williams didn't know how to react to this news. Her child would forever be legitimate. She could want nothing more.

"We will cry for our boy together," Mr. Williams said seeing the tears gathering in her eyes. Mrs. Williams stopped and nodded. She tried not to look horrified that she was being called on to mourn the man who had tormented her. Instead, she turned to her son who clung to his maid and said:

"Charley, this is your grandfather."

"Oh, you named him for your mother's father. What a wonderful way to honor that great man," Mr. Williams said, holding a hand towards the young lad, who looked to his mother twice before he shook it. After Mrs. Williams was able to release my hand, I left the two and turned to my brother.

"Miss Sadie Williams needs some wine," I said. "She looks ready to pass out."

"Of course," Richard said, "Can we see you to a room, Miss Williams?"

"I want to see my brother meet his grandson," she insisted, trying to stem the flow of sweat at her brow.

"You have done much for my Charley, haven't you Sadie?" Mr. Williams asked, looking up where he squatted in front of the boy.

"I did what I could for them. I have been working out of my stipend and between Adelaide and the many others…"

Mr. Williams looked down, so she shifted and said, "I have not done as much as I would like to have."

"You are very kind to us," Mrs. Adelaide Williams said quietly.

"I should have been funding your efforts. How careless of me," Mr. Williams said, "I will pay you back what you have spent, Sadie."

"It is of little concern," Miss Williams said. "What else do I have to spend money on?"

"The beads of crystal from China you like to thread," he said. "At Christmas, you said you gave that up, but now I see you were sacrificing it."

"It is of small consequence," she said.

"My father once said you were so good at it you could have sold them," Mrs. Williams said, realizing Miss Williams gave all she had for her.

Richard brought out the wine and insisted Miss Williams and myself drink it. Miss Williams could barely lift her cup and her brother insisted she lie down, but she said she would after he knew his little Charley. She feared to be alone.

The wine made me feel drowsy. Lawrence sat next to me on a sofa and felt me slouch. He shifted to hold the bulk of my weight with his side.

"Is that the surgeon?" Lawrence asked when a horse was heard riding up the drive.

Richard looked out the window.

"No, it is Rick," he said. "The nearest surgeon is in Dorchester. He will be a while longer."

We all waited, and finally, Rick came in.

"Is everything all right?" Richard asked his son.

Clara, who had been dozing off, became alert. Rick gave one slight serious glance to me, then his face broke into a grin.

"It turns out Millie was at her aunt's house all along. She did not mean to worry anyone. She just needed to get away from the neighborhood. Mr. Titus Williams took her for a ride to tell her he chose Clara after all. She went to seek solace at her aunt's. The message she sent her mother was somehow lost along the way, is all," Rick laughed.

"She is home?" Clara asked, tears rushing her eyes again.

"Safe and sound, there was no harm done. She is with her mother and her aunt. Mr. Clarke was even a little embarrassed he raised the alarm so quickly," Rick said smiling.

"It cannot hurt to be vigilant," I said.

"I am so glad she is safe," Clara said.

She and Mr. Williams both looked like they bought his story. Nobody else said anything, but Miss Williams looked so relieved, a few tears escaped. She looked ready to pass out, and I could see blood seeping through her bandage.

"Richard, I must go to my room. Miss Williams, your injury is deeper and has bled more than mine. Please let us put you in a quiet room, and clean out the wound again," I said.

"I confess I am not feeling well," she said.

Rick moved first. He came to her but smiled at her niece as he took Miss Sadie Williams by the arm. He almost had to carry her after she took her first few steps, but the strong young man did not seem burdened under her weight. Lawrence helped me up.

"May I carry you, Myra?" Lawrence asked. I laughed. Thankfully, he lost some of his gravity.

"No, thank you."

"Are you courting Miss Bolton?" Mr. Williams asked Lawrence curiously as he bounced his sleeping grandson on his lap.

"No, he is loyal to his late wife who died ten years ago," my brother said sarcastically, clearly put out at how tender Lawrence was being with me, though he still showed no sign of relenting.

"We are all old friends," I said to cover up the awkwardness. Especially when Lawrence said nothing but tightened his jaw and did not let go of my arm.

Chapter 33

Lawrence saw me up to my room. He tried to take me in, but the maid glared at him, and he promised to be just outside if I needed anything.

"Thank you, Lawrence," I said. Lawrence left the door open a crack, so he might hear my cry if I needed him. I was thankful to feel the heavy blood-laden clothes taken off me. I cleaned myself, then laid in the bed and dozed off. Eventually, I woke to hear Lawrence outside my door ask Richard impatiently,

"I thought I heard the surgeon."

"Yes, he is here," Richard said.

"Where?"

"I have taken him to see Miss Williams first. Her need seemed greater as there is much more chance of infection," Richard said.

"Not so. Your sister has a ball lodged in her shoulder."

"I have examined it. It is in the muscle. Myra will be fine. Come, it grows late. Do try to help me convince others to go to bed."

"I told Myra I would stay here. I cannot leave her door," Lawrence said.

"Very well. I will make the effort alone," Richard said.

I felt very drowsy and closed my eyes. With no concept of time, I awoke when the surgeon came into my room. Lawrence followed close behind him.

"Lawrence, you cannot be in here," I stammered barely opening my eyes.

"Please, do not ask me to wait in the hall," Lawrence said. The maid averted her eyes, and the surgeon pretended not to notice when Lawrence crossed to the other side of the bed, pulled up a chair, and took my good hand in his.

"I shall keep her steady," Lawrence said.

"Yes, my Lord," the surgeon said, clearly intimidated.

The surgeon worked carefully, digging into my shoulder to get the lead ball out. I tried not to show how badly it hurt when the surgeon pulled the bullet out. Poor Lawrence did not seem equal to witnessing my pain.

However, when the surgeon cleaned the wound, I could but close my eyes, tighten my entire body and cry. I felt Lawrence's tears hot on my hand, where he prayed for me. I wished I could say something to comfort him, but I could not.

The surgeon then stitched the wound and I felt certain I would pass out. The surgeon gave the maid instructions, then stood to leave.

"What are you doing in here?" Richard asked, seeing Lawrence in my room.

"I was assisting, keeping her still so she would not move," Lawrence said lamely.

"Come, it is time to take your rest before you compromise Myra's integrity," Richard said.

"Have this lady fetch me if you need anything," Lawrence said leaning over me.

"I think we will be fine until morning," I said.

"She will have whatever she wants, any slight whim," Lawrence snapped at my maid.

"Yes Sir," she said ducking her head with big eyes.

When the men left, the surgeon checked the wound on my back, but Mr. Black's aim was sure. The cut didn't even need stiches.

Chapter 34

I slept long and heavy barely able to wake from the concoction the maid put in my tea. She tried to give me more in the morning, but I refused it. It was hard to dress without the use of one arm, and the maid did her best to try and help but couldn't make me look the way I wanted to. Upon reflection, I decided I'd been through an ordeal. Why should I try to hide that? My true friends would understand.

I went down to the breakfast room to find Mrs. Williams and her little boy being entertained by Rick. Clara joined in the fun and they made a very pretty picture after the horrors of the night before. Mrs. Adelaide Williams seemed to lose some of her gravity and even looked her twenty and one years, instead of seventy and one.

When Clara noticed me, she ran to me and sat me down. She offered to pour my tea and get my breakfast. I allowed her to as my arm was of little use to me.

"Here, Aunt please allow me to cool your porridge," Clara said.

"Come now, child, it is a maiden aunt's job to protect her nieces. I must have you stop with this coddling," I said.

"Yes," Lawrence said, coming into the room, "as it is my job now, and I must have the pleasure of it. Myra, may I spoon the food into your mouth?"

I looked at him and found he was teasing me again, so I opened my mouth to see what he would do. He laughed heartily and sat next to me reaching for my spoon. I brushed his hand away and he snatched up my fingers and kissed them.

"I am glad to see you up and about," he said seriously.

"Thank you," I answered, blushing and pulling my hand back.

After breakfast, Mr. Williams came back to see about his sister. She sent word that she was recovering nicely but would not come down right away. Mr. Williams then wanted to know what his heir was doing. Mrs. Williams looked lighter every time he used the word to reference her child.

Charley romped in the nursery with the other children. He lived so long isolated; the four-year-old child only wanted to play with the older girls, who doted on him. Mr. Williams was extremely distracted by the boy's absence and even proposed someone check on the lad to be sure he hadn't taken ill from the previous evening. When it was settled that the boy was just playing with the other children, he asked:

"Adelaide?"

"Yes, Sir," she answered.

"Will you be able to come back to the parish to bury Titus?" It will be a bit of a journey."

"I…must I?" she asked.

"I am trying to legitimize your marriage, and you being among the mourners will be the surest way to show even those closest to us. You may have been young and enthusiastic in your marriage, but you were not indecent."

"Do you think… will that…?" She glanced at Rick who smiled and said: "It is the truth. No matter what followed, you ran away and got married. Nothing more, nothing less. You need not be ashamed forever of the action of young love."

"I cannot help that, but I will go… it pains me to admit… I have nothing to wear," she said.

"You are almost my size," Clara said. "I have my mourning dress for Lord Devon, and few lovely gowns you can use until you have your own made."

"That is very kind, but—"

"Please, I am desperate to do something for you. I am sure I did you injury. It was unconsciously done, but it was done, and I would feel better if you would let me do this small thing for you," Clara near begged.

"I… thank you," Mrs. Adelaide Williams said, taken back at her kindness.

"If you give me your measurements, I will order many fine things and send them to the house," Mr. Williams said.

"You can wear my mother's ring. It will close over your band and look very pretty on you."

"Thank you, Sir."

"I hope you all will come, Lord Grey Hull. I know it is a strange sort of request, and it is at a distance, but I feel like he is released from a trap he could not get out of himself. It will be a quiet affair but having a Marquess in attendance clearly blessing his marriage would soften the neighbors," Mr. Williams said.

"I will go," Lawrence said. "I promised Mrs. Williams I would look after her when she agreed to come with me."

I looked at Richard. I wanted so badly to be with Lawrence. I could not think clearly.

"I cannot go, I must see to my family. My wife returns in a day, and will wish to find her family at home," Richard said, indicating Clara would not be of the group.

Mrs. Williams looked to me hopefully. She had come to trust me. I saved her and her son in many ways. I could see she needed me.

"Perhaps, I will accompany Mrs. Williams. She will need a respectable companion until your sister can be restored to health," I said.

"And I will accompany my Aunt," Rick said, looking to me. I could see how important it was for him not be separated from the young widow. I looked at Richard and Lawrence. Richard nodded reluctantly to the arrangement.

"We can take my boat up the coast. It is a smooth ride, Myra," Lawrence said.

"Ah, perhaps you can invite Phineas. He is intrigued by steam power," Richard said, concerned at his son's fervor for the young widow. A level-headed friend could not be undervalued at such a time.

"It seems as good a plan as any," I said, wanting to be on an adventure with Lawrence. We talked about travel plans until the door opened and the nursemaid came in with Charley and Richard's youngest girls.

"Ah, my boy, my boy!" Mr. Williams' cried. The boy went and greeted his grandfather, while the girls came to Clara and me. Charley warmed up quickly to the man who doted on him. When the boy kissed his face or gave him the natural affections of a four-year-old, Mr. Williams seemed surprised by it. I wondered if he had ever received such affection from his son. I stayed with them as long as I could tolerate the pain. Eventually, I had to ask the footman to send a request for the cook to make me some more of her pain-relieving tea.

Richard came up as I was falling asleep and asked me how I wanted my pin money as I needed it to travel. I told him Lawrence would see to me. I needed him to do over his study. I did not wish to come home to a sickly green place smeared in blood. I doubted his wife did either. He tried to refuse, but I fell asleep.

Chapter 35

The next morning, we started out early and made it to the docks in a few hours. Lawrence agreed to carry the coffin containing young Mr. Williams on his boat as the elder needed to ride the train to London to settle a few accounts, order the grandest of clothes for his daughter and grandson, and get his mother's ring out of his London safe. He confessed to buying tickets for a whole carriage on the train, so Miss Williams might lie down on the bench, and at the end of her ride, have the benefit of a London specialist.

We sailed for the rest of the day. Mrs. Adelaide Williams and I sat on the deck enjoying the mild September weather. Rick played with Charley. Phineas and Lawrence almost fell into the channel examining the steam-powered wheel. Neither could speak fast enough about the power and I couldn't help thinking if Lawrence had a son, Phineas would be it.

I spent a night in the most luxurious apartment aboard with Mrs. Williams and Charley, and we were docked by the next morning. Many of the servants were out to market when Lawrence's stately ship docked. They came to gawk at a badge of heredity with a steam wheel on his schooner, but none of them could match Phineas' enthusiasm for the contraption.

We were careful to treat the remains of Mr. Williams correctly. Not that we felt honor-bound to do so, but at this point, every precaution taken was for the sake of Mrs. Williams and Charley. I took Mrs. Williams' hand in my arm and escorted her as if she were the grieving widow. Rick and Phineas each held one of Charley's hands. Lawrence acted with showy dignity in the role of the Marquess of Dorset. He even made his man wear his livery and his footman affix the Hull coat of arms to everything.

We were the very picture of all that was proper. However, it was all pretense and nothing like Lord Devon's solemn occasion. Lawrence hired a wagon to take the coffin to the Williams's estate, and we were moving toward a hired carriage when a maid exclaimed: "Why Miss Adelaide, whatever are you doing here?" she asked.

"Hello Nellie, I must bury my husband," she said reaching up and letting the ring on her beautiful long finger linger on the holding bar.

"Mrs. Williams, can I hand you up?" Rick said politely. She gave him her other hand and he helped her up.

"Well, don't that beat all. Here we was thinking you was hidden out in shame and you has been making friends with royalty," said servant girl, said nodding her head in disbelief.

It did not occur to me upon the onset of our journey that the young widow must know the place and the servants.

Mrs. Williams blanched and dropped into the coach. Rick glared at the impertinent girl and climbed in.

The coachman knew the way to the Williams' home. It was on an island of two thousand acres overlooking the ocean. The house itself was a huge Tudor style estate that took no effort to look authentic but leaned for modern and stately. The sounds of the ocean and the gulls relaxed me, but Mrs. Williams seemed incapable of calming down after her interaction with the servant girl.

Lawrence sent his man to announce us to the butler and housekeeper as we climbed from the carriage. His man returned and whispered urgently to Lawrence. Mrs. Williams blanched white.

"I'm sure it is nothing," Rick said quietly to Mrs. Williams picking up Charley defensively.

"Please, come this way," a footman invited while another came out to instruct the man who took charge of the coffin.

"They did not receive Mr. Williams' express until a few moments ago," Lawrence said smiling. "We are to be shown to rooms, but I believe it would be kindest if we admire the view so they may be made ready."

He stretched, then put his hand on my arm, just where it had been for two days, but he watched the North Sea. After we lingered as long as possible, we started toward the stairs.

"May I show you to your room?" a formal footman in his dark wool tailcoat asked, giving me preference because the Marquess held my arm. The footman had a broad forehead and condescending eyes trained in disgust on the young widow bride. Mrs. Williams flushed and did not know where to look.

"Mrs. Williams," I said glaring at the impertinent man then turning to my subject, "I suppose you will allow them time to air the family rooms before you take yours. Perhaps we may share a room for now. I understand your staff has been caught unaware."

"That would be best for now. It is not a sign of weakness to show your servants tolerance in such a situation," Lawrence agreed. He did not even see the interaction, but hearing my tone, he joined my quest in letting the man know his place. He did indeed flinch then bowed his head in respect and submission.

"Charley will need a bath and made presentable as soon as possible," Mrs. Williams said nodding to her child in Rick's arms, pretending she knew her place. The man nodded, then she took my sore arm, and I forgot everything else except the beads of sweat rolling down my back.

"Thank you," she whispered to me.

"What else are maiden aunts good for except meddling," I teased, but Lawrence flinched.

Mrs. Adelaide William's appeared to be clairvoyant. It was
not long after we were all cleaned up her parents came. It was
a very uncomfortable interview. Lawrence was certain to curb
her father's ire and her mother was at peace to have her
daughter in her arms.

     A cool light wind hinted at autumn when the
unfortunate Mr. Titus Williams was laid to rest. There was
not much of a funeral, but a simple interment. The Vicar was
a friend of the father, which was the only reason he performed
the interment, considering how the son died. Though it was
not proper, Miss Williams and I attended, leaving the widow
home with her parents.
     Sadie Williams needed to see her nephew put to rest.
Not in the way Lady Garrett needed to say goodbye to her
father. She needed to see Titus Williams' end, so she would
no longer have to carry him on her back. Only Lawrence,
Rick, Phineas, and Mr. Williams attended the body. The
latter did not notice anything beyond the coffin that held his
son.
     Moving from the carriage to the sturdy vault, I walked
behind the men and fought to be warm while the calm,
mesmerizing breeze from the North Sea insisted winter was
on the way. Peace reigned in the cool, cloud-covered sky,
like the sun took a well-deserved rest even though it was mid-
morning. It turned out to be a quiet affair, with none of the
pomp and procession of Lord Devon's funeral.
     Both were wealthy gentlemen, but those who were left
to arrange the funeral proceedings needed different send-offs.
I watched Miss Williams particularly. I could see in her
exactly what I felt after my father died. She seemed calm, but
guilty at the same time. A few times she squinted her face as
if trying to cry but couldn't manage the tears. I remembered

feeling so overwhelmed with relief after my father died I could manage little sorrow.

After the services, she and I rode back in the carriage alone together. I told her all about Baron Adlay, how he had come to claim me after my father died, and he meant to have me at a bargain.

"How did you endure such a thing?" she asked.

"Richard had already given me a choice. He'd already sent off a letter to Lawrence. I knew I would not have to endure the grimy old man who drank more than anyone and plagued me in front of the body of my father laid out on the dining room table," I said.

"Knowledge is a gift," she said, unsure why I told her this.

"Yes, but my point is that I did not mourn my father as I should. I felt guilty for it but looking back I must acknowledge he sent Baron Adlay after me. It was my father's fault Richard had to lock me in my room before the funeral even started. How could I mourn, knowing my escape was at hand? I was sent off to Lawrence's home. Until this year, Lord Hull had not known anything about Baron Adlay, so the very fact he was a Marquess must have kept the Baron from coming after me as if I were his property."

"That was kind of your brother," she said.

"Yes, Richard must have endured scorn, and torment for allowing me into servitude. And I feel sorry for that, but I still cannot muster much sorrow for my father dying so I never had to be that man's wife. My brother saved me all those years ago. Perhaps you should feel you have been saved along with the many other victims your nephew might have had."

"I was not a victim, I enabled his... his debauchery," she said, taking a deep sigh.

"How so?" I asked.

"I...I should have...."

"What? He tried to kill you when he found out you helped me. You may not have been hurt like the other women, but he hurt you. I don't believe his sin is yours. I made some heavy mistakes in my past, but they were mistakes only, and I believe I am on the way to forgiving myself for them. Can you do the same?"

"I...I do feel very guilty for the relief I have been given," she admitted.

"That is what he left you with. The mourning was done during the young man's life, and now it is time for you to recover. Do not fight with it," I said as the well-sprung carriage glided up to the estate and then came to a stop.

She nodded and finally her tears came.

The door opened rather abruptly. Mr. Williams had pushed his footman out of the way to get the carriage door. He helped his sister down and handed her over to Rick and Phineas. Then he reached in for me. Lawrence stood right behind him, but after I was safely to the ground, he did not relinquish my arm to the marquess but escorted me in himself.

"Thank you for your support. Not only of Adelaide and Sadie, but also myself," he said.

"It gives me purpose," I said dropping my head to him.

"I... now you must let me care for you. You do not look well," he said.

"I am feeling a little warm," I said. He asked about my symptoms and seemed so concerned about my wound, expressing a wish to send for his physician in London. He took me straight into the enormous ballroom set up with all kinds of refreshments for those who would trickle in to offer their condolences.

After we ate, I retired again, concerned with the throb in my shoulder. I had stopped sweating, but the heat inside my head only grew, I feared it meant I may be getting an infection. Thankfully, Mr. Spencer learned of my and

Sadie's wounds. He sent over his cook who practiced in medicine. I thought her crazy, but she reopened my wound with a knife and drained it of pus and blood. She cleaned it with something that I swore was burning me despite it being a cool liquid. After it soothed, the liquid that smelled like burnt sugar finally took the sting from my shoulder. Then she steeped a mixture of herbs and something that smelled like poppies in boiling hot water. I drank it and slept for almost twenty-four hours.

Chapter 36

When I woke, I was shown to the grand drawing room. I found the most pleasant scene. The family all sat strewn about on the golden flowers sewn into settees and armchairs. The room was lit with a warm fire to offset the splattering of rain, and the wind crashing waves into rocks outside the window.

Mr. Williams and his old friend, Mr. Spencer, spoke of politics with Lawrence. Mrs. Spencer shared the local gossip with her daughter. Sadie looked pink instead of chalky. Rick and Phineas taught Charley how to play chess. It wasn't going well.

Lawrence noticed me first. His mouth moved, but he didn't say anything. He looked relieved to see me. He stood at my entrance. He came quickly to my side and moved me toward a seat by the fire.

"Ah, my Lady, I am so glad you could join us," Mr. Williams said, standing and bowing, pulling a seat close to me.

I laughed.

"That is a very gallant sort of greeting," I said.

"But necessary. This morning's paper announced you, my lady, have been named a Baroness for life," he said.

"What?"

He handed me the paper.

"Oh, Eva!" I said closing my eyes.

"Myra," Lawrence said, concerned I might swoon.

"I am fine, thank you," I said sitting back in the chair. I read the short snippet in the society column that announced because of great service to the country, I was to be titled for life. After reading it again I closed my eyes and said:

"Oh, Eva."

"Are you not pleased?" Mrs. Adelaide Williams asked.

"I do not wish to appear ungrateful," I said looking to Lawrence who had grown quiet. "A title will change nothing in me, and everything in others."

"You are a superior lady, and I, for one, am pleased you will be recognized for it," Mr. Williams said kindly.

"Thank you," I said, blushing for him.

"Of course, she is superior, but she does not need the Queen nor anyone to affirm it for her," Lawrence said, growing moody.

"I remember my grandfather," Rick said quietly. "Though I was only eleven when he died, and they spent much of their time in London, I do not think Aunt can have too many honors bestowed upon her in this life to compensate for what she lived through with him."

I looked up at Rick and smiled at him. He had been noticeably quiet in the study when I made my confessions, but I could see he meant to show me he had not judged me harshly. Rick, as heir, was one of the only people whom my father treated decently. Yet, Rick grew into a man who did not appreciate my father diminishing those whom he felt were inferior, simply to make the select few feel superior.

"Perhaps Eva was more aware of... I am glad the world will respect you as you deserve," Lawrence said.

"I cannot see that I deserve such an honor over anyone else," I said. "But thank you all for your kindness to me."

"I disagree, but will not argue with you," Mr. Williams said, and he looked at me with affection. I bowed my head hoping he would stop.

"Myra, you must be hungry," Lawrence said.

"Oh yes, I ... I can wait until--"

"Nonsense, allow me to show you to the breakfast room. Come," Mr. Williams said standing, nodding to his footman while he held out his arm to me.

"Thank you," I said standing and taking his arm.

"You need not leave. Perhaps we could all be served some of those pastries your cook made for breakfast," Lawrence said.

"I would be happy to have them brought around," Mr. Williams said. Sitting me back down he nodded to another footman who left the room to catch the first.

"Cook often travels with me. She is French and has kept me in the finest circles. Everyone wants to sample her cooking."

The butler returned with tea and a crescent-shaped pastry I could not name. It was filled with nuts and a fruit paste. I was famished and ate two, though the pastry flaked and went everywhere. Everyone else pretended to eat but none of them was hungry, and I wished I had removed to the breakfast room after all.

When the refreshment was cleared, I turned the paper to the death notice of Mr. Titus Williams. It was a short tribute and was careful only to mention his wife and child, his accomplishments in school, and the prestige of the family he came from.

"I am going back to London tomorrow," Mr. Williams said when I put the paper down. "I will be back on Friday. There are a few matters I cannot put off. He looked at me. "I hope you will all consent to stay. At least until I can return over the week's end."

"I do not think I can be away so long," Lawrence said.

"Oh, you need not wait for us. I can escort my aunt back on the train," Rick said, feigning innocence, "I imagine there are many duties you must see to."

"I would not feel right leaving you here," Lawrence said.

"I can assure their passage home," Mr. Williams said.

"No, I would rather stay until Myra chooses to leave. After all she has done for my family, I could not, as a gentleman, leave her injured, and in the care of a person we know so little of," Lawrence said. Both Rick and Mr. Spencer smirked but said nothing.

We stayed another week mostly because Rick could not fathom parting from Mrs. Williams and her child. We dined with Mrs. Adelaide Williams' parents and found the Spencer house quiet and sad. Mrs. Williams' oldest three brothers joined the army, and the want of little niceties indicated the family was not as financially settled as their affluent neighbors.

I pictured sixteen-year-old Adelaide Spencer, seeing her brothers leave home to make their fortunes. What other avenue was there for a woman to make a living besides marriage? She must have thought herself blessed she had captured the attention of the only man in the neighborhood who could secure her situation. No doubt Titus Williams had seen it all and taken advantage of the girl.

When we finally loaded the boat and set sail with the evening tide, September was close to adjourning. Rick and Phineas would head back to school soon. I felt melancholy at the end of our adventure, knowing shortly it would all be over.

I slept in my lovely room. When I woke the next morning, I wandered about, enjoying the rhythmic jostle of the ship. I stood on the deck feeling the wind sting my eyes as I watched the English Channel trail by. There was no other way to travel. Lawrence quietly came and stood next to me as the crew worked around us.

"We are almost to Weymouth," he said. "We haven't even needed the steam. This autumn wind has been so steady."

"I almost feel like we should just keep going. There is so much world out there to see," I said.

"Where do you wish to go?" Lawrence asked.

"India, Paris," I said. "I have been nowhere."

"Yet, you have traveled more than most ever will even around England," he said, "but I am of your same mind. Let us away to somewhere warm, as the weather grows cold."

"Where will you go, Sir?" I asked.

"With you, wherever you go," he said putting his hand on my arm to steady me, as we were tossed a bit by the ship shifting.

"What are we going to do, Lawrence?" I asked turning to him.

"What do you mean?" he asked.

"Our final mission is completed. Our last little lark has played out. Where will you go after this?" I asked.

"I will stay with you, Myra," he said.

"At my brother's house?" I asked.

"If needs be," he answered.

"I am not sure that is prudent," I said. The boat jerked, and he put an arm around my waist. I leaned my head into his neck and smelled the warm sweetness of his skin. He wrapped his arms around me, making me sure they were the only home I'd ever know. I could fight no more. Just as I inched my lips toward his sweet skin, I heard a loud noise burst from the other side of the deck. Someone yelled my name.

I turned, startled that there was yet another tremor in the safety of my loved ones. Lawrence and I turned to the yelling when Rick came running toward us.

"Aunt, you must come to see this," Rick shouted, running around the deck pointing.

"What is it dear?" I asked terrified but saw before he could even point it out. A pod of dolphins raced the front bow of the ship. Lawrence wrapped his arm back around my waist instead of taking my arm to steady me as we all moved forward to the rail to see.

We chased the dolphins into the bay. Rick and Phineas shouted and flew about with the beautiful creatures.

When we landed everything moved exactly as it should for a marquess. I stepped onto dry ground and still swayed.

"That is a heady sensation," I started to laugh with Phineas while Rick imitated me walking with an extreme sway.

"Rick lost his meal when we landed in France," Phineas announced catching up to his friend who had outstripped us in his enthusiastic walk. Lawrence stayed with me. He took my arm and actually slowed our pace until we were in our own little space.

"Myra, let's go to India," Lawrence said.

"Okay," I shouted. "Did you hear that boys? Back on the boat, we're going to India."

Rick turned and goaded: "I promised Father you would not run away with Lord Grey Hull. Sorry Aunt."

"Isn't that just like Richard, putting such demands on me," I said, leaning against Lawrence's arm laughing, but it caught in my throat. I looked up at him to share my laugh, but he was serious. He looked down at my face examining me.

"Would you go with me, Myra?" he asked, his thick lips tempting me in so many ways.

"To the ends of the earth if there was but a way for you to keep your honor and make it so," I admitted. "But there is no such place for the two of us, not for us." Tears started in my eyes and he took my hands to his lips bowing over them.

I pulled away forcing my tears back and hurried quickly to the carriage waiting for us. I scooted to the far wall. Lawrence pushed Rick out of the way and sat next to me. Rick laughed, and Phineas smiled, but neither said anything else.

Phineas and Rick kept up a steady banter, but it no longer amused me. I was upset. Why did Lawrence make me admit such things out loud? It would only serve to hurt us both when we were divided.

With him forcing such sentiments out of me, I could only find two outcomes for Lawrence and me. Either he would give in and marry me, settling for me against his moral code, learning to resent me for years to come. I had seen that resentment once after he kissed me in his own home. He had looked at me in a way that felt...accusatory. I was in love with him, a falcon flying through the air, and with one jarring look, he shot me from the sky to fall.

There was no hope strong enough to wipe away the fear of him being ashamed of me.

I had almost let him kiss me again. I had almost kissed him. If he resented me, married or not he would use me ill like in the past. I loved only him. Would he marry me, only to shun me, and leave me to my misery when he finally mastered himself? I had lived in his house for six months after he kissed me, and he had gone out of his way to avoid me.

I was done being worked on by the Marquess of Dorset. I would no longer go on the defense. It was time for me to take control of my own life. If he really needed someone to follow him around in adoration, he always had Hetty.

When we reached my brother's home, dusk had settled. The sidelight of the setting sun had a sad sense of finality to it. This day would mark my commitment never to marry. I could not marry any man in good conscience. So, on the morrow, I would go to church and pledge my life to God and the betterment of those I could help and patience for those I couldn't.

Richard met us at the door with Mary, her arm in his. His face was calm and pleasant. He looked content with Mary at home. He took one long look at my face as I climbed from the carriage and away from Lawrence. He sighed in disappointment, but said:

"Myra, you must be exhausted. Mary, can we have her dinner sent to her room?" he asked.

"Of course," she said.

"That would be nice, thank you," I said, then turned to my traveling companions, "It has been a pleasure, my friends."

"The pleasure was all mine," Lawrence said with a bow as if I only spoke to him, which, if I must admit it, I did.

I walked into the house and noticed immediately the walls were white and gleaming.

"Look at this," I said, sticking my head into the drawing-room where the paper had been stripped, and the gold leafing pulled away. The whole place was white, and the furniture covered.

"I did not want to choose paper without Mary, so I had all the rooms made ready in preparation," Richard confessed.

"That was wise," I said, remembering the bloody mess I'd left behind. I walked to Richard's study and peeked my head in. It looked much the same as the rest of the house. I closed my eyes and took a deep breath in. It no longer smelt like blood. It smelled clean.

"It will be finished in a few weeks," Mary said coming to my side.

"No, I like it," I said laughing, but almost crying. The infection was gone.

I went to my room and a letter sat upon my dressing table. My sister Edith wrote asking how I'd been awarded a Baroness as Richard was not forthcoming with details. She insisted she would be in London for the little season and I was to come to her, so I might prepare to be presented as a Baroness. She was sure I could be spared since Mary came home. She would appreciate the companionship, and, as I was an heiress, we would need to revisit all my gowns. The distraction this letter promised was exactly what I needed. If

Lawrence did not mean to leave me, perhaps, I could leave him.

I ate whatever was on the tray sent to me, though I cannot be sure what it was.

I lay awake much of the night wrestling myself. My lips were so near Lawrence's neck. What if I could kiss the condemnation out of him until only his love for me was left. I felt so angry with myself I shifted my mind, determined to send him away. What alternative would I live with? What did it mean to love someone?

By morning, my agitation grew into anger again. Unfortunately, the plan I came up with was tinged in anger. And as my mentor, Henry Grey said, "Finding a rational path while wading through the bog of one's anger is impossible. Best to take a shovel and trench it out before making any decisions."

Chapter 37

I dressed splendidly for services. I wore my finest Turkish blue silk that curved with my figure. I fixed my delicious peach hair to flatter my face. I pinched my cheeks to have a blush. I took breakfast in my room as was the custom on Sunday mornings in my brother's home. I honed into the memories of my sixteen-year-old lovesick self, and even practiced giggling in the mirror a few times before I was called to load the carriage. The hitch came when I left my room. I felt ridiculous. Instead of gliding through the house and making a grand entrance, I moved quietly.

"Aunt, you look lovely," Clara said as I descended the steps. Lawrence, who stood in the entryway, turned to look at me.

"Thank you dearest," I said, avoiding Lawrence's eye. His mouth had dropped, and he hadn't managed to bring it up again. Well, good. Perhaps it was his turn to be a little miserable.

"You may snatch James Evans after all," Richard said teasing me or Lawrence, I couldn't be sure who.

"Perhaps I shall," I said taking the arm he offered.

"I would wager, Mr. Williams of the banking family is smitten with her," Rick said, "I think Mr. Evans has some competition."

"Yes, but Mr. Williams is far away and since he took his sister with him, Mr. James Evans will not be distracted by Miss Williams. Aunt's only competition here is Miss Clarke and Miss Dodgson," Clara said. I could see the clever little minx figured out the game and joined in on the scheme against myself and Lawrence.

"Shall we start taking wagers?" I asked dryly.

"The Spencer family also has a lover for her. Mrs. Williams' brother is a favorite of hers, and I believe her judgement impeccable," Rick said, glancing at his father.

"It is no secret why you would wish Aunt to marry into that family," Clara said, smirking at her brother.

"If that were all, Mr. Williams would do, and come to think of it, he is very astute. He may mentally keep her stimulated," Rick said.

"I would not give him so much mental acuity," Lawrence said, still looking at me, clearly put out with himself when he allowed his eyes to take in my figure.

Richard and Rick both grinned behind Lawrence whose face turned grim. Mary said little but watched. She could see what I was doing. She put a quiet hand on Richard's arm to get him to stop teasing me. Richard glanced at me with his misplaced triumph and I smiled sadly at my brother. His triumph faltered. He would see very soon I meant to send Lawrence home. I had to move on from this place I was stuck in.

"Come then," he said nodding to the footman at the door. He lost the mirth he'd been wrapped in only moments before.

At church, I paused at the cloakroom until the rest of the family entered the chapel. I peeked in and saw the commotion, the bowing and pomp that revolved around Lawrence. He slipped into the pew first to escape it all. Richard seemed to pause and turned to look for me. I could see his concern growing.

Only when Clara pulled her sisters into the pew after Lawrence did I walk toward them. Rick waited for me, but James Evans and his mother moved toward me as soon as they saw me. Lawrence turned pale and his jaw clenched when he saw the extremely handsome man coming to greet me. I tried not to notice the smirk on Richard's face when his old friend turned to Clara to ask who the young man was.

"Mr. Evans, Mrs. Evans, how do you do?" I asked.

"We heard you were injured. Are you quite all right?" James asked taking my hand. I took a deep breath, pretending I didn't know everyone watched us.

"I am doing excellent, and even considered wearing a gown to show off my wound, but decided against it," I said with a flirty laugh.

"Yes, we wouldn't want all the ladies swooning," James said mimicking my fake laugh, "I suppose now you will be a titled lady, you are above swooning."

"It is a pastime I am obliged to give up," I said, feeling the heat rising to my face.

"How is Miss Williams fairing?" Mrs. Evans asked.

"Her injury is healing, and she endured her nephew's death with fortitude," I said quietly.

"We are going to enjoy the last of the blackberries in three days. Would you like to join us?" James asked, rapidly changing the subject.

"I must consult with my brother, but..." I felt someone take my arm. I looked back surprised to find Lawrence at my side. He glared at James.

"Oh, excuse me, Mr. James Evans, this is the Honorable Marquess of Dorset, my Lord Lawrence Grey Hull," I said.

"That is quite the title," James said glaring back at Lawrence.

"Yes, it is, I'm sorry I didn't catch yours," Lawrence said, glowering down at James.

"Mr. James Evan," James said slowly as if Lawrence might be hard of hearing.

"Myra, I think the preacher is trying to start," Lawrence said, growing so bold as to put a hand at my waist to turn me. Then he took my arm pulling me toward our pew. I glanced back slightly to bow to James and his mother. They looked startled.

I happened to look up behind them, glancing at Mr. Clarke, who stood at the pulpit. He looked furious. No wonder. His niece sat at her pew alone and looked ready to cry. Perhaps this was a cruel sort of game to play after all. Lawrence escorted me to the end of the pew where he sat too close to me. Was he fighting James Evans for me? I glanced at Lawrence, but he seemed content to sing the hymn, so I opened my book.

I didn't sing. Instead, I watched Miss Clarke, and felt guilty. I hadn't even thought of her role in my game. I didn't mind toying with James a little, the man was growing insufferable; but Miss Clarke was kind enough and fragile.

Watching Miss Clarke, I realized that pretending to be enamored with one man to put off another really wasn't the best way to handle the situation. The more I watched Miss Clarke, my guilt softened, and I started to suspect her pain from a different source. Her eyes were in the direction of Mr. Davies and not James.

The woman spent more of our escapades with Mr. Davies then James, who had often been engaged with myself or Miss Williams. The two seemed comfortable with each other, and Miss Clarke had never relaxed around James. No matter how often she looked at Mr. Davies she could not catch his eye. Did they quarrel? Was he at wits end being set aside for his handsome friend?

I looked over at James and noticed he caught Miss Clarke's eye and winked. He meant to keep her in his pocket, while he courted me. But then, wasn't I using James to make Lawrence think me settled so he'd leave? Well, it was a stupid and unfair plan, not to mention it didn't work. Despite Lawrence once assuring me that when I was settled with a respectable man he would leave, he got feisty and combative.

"Are you cold, Myra?" Lawrence whispered.

I looked up at him. He did not look back. He looked out at the preacher, but his whole frame leaned against me.

He knew me. He knew my dress was not cool weather appropriate, and that I would be chilly.

"I am fine," I said pulling my arms in, wishing again for a shawl. Richard had known, as I should have known, Lawrence would always fight. Perhaps I did know. Perhaps deep down I wanted to manipulate Lawrence into trying for me. When I dressed so prettily, I thought only of him. When I flirted with James, I made sure he saw. I could not be shocked when he responded.

I took a deep breath. Was I as bad as James, playing games? Was my love for Lawrence so ungenerous that I would sink to hurting him simply to force him to betray his feelings for me? If he did admit his love for me, would it change anything? Was there enough balm in his love that could heal me even when his shame came upon me?

I would not play this game. I would honestly tell Lawrence I did not mean to marry, and he needed to let me go. I could not tolerate looking at him day after day with no hope. If I simply asked him to leave, would he? Could he return home safe in my steady outlook as a spinster? It would help that I was leaving. I'd already written to my sister. I would go to her as soon as could be. Then I would heal. First, as any good spinster should, I would interfere with Miss Clarke, because Mr. Davies was an honorable man who deserved a chance.

"We must have a little scheme for Miss Clarke," I whispered to Lawrence.

"What?"

"Look at her, she loves Mr. Davies, but thinks she must continue with Mr. Evans for some reason," I said.

"She is ... you are going sink her as a rival, and you want me to help," Lawrence asked quickly glancing at me this time.

"She is not my rival as I am not interested in James. I just think she ought to marry whom she fancies," I said.

"You are not…"

"Lawrence, I charge you to speak to James Evans for twenty minutes after the service ends. You may see for yourself," I whispered. Lawrence stared at me and stammered. I lifted my smiling eyes to him, but Mr. Clarke looked in my direction and glared. I stopped speaking to hear Mr. Clarke saying loudly:

"And I quote, 'Whoever lives in love lives in God, and God in them, Ephesians 4:2.' This is proof that God expects us to love, but it must be done in his way." Mr. Clarke stopped to glare at Millie Fielding and even Clara. I glared back at the preacher. Did he really blame any of this on the the first young girl, who dabbed at her eyes or Clara who turned bright red? That wasn't fair.

I was about to mention insult to injury to Lawrence but realized he was listening too attentively to the preacher. Mr. Clarke went on to preach about marriage and the proper way to court a lady. This time he sent his barbed looks to James. I was soon caught up in the sermon. I felt very wrong playing tricks on Lawrence when Mr. Clarke quoted kindly to his niece,

"Be completely humble and gentle; be patient bearing with one another in love. 1 Peter 4:8."

She ducked her head to look at Mr. Davies. Lawrence glanced at me. I smiled. He looked frightened. I put my hand on his arm and smiled again. This time he smiled back. I would be kind. He would never have anything to fear at my hand again.

After services ended, I sought out Miss Clarke. Lawrence followed me. James soon joined our group. Mr. Davies gave a glance, but seeing James engage Miss Clarke in conversation, moved toward the door, looking rejected.

"Oh dear, I did want to ask Mr. Davies where he picked you those hazelnuts," I said to Miss Clarke.

"I am not certain. He said he collected them himself," she said, straining her neck to find him.

"Lord Hull has a grove out near his house. We would collect them about this time of year. Now that I am settled here, I would love to know where they are to be found," I said.

"I will undertake to find them for you, Myra," James said.

"We could always go to Grey manor for a day and collect them," Lawrence said quietly as we all followed Mr. Davies out of the church.

"It would be more prudent to find them here," James said. "Miss Clarke, you would not mind asking Mr. Davies where he procured them?"

She looked from me to James and nodded seeing herself excused, as she had always been. She did not look sorry but instead hurried up the aisle to catch up with Mr. Davies.

"Myra, you will join us blackberry picking, won't you?" James asked.

"My sister wishes for me to join her in London. I will be arranging for that trip, but I may be able to. Can I write to you tomorrow after I've spoken to my brother?"

"Of course," he said, "but I would not take too long. I know Miss Clarke is most anxious to know who is of the party. She is providing the picnic lunch. She is quite good at arranging such matters."

"I have no doubt," I said bowing. He was not satisfied with my disinterested objectivity.

"I might safely say she may be one of the finest arrangers in the county," James said eyeing me seriously as if I must worry about this.

"Arranging outings, or just in general," I asked flippantly. As James thought about this I glanced at Lawrence. He was not as amused as myself.

"I...I would say primarily outings, but ... I cannot see why that would not extend to arranging other matters," he said, thinking hard.

"I have a housekeeper who arranges matters masterfully," Lawrence said glancing at me, finally realizing I was teasing James. "Do you think Miss Clarke could rival her?"

"I have no doubt," James said.

"I think it would have to be tested," I said. "Perhaps we could bring Hetty here and have some outing, at which point we could put it to a test."

"I think it might be worth a try," James said, grinning.

"What might be worth a try?" Mr. Clarke asked, coming up behind us and glaring.

"We are to test your niece's skills at arranging against Lord Grey Hull's housekeeper," James said. Lawrence and I went silent. We, of course, had been kidding. Poor James did not see it.

"Do you think it appropriate to pit a gentleman's daughter against a paid servant in such a degrading way?" Mr. Clarke asked, astonished with James.

"I cannot see why not," James said as if it were a challenge that I should rise to instead of an insult she was lowering herself to. James said to me, "She will do whatever I ask of her."

"To her detriment if it is degrading," I said trying to hint to James that he might be offending the rector.

"Nonsense. Women like a little competition," James said.

"I think you may be mistaking women for show dogs," Lawrence insisted.

"Yes, I agree. I came to tell you your mother needs help with your children, Mr. Evans," Mr. Clarke said angrily, and he stomped off to find Miss Clarke.

"Miss Bolton, you have such a rapport with Sally and Jim, perhaps you could help--"

"Her brother is ready to leave," Lawrence said, pulling on my arm.

James looked confused as we were in the front of the crowd exiting but turned to find his mother. I quickly followed Mr. Clarke, pulling his arm to stop him as we exited the chapel. Miss Clarke, engaged in conversation with Mr. Davies, did not notice us.

"Mr. Clarke, I have never seen that look upon your niece's face. She is positively glowing," I said.

"Yes, she does look much happier," he said squinting as he moved toward her.

"I certainly don't remember such fervor when she talks to Mr. Evans," I hinted, tugging his arm again.

"Nor do I," he said stopping short, realizing he had misinterpreted her depressed spirits earlier. He turned and looked at me, really studying me.

"Miss Bolton you are a strange creature as far as women go," he said.

"I am only an observer of people. If it falls within my privilege to be God's hands and nudge them, who am I to refuse? After all what else are spinsters good for?"

He laughed.

"I will ask Mr. Davies to be sure she gets home safely as I must finish up here," Mr. Clarke said, then glancing from me to Lawrence with a little grin like he knew how to play my game, he gave us each his hand in turn then said, "I suppose you will marry Mr. Evans, now Miss Bolton?"

"Oh goodness no. I do not like to be equated to a show dog any better than I do a horse," I said grinning and looking emphatically at Lawrence. Mr. Clarke laughed again at my facial expressions, though he didn't get the joke. He turned to shake hands with his next parishioner. Lawrence scowled and took my arm.

289

When we were clear of the crowd Lawrence growled, "I'd rather be compared to thoroughbred racehorse than a show dog myself."

I laughed heartily until he could not help joining in.

Chapter 38

As we rode up the drive to the house, we found a hired carriage, being jostled by two horses. A servant in livery was trying not to be trampled by the horses.

"Is that Duke Garrett's man?" Richard asked.

"Eva," I cried alighting the carriage. We all rushed in except Rick, who struggled with the stillness of the sabbath and looked delighted at the idea of wrestling a pair of post horses with miles of run in them still. Sitting in the stark white drawing-room were the Duke and Duchess of Surry. Thankfully, the housekeeper uncovered the furniture. The whiteness of the room caught the chandelier, and I thought it lovely.

"Eva, darling, what are you doing here?" I cried.

"We are in a bit of a quandary. Our ship went off course in a strong wind and delayed us a day crossing the Channel. We found ourselves traveling on the Sabbath by mistake. Everything is closed. If we had not offered an obscene amount, I do not think we would have been able to hire a carriage. I do hope you will excuse the imposition we make on you," Eva said to Richard.

"Not at all! I invited you. You are always welcome," he said, and Mary echoed his welcome with such warmth, Eva and Jonah relaxed and took the refreshment offered.

"How was your trip?" I asked. She could not speak fast enough of all the wonders they had seen in France. She brought me back a lace shawl that was so fine, it could fit through her wedding band. After she finished talking, she asked,

"And what adventures have you had?"

"I was shot," I said.

"What?"

"I was shot," I said again.

"Surely you…" she looked to her father who just nodded. He looked miserable. He was reunited with his dear girl: his slumps would not last long. We told her the story of Clara's beau turning out to be a mad man. She was the perfect audience gasping at just the right moments and trying to find sorrow in the lost life of a man who caused so many problems. After our exciting communications, we took a leisurely Sunday walk. Then Richard led us in the scriptures. When he closed the family bible Eva turned to her father.

"Well, I suppose you will not be sorry to see us back to Grey Manor tomorrow morning," she said and looked out the window of the drawing room but saw only her own reflection.

"I…I have just been thinking about that," he said, glancing at me. Only then did I realized Eva coming meant he had no choice but to leave my brother's home with her. In the depths of my very being, I began to mourn, but I knew it was for the best. Being so near him with no promise of a future could never heal what broke over and over in my heart.

"Jonah, the lake is stocked, and the fishing is extremely good here," Lawrence said.

"Yes, well, we might stay a few days if our host would not mind being imposed upon," Eva said, noticing her father's despondency. She looked to her husband to see what he thought of this. As any cow-eyed lover, Jonah would not fight Eva on anything in this young fresh love they shared.

"You may stay as long as you wish, my lady," Richard said, and I thought Rick might burst out laughing. So much for decorum, "though, my son is heading back to school in three days and I will be obligated to take him to the train."

"It would be our pleasure to take him on the way to Grey Manor. In fact, Lawrence, perhaps we should all come for a holiday," Jonah said glancing at Eva and then at

Lawrence in a way that told everyone in the room he was actively plotting against the Marquess of Dorset.

"Yes, yes that would be best," Lawrence said, glancing at me in a relieved way.

"I meant to tell you; Edith invited me to come stay in London. Perhaps in three days, I will ride to London with Rick," I said. This statement was greeted with silence. Richard deeply exhaled, frustrated with me.

"Well, we would be delighted to transport you," Eva said. She looked determined.

"That would be ideal. Thank you, Your Grace," Rick said.

"Please call me Eva," she said.

No one said anything for a time.

"It sounds as though we will have three days," Eva said, looking to me, disappointed.

"We shall have a lovely autumn day tomorrow. I have heard the blackberries are on," I said. Lawrence threw his eyes upward in annoyance.

After supper Lawrence, asked my brother if he had anything stronger than wine to partake of. Eva scowled at this and instead of acknowledging her father's thirst, she turned to me, though I sat at a very inconvenient distance and asked: "Myra, you look so lovely today. How is your old friend, Mr. James Evans, I believe his name is?"

"Yes, he is very handsome," Clara gushed.

"But he is not her only admirer anymore," Rick put in, "I will wager the invitation Aunt received from Aunt Edith Leigh will turn into something more to her advantage."

"Does your sister have a beau for you?" Eva asked me.

"No, I already confided to you she wishes to share in the pomp of my being awarded a Baroness," I said, glaring at Rick.

"I am not sure I follow you," Eva said to Rick.

"Well, Mr. Williams asked her to write to him when she was to be presented as a baroness. He said he would show her every lovely site imaginable in London when she was in town next. And now she has an excuse to go."

"Rick, I did not know you overheard," I said, blushing.

"He did not make the effort to be secretive about it," Rick said. Turning to Eva, he finished, "he may very well write and offer to her. He is a busy man."

I could not deny this. Mr. Williams had mentioned he would send a messenger to be sure I made it home all right. Lawrence stood and walked over to my brother's selection of liquor, meaning to help himself. I knew there was only one comfort I could offer.

"Well, I am not … I am not so interested in marriage as I once was," I said glancing at Lawrence, "I have found purpose in the role of spinster Aunt. I do not mind this life I have settled into. I would even like to come to stay with you at times, Eva. I could not do that married to Mr. Williams. I would also like to be a part of who Clara, Rick, and the other girls become. Perhaps I will even have Sally Evans over for tea since she learned not be so insolent. For me, this is enough."

"That is not enough," Lawrence said slamming a jar of amber liquid onto the cart. He had both hands in front of him, his head was bowed. He rarely lost his temper, but as he turned slowly to me, he looked angry.

"It… it will do for me," I said standing and trying to hide the tears. Hadn't I tried to do the right thing? Wasn't I trying to let him go? Lawrence crossed the room in three fast steps and swooped down on me in one motion. He took my good arm and pulled me.

"Richard, I need to speak to Myra. Come," he said, we walked quickly from the room. I looked at Richard feeling panicked. He gave me a delighted grin. I rolled my eyes at him.

Lawrence led me into the breakfast room. It was dark. The only light came from the full moon shining through the three checkered panel windows making everything in their path silver. The rest of the room faded into blue and then was blotted out in inky black. Lawrence stopped in the luminosity of the moon and turned me to look at him, putting a hand on my good shoulder so I did not squirm as he knew I wanted to.

"I cannot leave you," he said.

"You won't. Not really. I will be in Eva's nursery," I said fighting the tears, "Please do not forget to send for me when you come to visit."

"Myra, that isn't fair to you."

"Tell me what to do then! Tell me what to do," I said pushing him back into the darkness, "I pretended I would marry, you did not like that. I did it so you could move on, but you did not. Now I honestly admit I never mean to marry and that won't do. Tell me what you mean for me to do. I will gladly do it."

"I am not your master, Myra," he said stepping back into the beam of light with me.

"You have mastered me, body and soul," I said hysterically going to push him again, but he grabbed my hands and pulled them to his chest. I rested my head on it and finished, "I do not know what to do next. Would you have me pretend I have some part of my heart to give? Should I marry a man who is willing to share his life with me, when I cannot give him my adoration?"

"No...I do not," he stammered releasing my hands he wrapped his arms around me. I pulled away and shook my head astounded he dare hold me. His eyes alternately watched my mouth move. He said nothing intelligible, but a fiery passion came from his eyes that I could not face. Frightened by what I saw in him, I said:

"Very well sir, you live by your code, and I will live by mine." I turned, unable stand the fire erupting inside me. He came up behind me and threw his arms around me, burying his head in my neck. I started:

"Please, I must..."

He turned me to look at him putting both his hands to my face, silver in the moon. Before I could say anything more, he released his craving and pulled my face to his. He kissed me. Everything in me erupted. He kept kissing me and wrapped his arms about me, until I could do nothing but kiss him back.

I did not think. I did not consider the ramifications of waking up on the morrow having had his passion igniting my own. I did not remember his condemnation for allowing it. I simply kissed him knowing if I only got this one moment in my whole life to feel so complete, I would take it. A knock sounded at the door and winded, Lawrence pulled away. The door opened, throwing a panel of harsh brightness over the path of the silvery moon-lit room.

"Myra," Richard said entering the room, "I do not wish to interfere, but I cannot allow your reputation to be tarnished."

"I have imposed upon her I am sure," Lawrence said not moving his eyes away from my face. "We will have to be wed tomorrow."

I laughed and said, "I do not think it that serious, Sir."

"No, Myra it is. I took you into my home. I made you the mother of my child. I love you like a man should love a wife, and yet, I have not done the honorable thing and married you. I cannot go home without you. So, either I will stay here, until I must follow you to London, and then where ever else you choose to go, or you will marry me, and we will go home together."

"I ... I thought you..." I stammered looking over at Richard.

"Perhaps you need another private moment," Richard said, turning away, "Two minutes, upon your honor."

Lawrence nodded. When the door shut, Lawrence leaned over me, and I watched him, so perfect in his intensity.

"Will you marry me, Myra?" he asked.

"What about your promise to…"

"To forever be miserable, only to keep a young man's fear. It is not my ideal, or promise, it is fear that keeps me from trying again. It is like the preacher said. I am supposed to grow wise with age."

"I am certain he was talking to James Evans," I said.

"No, he spoke directly to my heart."

"What if in a year or two you resent me. What if you learn to hate me for the loss of your honor?

"What honor is there in leaving you like this? I love you, Myra. There is no shame in that, no resentment."

"You resented me last time," I said letting out an unattractive sob. He put his hands on my shoulders and stammered so confused. I looked up at him.

"It was not resentment toward you last time, but myself. That was a different situation, Myra. You were under my protection. I should never have," he shook his head and I saw the look he gave back then.

Perhaps it was more directed toward himself. I did not know what to think.

"Now we are both free of that. Your brother has made it noticeably clear to London, nay the world, he is your guardian, which leaves me free to court you. I will love whom I love and be grateful I am capable of the emotion. Please marry me," he said, then not even waiting for a response he picked up my face and kissed me again pulling long and hard on my mouth. The fire within me grew and I kissed him back. Richard knocked at the door when our two minutes were up. Lawrence pulled away. Richard opened the door, letting in the hallway light again.

"I have almost convinced her, I think," Lawrence said not looking away from my face.

"Put the poor man out of his misery, Myra," Richard said, taking his friend seriously.

"I will marry you, Lawrence," I said reaching up and cupping his face in the palm of my hand.

He turned his face into my hand and kissed it.

"Very well, it is ... please let us rejoin the group," Richard said because Lawrence kissed my wrist in a way that was too intimate to be witnessed.

Lawrence kissed my wrist one last time, then gave way.

"I would like to be the one to tell Eva. It must be done delicately," Lawrence said looking me in the eyes seriously, like I may argue with him. I nodded while Richard smirked behind his back. As Lawrence turned, I glared at Richard. We walked together back into the drawing-room. Lawrence did not let go of my arm. Eva took one look at our stance and asked, "Is there finally an understanding between the two of you?"

"I..." Lawrence evaluated his daughter.

"Come now father! You have loved Myra for years. It is time you do the honorable thing and marry her," Eva said.

"It will impact you, possibly your inheritance--," Lawrence said.

"I do not care. Knowing you are happy and not alone is all I want," she said.

"It does not mean I stopped honoring your mother," he said.

"I do not think my mother would like you feeling so alone you must drink to stave off your discomfort," Eva said pointedly.

"You are right, I am sure," he said and sat next to me on the sofa. For the first time since Eva married, he appeared content. And in his contentment, I let go of the guilt of practically forcing him to propose, though I'm not sure what I did this time. Perhaps, no matter what I did it would have come to this end. No manipulation could have helped or hindered it.

We watched and listened to everything happening around us. Eventually, Lawrence discreetly ran a finger over my hand tracing a pattern there. I was exquisitely happy.

Eva and Jonah retired early. After a time, everyone else trickled out. Finally, when only Richard was left with us, he said, "I cannot chaperone the two of you all night."

"I do not know how I will endure the separation," Lawrence said.

"What a sap you have turned out to be," Richard said. "You owe me a hundred pounds."

"Give me your sister's hand tomorrow and I will give you two hundred."

"I thought this would be a more enjoyable gloat, but you are too sentimental to enjoy pestering."

He turned disgruntled, and Lawrence kissed my hand.

That night I went to bed in a dream, unsure what I would find the morning, but at least I had the dream. I quickly dressed the next morning and went into the breakfast room. Lawrence looked to be waiting for me and stood at my entrance. He moved to me quickly and kissed my hand. His lips lingered on my skin.

I was extremely glad to see his affection had made it through the night.

"My Lord," Rick complained, squinting and covering Clara's eyes.

"Stop that," Clara swatted at his hand.

"All right," Rick said. "But I cannot be responsible for what you see."

"Oh, come now. It is our wedding day. We must be allowed as much sentiment as we please."

"Lawrence," I said. "We have not posted the banns
…. There are a few things we must consider."

"Well Rick, there you have it, you will have to see us
being affectionate for more than just today," he said.

"Thank goodness I'm going back to school soon," he
said.

I grinned at my nephew. He did not seem to mind my
happiness. He kindly did not notice my red face when
Lawrence ate his breakfast so close to me, that he hooked his
foot to mine under the table. That morning I received Mr.
Williams' proposal. Lawrence wished to help me write my
refusal, but I did it in private because I felt the language he
used a bit strong to refuse the honor of a man's affection.

James also wrote, to admit our outing would have to
be delayed. Miss Clarke had accepted a proposal from Mr.
Davies and was taking a trip to her father's house to introduce
the young man. Throughout our acquaintance, I learned her
father was a man of means and meant to settle upon Miss
Clarke a decent sum. It would certainly go to good use within
the Davies dilapidated estate.

James, of course, asked if he could call on me as he
had business we needed to settle. Now that I was his only
option left, he meant to give in and propose. I wrote him back
and let him know that I could not be called on as I was
planning a journey with my own intended. I hinted that
perhaps he should take more care to focus on the one lady he
meant to court so that they might not all slip through his
fingers.

Two days later we all traveled to Grey Manor on the
way to drop Rick and Phineas off at the train station. Richard
was ever the vigilant chaperon until Mary took to scolding
him when he followed us around too closely. Once we settled
in at Grey Manor, Richard soon found Hetty could do more
than he could anyway, so he set the housekeeper on us like a
bloodhound. She did not manage her disappointment well

and found destroying any romantic tension between Lawrence and I the perfect outlet. Hetty was nearer bloodhound than a woman.

Lawrence hired a local artist to paint my portrait in front of his father's peach roses.

"Are you still happy?" I asked him as he watched to be sure I was accurately portrayed.

"I am," he said looking so content I believed him. He moved to pull a rose from behind the bush. Turning to me said, "It is almost unfathomable I would turn from my happiness when I only had to take hold of it, just as it would be unthinkable for my father to burn this bush when the roses turned such a rare peach instead of pink."

As he said this, he handed me the rose and kissed the hand I used to reach for it. In return, I grinned at him with the happiest of smiles.

"And now, I will spend the rest of my life earning that smile," he said, "I swear it disarms me every time I see it."

Epilogue

Lawrence and I married quickly. It caused a bit of a scandal, but neither of us made the effort to care. Upon our marriage, Lawrence settled ten thousand pounds on each of my nieces and a lucrative piece of worked land on Rick so he could be independent before he inherited. He called it a wedding present for me, but I suspected he always meant to set his old friend's family back to right.

We went to India on our wedding trip. I rode an elephant to hunt with a Baron and his lady Lawrence knew from school. With Lawrence's arms always around me, I did not feel frightened once. We behaved shockingly like young lovers. We did not have to keep to anyone else's schedule and could come and go as we liked while being established in the finest house in Bombay. Lawrence had matters of the crown to undertake so he could not always be with me, but took me with him whenever he could.

I once promised Miss Williams I would look out for her when everything fell. I did not, and she was stabbed. I meant to make it up to her.

A day or two before the heat drove us from the country, we happened upon the infantry we'd come specifically to Bombay to meet. Lawrence, of course, had to make his way down the ranks. He started with the Governor-General. The problem arose when dealing with the East India Trading Company which had established an army led by British Officers but filled with natives. The company reached far and wide in Bombay and distinguishing the Queen's Army from the Bombay Army became more challenging than he thought.

All three of Adelaide Spencer's brothers, having gentry education and a commission, came to Bombay, not only that they might serve within the vicinity of each other, but to find fast growth opportunities. Lawrence finally found a Captain Spencer who happened to command a company that incorporated two separate troops commanded by lieutenants of the same surname.

Lawrence claimed his interest in them was to help their careers along, and so he did with the Lieutenant Colonel. He was unable to contact the brothers personally. Lawrence, having a significant number of shares in the company, ended his last few days of our wedding trip being pressed by the director to help in all sorts of business matters. It was left for me to meddle, and so I invited all three of Adelaide's brothers to tea.

When they walked in, they looked uncomfortable, and I was not certain a person could stand as straight as the oldest brother who had dark hair and blue eyes like his sister and introduced as:

"Captain Victor Spencer."

Next came the middle son, the storyteller. He looked like a mixture of the father and mother. He was handsome enough, but not in the obvious way of his brothers. His name was Oliver Spencer. The youngest, who could not be much more than two or three years older than Adelaide, looked as though he could be her twin instead of her older brother was Noah.

They were extremely handsome, well-disciplined men. The oldest, most rigid of all, watched his brothers in the Marchioness' presence just to be sure they behaved correctly.

The men had heard nothing of their sister nor what happened at home. Communication took months for soldiers in India. And they could not fathom why the Marquess of Dorset was advancing all their careers.

After I finally persuaded them to sit, the younger two looked to the eldest brother to learn why fortune was smiling on them so.

"I suppose you have… you have news. Did you say your nephew is a friend of our families?" Captain Spencer asked, confused.

"Your sister of course," I said nodding to the maid to serve the men.

"You have news of Adelaide," The youngest asked, his blue eyes terrified, glancing at his oldest brother.

"Your sister Mrs. Adelaide Williams is a great friend of my family," I said.

"Mrs. Williams," the captain said, "the scoundrel married her after all?"

"Yes, he only lived with her for three months, long enough to sire a child. Then he left her in Scotland while he finished his schooling. Thankfully, his Aunt Sadie took care of them. It is Sadie who…well, introduced us of sorts. Now we are all such great friends," I said, fanning myself and looking again at the maid. Most days she brought cold lemonade as a treat for me but had not yet.

"Sadie Williams…is it still Williams?" Captain Spencer asked, watching me.

"Yes, of course. She spent the last five years caring for Adelaide. It left no time for marriage," I said pretending I knew nothing of his love affair with the lady. I nodded to the maid again to get us all drinks, and she finally left the room as if she might.

"I forgot, you must have grown up with Sadie," I said innocently.

"Yes, but how do you know her" the middle son, Oliver said.

"We had such a time of it. Rick, my nephew, was in the habit of thwarting Mr. Titus Williams at school. Mr. Williams came into our parish, and in the act of getting revenge on Rick when we met Sadie and your sister. Your sister, of course, was married to him, but Mr. Titus Williams thought he may want to marry my niece. I believe he meant to kill your sister so he might," I said.

"Is she … is Adelaide all right?" Noah, the youngest brother, asked.

"Yes quite. We took her into my brother's house to keep her safe. Now, she is living five miles from your parents and they are together very often," I said.

"Oh, Mama must love that," Noah, the youngest said. His smile was broad, and full of pleasure at my statement.

"I believe she is very happy," I said, smiling at him.

"I feel very… confused by this. Did my father… Is he in habit of visiting my sister?" the Captain asked, his brow furrowed grimly.

"Of course," I said, "If Mr. Williams had not forbidden her from leaving Scotland and going home, I believe your parents would have been saved much of their concern."

"I am sorry, can you... I don't suppose you can tell us. You are sure Titus meant to kill Adelaide?" Oliver asked, horrified.

"I am. He..." I took a deep breath. I saw the captain meant to be severe on everyone involved. I decided I would invoke his pity if I could. I said, "he stabbed Sadie in anger, just for telling us where Adelaide was. I do not doubt he would have done the same to Adelaide if Sadie hadn't warned us."

"Is... is Sadie all right?" Oliver asked, seeing the captain had turned white.

"Oh yes, it was Sadie who saved the day. She was quite brave. She got stabbed, but still ran three miles bleeding the whole way to my brother's house, just to warn us."

"That Titus would try to kill Adelaide," Oliver asked.

"Yes, and that Titus Williams was going to try and take Clara," I said.

"The scoundrel," Captain Spencer said.

"I will hunt him down and teach him some manners," Oliver said.

"You may be my second," Captain Spencer said tersely. Oliver nodded.

"Oh, none of that is necessary. In the process of trying to take Clara, Mr. Williams met with the father of another young lady he had hurt. He was killed," I said.

"And Sadie is she... is she hurt dearly?" Captain Spencer asked, fixated on this one point.

"She was recovering though I haven't seen her since autumn of last year," I said, "but since Titus Williams no longer stands as an impediment, she and Adelaide are recovering together at the Williams estate. Your father even sent her a cook who is quite medicinal."

"Cook is very good," the youngest brother said. I could almost see growing up he must have merited the cook's services more often than the others.

When tea ended, I stood and said, "I had Adelaide in mind when I asked Lawrence, my husband, to pull a few strings to get you early leave. If he were here now, he would offer you passage on his clipper to go home for Christmas, but he is not, so I suppose I must do it."

"I don't have leave," the youngest said.

"You do dear, it's all arranged. After all, your sister's husband just died," I said.

"You should not have imposed so on her Majesty's armed..." Captain Spencer started. I raised my eyebrows at him as I had his father. He stopped speaking and looked embarrassed.

"You cannot worry about that," I said. "It is your family's turn to need a little extra time. When one of your comrades needs leave you will step in to help, will you not?" I asked.

"Assuredly," he said bowing.

"I... suppose my sister mourns..." Oliver said.

"In many ways. Her life has been full of sorrow. She does mourn, but less so for the loss of the man who abandoned her. She is slow to trust and will be for a time, but she has the most agreeable little boy to keep her busy. He keeps her sweet. Thankfully, she will also have her noble brothers at her side." This time all three bowed.

The three left at the utmost proper moment, with much to do before they could leave the country. I doubted all three would take our offer for a ride home for the holiday.

The eldest appeared uncomfortable without a Spencer left to defend the bay.

However, when the gray of the early morning began to dawn over the harbor, all three officers were present. I thought I sensed friction between them. I quickly imposed on them to help with my trunk and the crates of gifts I brought home for all who had ever crossed my life for good. The distraction did them good.

When the clipper moved out among the small fishing boats, Lawrence and I stood together on the deck.

He often had his arms about me, like he spent so long resisting our attraction, that he had to now honor it by always giving into it.

"Are you content you have made amends to Miss Williams by bringing home her beau, my darling?" Lawrence asked.

"Very," I answered, "I am glad to know I can still meddle in people's lives, though I am now married."

"I admit to being distracted since I am no longer a widower," he said leaning down to kiss my neck. I smiled and leaned into him so his kisses could move upward toward my ear.

Made in the USA
Middletown, DE
09 May 2023

30285580R00187